PRETTY BOY DEAD

PRETTY BOY DEAD

A Novel

Joseph Hansen

Gay Sunshine Press
San Francisco

This novel was published originally in 1968 by Brandon House, North
Hollywood under the title *Known Homosexual*. It was re-issued in 1977 by
Major Books, Canoga Park, CA under the title *Stranger to Himself*.

Library of Congress Cataloging in Publication Data:

Hansen, Joseph, 1923
    Pretty boy dead.

I. Title.
PS3558.A513P7   1984   813'.54   84-13764
ISBN 0-917342-48-8

Gay Sunshine Press
P.O. Box 40397
San Francisco, CA 94140
Complete catalog of books available for $1 postpaid.

Every man has in him
a night that is unknown
to him.

—Jean Cocteau

PROLOGUE

H E WAS NAKED IN A STRANGE BED, one of those beds that stands in a closet all day, like a bad child. At the far end of the room, gray early light fogged a bay window edged with scraps of colored glass. Close to his face, a poster for an old Bette Davis movie was taped to the wall. He rolled onto his back. The ceiling had golden oak beams, the plaster between them rain-stained. There was a black iron chandelier with only one bulb. He had never seen any of it before.

He moved his hand. Beside him the bed was empty. He raised himself on his elbows. On a cushioned seat under the window a boy lay asleep, one knee up, one arm flung out, a fragile-looking kid of nineteen or twenty, sunburned skin, sunstreaked brown hair, genitals neat in their shadowy crotch. Who was he? Name? Steve shook his head. Hell, he couldn't even remember the face. Where had he met the kid, how had they got here?

Wincing at the dull ache in his head, the taste in his mouth, but careful not to rattle the bed, he swung his feet to the floor. It was covered with grass matting from Akron's. Strewn across it lay his clothes. Unsteadily he picked them up and put them on—white Levis, white gym socks, white canvas shoes, blue turtleneck sweater, red orlon jacket.

The boy on the windowseat stirred, and Steve paused and stared at him, not wanting him to waken. He looked like a nice enough faggot, but Steve didn't need him. He needed Coy Randol, needed him the way he needed air, food, water. He had to get home from wherever this was and tell him so, tell him that no matter what he'd done, Steve Archer couldn't live without him.

His keys, wallet, change, cigarets lay on the peeling veneer dresser. He stuffed them into his pockets, threw the sleeping boy

7

a grimace of apology for the nothing night he must have had, and eased out of the room. The bathroom at the end of the hall was bleak and green, the paint flaking, amber plastic pasted over the window. The place reminded him of suicide. He did what he had to and got out.

At the foot of the golden oak staircase the front door stood open. There was a heavy-raftered porch, half smothered in vines. The yard was choked with overgrown shrubs and the grass, the weeds, were dry. He didn't recognize the street, didn't bother to look for its name. It was steep and therefore in the hills, some section of the curving miles of hills that cradle Los Angeles.

Hibiscus bushes, flaming with blossom, crowded the sidewalks. Their fallen red flowers were slippery underfoot as he started downhill, walking fast. Because these hill streets twisted a lot and came to dead ends sometimes, it took him twenty minutes to find his way out. Hollywood Boulevard. The store fronts looked dismal without their neons, like female impersonators stripped to their jock-straps.

He found a cafe, a gleaming white plastic cave, and from the worn boy behind the counter ordered coffee. He gulped it black and hot to still the uproar in his gut. He lit a cigaret and, scowling through the smoke, marveled at himself of last night, himself of this morning. Not that the contrast was new. That was what was so stupid about it. When was he going to learn that you can't transform someone you love? To expect ethics, scruples, brains of Coy was irrational. He was a beautiful animal. That was all he ever would be. And it didn't matter. When would Steve get that through his head? Not till it was too late? After last night, was it already too late? He got up quickly, dropped a dime on the counter, and left.

When he jumped off the bus at Silverlake, it was already warm. The day would be hot. The April sky was perfect blue. Here Sunset Boulevard curved between steep green hills, crowded with white buildings roofed in red tile. He crossed Sunset with the signal and began to climb Kean Terrace. He grinned. Coy would be asleep, his honey-colored nakedness sprawled cattycorner across the bed in the dim, rosy glow that filtered through the Madras curtains. Steve knew just how to waken him.

As he rounded the first bend in the street, a brown Police ambulance passed, headed downhill, moving soundlessly. He squinted at it, then automatically looked in the direction it had come from. His heart turned over. At the foot of the long cement steps that climbed between hedges to the apartment he and Coy shared, stood a gray, late model car. It was unmarked. But it had a buggywhip aerial. It was a Police car.

Steve frowned, feeling cold inside. What the hell went on? He glanced at the ambulance again, where it waited at the intersection below. Then he turned and began running up the hill, heart pounding. He raced up the stairs, somehow very scared, panting under his breath, "Coy... Coy..." The narrow front terrace, fenced by ivy-covered wrought iron, was empty. He ran along it and found the front door open the way he'd left it. He walked in.

A man got up from one of the basket chairs, a tired-looking man of forty, with faded red hair. He stared expressionlessly at Steve. "Are you Stephen Archer?"

"Yes. Where's Coy?"

There were things wrong with the long, white, sunlit room. Some kind of powder was sprinkled on the coffee table. The martini glasses and ashtray were still there, cigaret pack, match book—powder on them all. At the end of the couch, where he had tossed them last night, lay Coy's little blue shorts with the white piping. But there was something else on the couch. Splatters of reddish brown. Blood? Coy's blue and white rubber go-aheads were on the white rug. Beside them was a big ugly reddish brown stain. He looked at the man's impassive face. "Where's Coy?"

The man studied him for a moment, then, with a whispered sigh, sat down in the basket chair again. He nodded at the other one. "You better sit down." It took Steve a minute to understand him, then, dumbly, he obeyed. The man took a wallet out of his neat tweed jacket and held the wallet so it fell open and showed a Police badge. "Detective Sergeant Cummings." He put away the wallet. "Homicide Division."

Steve stared at him. "Homicide?" He could feel his heart beating hard and slow, but from a distance, as if he were remote from his own body. He also felt very cold. He looked again at the stain on the rug and then again at Cummings. "Is it Coy?" he whispered. "Is it Coy who was murdered?"

"Randol," Cummings nodded. "Jesse Coy Randol."

"They took him away in that ambulance?"

Cummings nodded again. He glanced at his wristwatch. He looked toward the door to the hall that led to the bath and bedrooms. The phone was in the front bedroom. He must be

9

expecting a call. He asked, "Do you know who his next of kin are, his family?"

"They've got a little ranch outside a town called Dead Oak," Steve said dully, "down the coast, La Paz Valley. Lemons, grapefruit, limes. They're large in the evangelical church there—Berea Church. Father, mother, sister. Half Steinbeck, half O'Neill. Too much. Listen . . ."

Something was going to happen. Was he going to throw up? Was he going to pass out? He tried to stand. Quickly Cummings stood too. "Listen," Steve told him, "I'm sorry, but I'm afraid I'm going to . . ." To cry? No, not that. Surely not that. But that was it. That was what happened. His belly muscles jerked in, hard and suddenly, doubling him over so that he sat down again. Sobs tore up out of him, loud and hoarse. Tears scalded his eyes. He folded forward, covering his face with his hands. He bit his lip and shook his head, but there was no stopping it. Poor Coy—poor, pretty, innocent, corrupt little Coy!

At last the phone rang. Steve heard Cummings jump up and run for it. Choking, shuddering, Steve forced himself to sit straight, to drag in deep breaths. He wiped his face on his sleeve. The orlon wasn't absorbent. He used his hands, wiped his hands on his Levis. He groped shakily in his pocket for a cigaret and set it in the corner of his mouth. Match? The book on the table. He stood up.

From the kitchen, somebody said, "Just wait."

"I'm waiting," Steve snarled. He lit the cigaret and saw another detective staring at him from the kitchen doorway. A big man in a wrinkled blue suit, the knot of his necktie crooked. Behind him, moon-faced, wide-eyed, Brubaker, the landlord, goggled at Steve as if he'd never seen him before. He lived upstairs. He would have heard the row last night. A witness. Excitement. Steve turned away, and there was Cummings standing in the hall doorway, looking at him. Steve blew out the match. "Well?"

"You're under arrest, Archer." Cummings came toward him. "Let's go."

1

SHE CROPPED HER HAIR SHORT like a boy's. It was yellow hair. Her eyes were blue. She didn't draw the Charlie Chaplin lines around them that were favored by the other chicks at Terra Rosa High. She wore only lipstick. Her figure wasn't good—too thin, boyish, pelvis narrow, breasts small, shoulders square and spare as a ten-year-old boy's. The cheap cotton dresses she wore hung on her. Even in hot weather like this—June, graduation just past—she wore cardigans. She looked starved, chilly and pale.

He asked, "What happens to you when you get out in the sun? Like at the beach?"

She turned her head on the pillow and her eyes smiled. "I sunburn." She ran her small, thin hand along the blackness of his chest and belly. "You don't sunburn."

"I started out sunburned." He took her hand and guided it down. "There now. Hold that."

"It's a pleasure."

They lay on her bed, that was made for only one sleeper, but they weren't sleeping and they were, most of the time they were on it, close enough for one. The room was cramped. Like the two thousand identical houses around it in the flat section of sprawling Los Angeles called Terra Rosa, the house was cramped, every room. It was new, but the smooth plaster was already cracking. The windows, arranged high and in a line next to the ceiling, were warped and wouldn't slide. From the bathroom they could hear the drip of the shower. In the kitchen, the refrigerator hummed.

The clock beside the bed was tin and ticked loudly. Steve looked at its hands and then turned from her and sat up. "I've got to cut out. Your Mom will be home." He reached for his clothes, feeling her sit up too, kiss his shoulders lightly, then run the tip of her tongue down his spine. He grinned and shivered.

"Mmm," she murmured, "salty! You sweat."

"You bet." He pulled on his T shirt and stood up to kick into his chinos.

"Wait, hold that pose." She kissed him. "You have the most beautiful butt in the world."

"Thanks. I like yours, too." He grinned down at her where she sat on the side of the bed. She looked down at herself and sadly shook her head.

"I'm too skinny," she said.

He kissed her hair. "You're beautiful. You also taste good." He touched between her thighs. "What is it the guy calls it in *Candy?*" She didn't read much. He had read it to her.

"Honeypot," she giggled.

"Right." He sat down beside her and pulled on his socks and pushed his feet into his loafers. "I've got to split." He kissed her mouth hard and stood up and was out the bedroom door when she called sharply, "Steve!" There was a new note in her voice, something he hadn't heard before. He swung around. Suddenly she was looking very serious and scared.

"Steve . . ." Her little pink tongue moved over her lips. She lowered her eyes and mumbled the rest in a rush, as if she were telling it to her dim reflection in the waxed linoleum-tile floor. "Steve . . . I'm gonna have a baby, Steve. And so I guess we have to get married, don't we, Steve? Don't we?" She jumped up and came to him in the doorway. She put her arms around his neck. He held himself stiff, shocked. He used condoms. How could it have happened?

"You sure?"

She nodded. "I've missed my period twice, now."

"Christ!" he whispered. He wanted to sit down.

His father's office in the shiny new clinic glowed with fluorescent light. Pumpkin colored walls, chairs in chalk blue naugahide. White floors, white ceiling, white desk and file cases, white plastic anatomical cutaway models on top of a white bookcase full of medical texts.

In these surroundings, and wearing the starched white cotton jacket, his father looked very black. Gaunt, hard as wood, like a Gold Coast image, he sat back of the desk and his long hand, with its big pink nails, toyed with a hammer that was a wedge of gray rubber caught in a bright loop of steel. He bumped it rhythmically on the prescription pad in front of him.

"And of course," he said, "this is a white girl?"

Steve nodded.

"And of course of a lower income family?"

"Tire workers get almost three dollars an hour."

"When the plant functions. But that's irrelevant. The relevant thing is that you couldn't choose someone of your own quality and breeding." The whites of his eyes were like stained porcelain.

"How old is she?"

"Seventeen, eighteen."

"And you are . . .?" His father waited.

Steve nodded at a filing cabinet. "You could look it up."

His father threw the hammer. It clattered in the corner, hopped crazily, stopped. He was on his feet. Face twisted, he started to round the desk. Then he checked his stride and took a breath. His fists were clenched. He kept his voice low, but it shook.

"I worked, drove myself, deprived myself when I was your age to get someplace in a world and time when a black man wanting to be a doctor had every strike against him, when a lot of them would rather see you dead than with a decent profession and some importance in the world.

"Do you think I took all their insults and contempt, all their political tricks and red tape, and worked and worked and built all this—" His long arm swung savagely. "—to have my one son end up a cheap nigger, a raghead cotton picker with only one thing on his half-wit mind—where to stick his big, hot, black prick?" The words ricocheted in the bright room like a shot. Slowly, sweating, his father sat down. For a moment he stared silent at the prescription pad. Then, grimly, hoarsely, he went on, "I warned you last time, when you got mixed up with that Smith Tyler boy. Didn't I? Promised that if you let this kind of thing happen again, I was through with you."

"This is a little different," Steve mumbled.

"It's no different!" His father slammed his open hand on the desk. "It's still sex. I'm not interested in what kind. You're obviously doomed by it the way an alcoholic is doomed by liquor. This time it's a girl. So much the worse. She's got a claim on you as old as the world. White slut—I know the type. But decency, if you've got any, forces you to honor that claim."

"She's not a slut, and I will honor it."

"I should hope so. Just don't expect any help from me. Don't expect anything from me. You were going to Stanford. Best money can buy. Now you'll go nowhere, nowhere. If you're lucky—on the strength of being the son of Abel Allen Archer, M.D., you can maybe get a Civil Service job. God knows, every colored in Los Angeles seems to take that route to respectability.

"But it won't make you respectable in my eyes. Never. I'm through with you. From now on, I'll build my hopes on myself. The Urban League wants me in the chair. I've been asked to run for Assemblyman from this district, and next time I'll do it. When I had your future to look after, I couldn't risk the time, had to keep building the practice. But you're not in my future any more. Negroes like you aren't any part of my future." He looked down at the desk top for a minute, shook his head. "Nothing but sex on legs," he muttered, " running down a long hill." He looked up again. His voice was soft but he meant what he said. "Get out of my sight. I never want to see you again."

"Mama, Daddy—this is Steve." Her hand in his was cold and damp. A little smile edged her mouth for a second, then died.

The man and woman stared at him. The man sat in a meager easy chair facing the television set that was rasping. The woman sat crocheting on the couch that matched the chair. Her pink and yellow doilies were all over the room. Above her head, in a molded white plaster frame with shelves, stood nine cheap little china figurines, fawns, lambs, bluebirds. The woman was flabby, with uncertain eyes and a wet mouth. She wore curlers, a sleeveless blouse, denim pedal pushers. The man was shrunken and hard, like dried beef, the color of dried beef. Though he was probably no more than forty, his face was creased like an old man's. His two upper front teeth were missing. On the arm of his chair stood a beer can. He smoked a handmade cigaret, the smoke making him squint.

Steve said, "Pleased to meet you. Lacey's told me all about you." The woman worked, the man lived in taverns.

He got up and turned off the television set. He was short and his walk was jerky, the elbows crooked. "She didn't tell us all about you." He had an Oklahoma accent.

"Tsk, tsk, tsk." Watching her bright, fierce needles, the woman on the couch shook her head.

"Didn't tell us a thang." The man glared at the girl. "Never spoke your name till today, tonight. Sure as hell never told us you want white.

"Harry, now . . ." The woman had sat with her legs tucked under her. Now she put her feet on the floor.

"I'm not white," Steve said. "Nothing I can do about that."

Lacey said, highpitched, "I don't care what color he is, I love him."

"Shut your mouth," her father said. He looked at Steve, eyes hard and bright. "I got a double hernia," he said, "but if I didn't have, I'd beat you till you couldn't stand up, then I'd kick your head till you crawled in circles, and then I'd pick you up and throw you out in the street, and let the cars run over you till you want no more than a black spot on the white ce-ment."

"Harry, now—" The woman stood up.

"Don't you say nothin'." He bent to stub out his cigaret in a tiny china ashtray rimmed with rosebuds. "If you was any kind of ma to her, this'd never happened."

"If you was any kind of pa to her, you'd got out and made a livin'." She picked up the ashtray, emptied the one butt into a flower-painted pink waste basket, wiped the ashtray out with a pink tissue. "Then I coulda stayed home and looked after her like I wanted."

"I'm sick. You'd like it if I worked right on into the graveyard, I guess. You'd like that fine."

Steve squeezed Lacey's hand. When he had phoned, she'd asked him to come and get her. "We better go," he said to her quietly now. "Your clothes all packed?"

Crying, she ran out of the room. In a minute, cheap little blue cloth coat over her arm, suitcase in her hand, she was back. "Mama," she said, "goodbye, Mama." Tears smeared her white face. The woman sat on the couch again. Lacey kissed the plastic rolls of dyed red hair, turned to the man. "Daddy, darling, don't look like that."

"Dear Lord Jesus!" the man said, staring at her. Then he turned his back, shoulders hunched, knobby fists clenched and trembling at his sides. "What'll it be next? Looks like God ain't never gonna let me be."

"I'm sorry," Steve said. "Come on, Lacey." Gently he took her arm, pulled open the warped front door, and led her out into the darkness.

"Those are extremely disagreeable people," his mother said. The Literature Department of the Public Library was a big room, high-ceilinged, hushed. She stood facing him in the center aisle between heavy refectory tables. He held on to the cart of books he was shelving and listened. She looked, as always, very smart. Pale green linen suit, lavender bag, gloves, shoes, hat with a little veil on gray hair freshly set. She was not so dark as Steve's father, ten years younger, had been a beautiful girl—there was an oil portrait over the fireplace—was still a handsome woman, though growing a little heavy lately in the breasts and hips. Her voice was musical. "But at last they told me where you were living." Her smile was wan. "Your Lacey's a funny little thing . . .Steve, couldn't you have seen—" She glanced, annoyed, at the librarian who came and opened little wooden file drawers nearby. "I lie awake nights," she whispered bitterly, "blaming myself. . . ."

"Don't do that. I'm all right. We're all right."

"No, but for not telling you, not warning you."

"Of what? That girls get pregnant? I knew that."

"No," she said sharply, "not that. Of the fact that there are white girls who—I find it difficult to say, now. Driving down here, all the way, I promised I would. But after all, what's the use? The damage is done. If I tell you now, you'll only—"

"Steve Archer, please." From back of the counter at the end of the room a bald man called him. "Telephone."

"Excuse me." Steve hoped she'd go while he talked. He made meaningless jottings on a note pad while in his ear Lacey's voice whimpered, "She came—your mother—and she's coming there to see you, Steve. I tried not to tell her where you worked, but she made me."

"Yeah, Lacey, she's here." What was the use of scolding her? He should have known she'd never be able to stand up to a woman like Mrs. Abel Allen Archer, should have known better than to expect it. Only, he hadn't wanted his mother to find him. "It's okay. Forget it. I'll see you later."

When he came back, his mother was impatiently fumbling in her handbag. "Have you a cigaret? I can't imagine—"

"Can't smoke in here. Have to go outside."

With its towering gray walls, the Library patio was like a prison recreation yard. A pale small boy lay on his stomach on a cement bench, poring nearsightedly over a brightly illustrated book. On another bench a bearded old man slept like a propped corpse. Clumps of banana trees cringed in the corners as if driven there. High overhead, pigeons made their tragic love noises. Steve gave his mother a cigaret and lit it for her.

16

"Thank you. What I ought to have told you, and really scold myself for not doing, is that there is always a certain type of white girl lying in wait for boys like you . . ."

"I knew that."

"You didn't act like it. That girl—I've seen her now and I understand. She's a poor little thing. She could never have found a white boy—"

"Mother, you don't want to say these things."

She blinked her eyes quickly, angrily. "It's true and you know it's true. Had she ever had another boyfriend?"

"If she'd wanted them, she could have."

"No, Stephen, she couldn't. No figure, no face, no personality." She took a step away from him, then turned back. "I was so certain we'd raised you free of the whole white superiority concept. Instead, you've given one of the most heartbreaking examples of—" She dropped the cigaret and ground it out under her delicate lavender shoe. "I never thought you'd be so misguided." Her eyes reproached him.

He turned from the look. "I'm supposed to be working."

"Yes." She bit her lip. "Of course." Her smile was mannerly, patient. He held the door for her. They went down the long, quiet corridor. "As I told myself, there's really no point in mentioning it. But I do love you, Stephen, and I hate to see you hurt. And this girl will disappoint you. She has nothing to offer. Be prepared."

They stopped at the door to the Literature Department. She took his hand in her gloved ones. "You look so tired."

"I'm all right."

"Steve, please take this." She pulled something from her purse and pushed it into his hand. "I'll try to send more later."

He frowned. A twenty dollar bill. "What am I going to do with this? They pay me here."

"Well, that dreadful car of yours is always demanding some sort of repair work. And clothes. Did you take any clothes? All I can find gone are books and the typewriter. Now, do take that—" She folded his fingers over the bill. "And make me feel better." Tears made her eyes glisten. She touched them with a lavender hand-kerchief. "I'm so sorry it all happened. Your father—"

"He's all right," Steve said harshly. "He's got his own life to lead. I was only in his way."

Instantly she grew defensive. "Now, that's not fair. You have no call to be bitter towards him. It was you who made the mistake,

Steve, after all. You *were* in the wrong."

Arguing would do no good. He folded the bill and pushed it into his pocket. "Thanks. And if you can, would you wrap up some shorts and things and mail them to me? Look, thanks for coming. I wish I could make it all different so you wouldn't feel so badly. But I can't.

"Ah, Stephen, Stephen." She patted his face, looking into his eyes, hurt, but not, he thought, mortally. Then she turned and, with her graceful, easy walk, moved toward the doors.

2

THROUGH THE THIN APARTMENT WALL came the thud of drums, the ramp of brasses, the shriek of reeds. An electric guitar snarled. Feet stamped and there was a crazy bray of voices. The music was recorded. The stamping and the voices were live. "Christ, aren't they ever going to stop?" Steve rolled over on the creased, sleepless sheets and groped for the clock. Its hands glowed green at 2:20. "This is the third time in seven days."

"I know," Lacey sighed. "I know it."

"You been awake all this time?"

"Mmm." It was a noncommittal sound, but he knew she slept poorly under the best conditions, that she was scared about the baby, and guilty, and maybe, except when they were making it, sorry she loved him. She never said so. He had to guess it. But it worried him and made him sore, at himself, at her, at the world. He said with bitter irony:

"This is what you get when niggers move in next door."

"Steve." Lacey put her hand over his mouth. "Don't talk like that."

"I'm going to talk like that to Hoxie." He sat up and swung his feet to the floor.

"No, Steve, please. He'll be drunk. It won't do any good. It'll only make trouble."

"Don't worry." He pulled on his shirt, stood up and kicked into his chinos. "I'll be back in a second." He ran barefoot across the little living room and out the front door. He nearly stumbled over a couple squirming half naked on the narrow gallery. He saw a gleam of eye whites, a show of teeth, heard a startled, drunken giggle. He didn't slow.

Hoxie's front door was open. Even out in the fresh night, you could smell the smoke, the reek of booze. He stepped inside. The room was yellow. Spheres of rough, brick-red glass pierced with fine bubbles furnished the illumination. There were gaudily striped modern couches in orange and yellow, piles of pillows, blue, green, purple. Along one wall stood a sleek mahogany sound system, its twenty speakers blaring through their covering of gold-threaded rope.

In front of it, dressed only in sox, shoes, and jockey shorts, and with a red towel wrapped like a turban around his head, the squat, sweat-shiny Hoxie frugged with a tall, willowly yellow girl wearing a platinum blonde wig and beaded eyelashes. The place was writhing with people. Most of them carried drinks. Those that smoked weren't smoking Camels and they tended to clot, sleepy-eyed, low-spoken, in the corners. This was a bigger apartment than Steve's and Lacey's. From its recesses someplace, in the moment's silence while the expensive tone arm moved from band to band on the record, came a woman's highpitched cry: "Now, now, NOW!"

"Now," Hoxie laughed, "yeah!" Then he noticed Steve standing just inside the doorway, staring at him. He came wiggling through the pack of narrow-shouldered glossy mohair suits and smart frocks, swiveling his beefy pelvis to the music, rolling his eyes. "Yeah, man! Hi, Steve, hi, neighbor! Rock, man," he yelled over his shoulder to the saxophonist on the record, "oh, rock, you knocked-out son of a bitch!" Then, to Steve again, eyes glittering—he wasn't only drunk, he was hyped up to his turban—"Honey, where's your drink, man, where's your roach?"

"Hoxie," Steve said, "it's two-thirty in the morning and I've got a pregnant wife who needs to sleep, and I've got to work at eight o'clock tomorrow morning, and your parties, man, they're too loud, Hoxie. Too loud and too long."

Hoxie's shine seemed to fade. He looked grave. "Yeah, man. Okay, now you voted." He glanced at the crowd, then back, and grinned. "But you kinda outnumbered, neighbor."

"I'll call the fuzz, Hoxie."

Hoxie's eyes bulged. "You'll what?"

"You heard me."

"Man," Hoxie scowled, "what are you, anyway?" 'Cause you can't be black. You got this white chick. You mixed up is your problem. Ain't black, ain't white. You ain't nothin'. Why don't you take a drink and relax, baby?"

"I'll relax when I can go to sleep. And that'll be when your party breaks up. And that'll be in about ten minutes, when the patrol car arrives." He turned to leave.

Hoxie caught his arm. "Don't do that, honey. Don't fink on Hoxie. I'll punch your little girl in the stomach if you do that to me."

A huge man in a suit of watered silk came to stand beside Hoxie. "What's on this lovely young stud's mind?"

"Just a little peace and quiet," Steve said.

"Peace and quiet's for dead people," Hoxie said. "You don't want to be dead, neighbor."

"About as much as you want a jail term," Steve said.

"Man," Hoxie winced, "you don't even talk right." His fingers daubed playfully at Steve's face. "You sure that color ain't Shinola?"

"Are you going to send these people home, or do I call the police?"

"Neither one. We gonna move the party." With surprising quickness, Hoxie wedged his squat bulk past Steve and pushed out the flimsy aluminum screen door. "What's wrong with this party is it needs more colors. I'm gettin' me a white chicky-baby."

"Crazy!" The giant in the silk suit shifted Steve aside as if he was a stuffed toy, and lumbered out after Hoxie.

"No," Steve shouted, "wait."

But the squat man had already disappeared inside Steve's front door, his big friend after him. The couple who had been making it on the gallery floor were gone. Light sprang up as Steve plunged into his own front room, light from a dimestore pottery lamp that stood on a card table with his typewriter and the pages of a play he was trying to write. A couple of iron-framed canvas sling chairs made up the rest of the furniture. And books—his own, library books, paperbacks, Lacey's movie and confession magazines.

"Cool it, Hoxie," Steve said, "get out, go home."

"Naw, man." Hoxie swung round with a wide, wicked grin. "You can't come by my party and leave your little ofay frau all by her lonesome. Old Hoxie spread joy, man." He turned, calling falsetto into the darkness beyond the living room, "Baby, where are you?"

"Lacey!" Steve yelled. "Get in the bathroom. Lock yourself in."

"Oh, man," Hoxie said reproachfully. "You anti-social." He ducked into the dark. Steve started after him, but the big man caught him and held him. He reeked of perfume. Steve kicked.

"Let go, you overgrown faggot."

The man's huge fist cuffed him above the ear. His head rang, lights danced in front of his eyes. He kicked again, missing, and got hit once more for his trouble. Then there was Hoxie, tugging Lacey, shivering and blinking, into the light. She hadn't a stitch on. Her little belly already showed round where the baby was.

"Lacey, get away from him."

"Man," Hoxie complained, "what you tellin' her? This little party of ours only started. Come on, baby, you kinda skinny but you sure white." The fat hands with their sparkling rings ran over her. Big-eyed, she cringed away, Hoxie, chuckling, keeping close, forcing her back into the room's blind corner, dragging at the elastic of his shorts.

Steve struggled in the big man's grip, managed to turn halfway and ram his knee up into the man's crotch. There was a grunt and the man let go. Steve lunged at Hoxie.

"You son of a bitch, get off her!"

Hoxie turned at him, snarling. But his shorts were down around his ankles now and he tripped over them. Steve grabbed at him as he fell and slung him aside. The lamp went over with a crash and the room was black. He groped out for Lacey, found her fragile little wrist, and ran with her toward the rectangle of gray that was the door. Blundering on his knees, the big man pawed at them. They dodged him.

Then they were out the door and running for the stairs and the car.

"Who is it? What you want?"

His grandmother's little frame house stood behind hollyhocks and a patchy lawn on a night street of houses like it, cheap, one-story, old. The neighborhood had been a Negro section for a long time. In spite of his father, she wouldn't leave it. Now, at three in the morning, it slept under its remote corner lights, silent. The cars at the curbs were not flashy like those in Hoxie's neighborhood. They were old here, dented, dulled, sunk on their wheels.

"It's me, Grandma. Steve."

"Steve?" The thin door opened a crack. The face of the tiny woman who peered out was intensely black, withered, the eyes bright. She wore a cheap flannel bathrobe over her cotton night-dress. On her bony feet were big, felt carpet slippers. "Why, Steve, honey, what in the world...?" With a smile, she opened the door wider. Then she saw Lacey, who was shivering in a blanket from the car, her thin shoulders hunched up, hair uncombed after bed. The old woman's smile vanished. Her eyes narrowed. "What goin' on here? Who this white girl?"

"It's my wife, Grandma. Don't act that way. Lacey, this is my Grandma. Can we come in, Grandma? It's sort of chilly out here." But the old woman kept glaring at the girl. "Child, why ain't you got nothin' on? Where you clothes, girl?"

"Grandma, please, can we answer questions inside? We've had a little trouble and we need a place to sleep. I can't go home. You know that."

"I know what your father say." Grimly, grudgingly, the little woman backed from the door and with a jerk of her whitehaired head indicated she would let them come in. "He say you acted carnal with this white girl and got to marry her, but he sure feel bad about it, Steve. You done broke his heart." She shut the door and glared at Lacey again, who shivered, scared, and moved close against Steve. "What the matter you come here?"

Steve told her while she peered up at him, her misshapen hands, all bones and knotty veins, twitching the neck of the dressing gown. "So we . . . we'd like to stay here . . . tonight, if you'd let us."

"It wrong, Steve." She shook her head, scowling. "I don't understand you turnin' out sinful when you liked the church so much when you was little. Liked the songs. Used to sing . . ." She was telling Lacey, forgetful for a moment of her disapproval, showing off her grandson. "Up high . . . so pretty, like a little bird . . ." She scowled again. "But his marryin' . . ." She clamped her wide mouth tight and shook her head. "That wrong, Steve. You know it ain't right."

"Aw, Grandma, colored and white get married all the time now. You're not a girl in Natchez now, Grandma—you're up North. This isn't 1910, it's 1966. People don't believe that race stuff anymore. Not good people."

She lifted her chin. "Bible don't say it's right."

The little room was oppressive with day heat and long living in it. It was neat and clean but there was a darkness about it, dark paper, dark woodwork, dark rug. The weak bulb of the old silk-shaded floor-lamp showed weary overstuffed furniture with faded, mended slip covers. Only the television set and the platform rocker that faced it, where his Grandma did her sitting and

23

Bible reading, her praying and singing with the TV evangelists, were new. Steve wished they hadn't come here, but he'd left his money on the bedside table in the apartment and was afraid to go back for it, so there was no way to pay for a room.

"Grandma, are you going to help us? We only want to sleep here. We'll find another place tomorrow night."

"What folks gonna say?" the old woman demanded. "They gonna know you here. Mizz Hickam, next door, she gonna snoop out the winda. 'What you doin' with that white girl and you grandson there all night?' Oh, she scandalize . . ."

Lacey sneezed, hard, again, again. When she rubbed her nose with the back of her hand, the blanket fell open.

"Why," Grandma said, "you in a family way, child!"

Pulling the blanket around her again, Lacey nodded dumbly, tears in her eyes.

"Aw, come on, Grandma," Steve chided, laughing. "You *knew* that."

"I never!" the old woman blazed. "Nobody told me—not your father, not your mother. Course not her—she too stuck up. Now, listen, child, you get into that bed in there. That my bed, but it nice and fresh today . . ." She bustled Lacey away. A drawer opened and closed. "Here's a nightgown. My, you tall, ain't you?" Steve smiled. Almost anybody would seem tall to his grandmother. "Now, you snuggle down under them quilts and I'll fetch you some nice hot milk." Steve went to the doorway and looked at Lacey in the big, old, mahogany carved bedstead his grandmother had salvaged from some decaying mansion fifty years ago. Lacey stared at him wide-eyed, as if she was about to cry.

"You do what she says," Steve told her gently. "I'll be along in, in a few minutes."

But his grandmother, passing him in the doorway, said, "No, you will not. Not in my house. You sleep there, on the sofa. Things gonna be decent in my house." She flip-flapped in her big slippers toward the kitchen.

Steve followed, grinning. "That's segregation, Grandma."

"I don't care nothin' about all that political stuff. I knows right from wrong. I'm old. You be what you wants to be outside. But in my house, you gonna be Christian."

And that was the way it was.

24

3

P IKE SAID, "I'll level with you. It gets cold. It's big and it gets cold."

It was a white room full of sunlit space, a notch out of it in one corner to house toilet and shower. There was a sink, a boxy white cookstove, and a little refrigerator.

"There's gas," Lacey said. "Here's the outlet."

"Is there a heater?" Steve asked.

"I'll get you one." Pike stared out the broad window over roofs that were lower down the slope to the ocean. He shook a cigaret from a blue package—Gauloises. Lighting it, he said, "But even with a heater, you'll be cold."

"Come on, Lacey," Steve said wearily. It had been a long day, a long, hot Sunday of househunting, meeting hostility where the place was decent enough to live in, welcome where it was not. "Back to the ghetto."

"What's the matter?" Pike asked.

"You don't want a Negro tenant," Steve said.

"Man, I'm only trying to be honest, and I know this pad is cold. I lived up here as long as I could stand it myself, then I boxed in one of the garages downstairs and moved in there. Hell, my car was keeping warmer than I was." He loved that car, a silver-gray Jag; he'd shown it to them before leading them up here. Now he glanced around the room. "Man, when that fog comes in, when it rains . . ." He shivered in retrospect, a lean young man, blond beard, paint-dribbled sweatshirt, meager black dungarees, bare feet, a suntan that made his blue eyes dazzling. "And if the wind's from the North during a storm, the skylight leaks."

"Shit," Steve said.

From the time he was six, he had hated the white neighborhoods his parents always chose, the big, somewhat outdated but

25

expensive houses, the private schools where he was often the only black boy. He'd been allowed to attend public high school, but that had only increased his yearning to live with Negroes. Now six weeks at Hoxie's had taught him it was too late. He couldn't cut it. The life, the language, background, tastes, clothes—he was alien to them all. Hoxie was right. He wasn't white but he sure as hell wasn't black. Yet if it was easy for a rich professional man like his father to move into white sections, it was hard for a nobody kid. He started toward the door.

"Steve, I'm tired." Lacey clung to his arm with both hands, looking up at him, pleading. "And it's so clean, and I love being at the beach. Look at the seagulls."

"Sure, it's great for seagulls. They're white."

"Oh, man," Pike said disgustedly, "what do you want? You want me to kiss you?" He stepped close suddenly, put his hands on Steve's shoulders and kissed him on the mouth. He smelled of turpentine. Stepping back, grinning, he asked, "Okay?"

Lacey gave a squeaky gasp and clapped her hands over her mouth, eyes round and staring.

Steve's laugh was wobbly. "Man, what do we do now?"

"You are my brother," Pike said, "that's all. But the rent is still eighty-five a month, payable in advance, and you're still going to be Christ cold up here in the winter."

The small paved yard back of the place was piled with steel scrap, slabs of auto bodies, chunks of machinery. In the fog and rain, rust had run out of it and dried on the asphalt. When he wanted to make a piece of sculpture, Pike used a blowtorch to cut up the junk and then to piece it together. He wore a mask and moved in his cave-like quarters like a displaced Hell King from a 12th century morality, eerie in the angry blue-white glare of his scepter. When he wanted to paint, he enameled six-by-eight foot flats of masonite black, traced the rain puddle designs off the yard floor, transferred them to the masonite and painted them rust color.

"I used to." It was the Sunday after they'd moved in. He'd stopped them when they came downstairs, haled them into his place, set them down in his bed that was the only real piece of furniture in the room. He poured red wine from a half gallon bottle, watered it at his paint-stained sink, handed it to them in glasses that were the cut off lower halves of brown beer bottles.

"But that kind of painting's a complete wipe-out now. Representationalism's back." At the base of a tall green bronze, cast from welded gears and piston rods, he found a corner for his rump, sat, and narrowed his eyes at Steve. "I'm going to paint you. Naked. Shadow Apollo. Umber and ultramarine on black."

"Thanks," Steve said. "I think."

"Stand up. Take off your clothes." Pike set down his wine and went to rummage in a battered plywood chest.

"Now?" Steve looked at Lacey but she was no help. She only bit her lower lip and blinked at him.

"Yeah, now." Pike's voice came muffled. "It sure as hell couldn't be much hotter, and you want to paint a nude you pick a hot day. Besides, Sunday's your day off—"

"And Monday," Steve said.

"Monday I teach," Pike said. "And don't say nights. Artificial light's no good to paint by." He turned from the chest with a big drawing pad and sticks of charcoal. "Come on, man—strip."

"Isn't this a little sudden?" Steve laughed shakily, and gulped at his wine. "Why me?"

"Because you're beautiful." The easel Pike set up was mottled with color like a bird's egg. He dragged up an orange crate to sit on. "You want to paint Apollo, you don't ask the garbage man." While he talked, he tacked a sheet of heavy white paper to a board, set the board on the easel, tightened it there. "Come on, stud, I've got to do at least a few preliminary sketches till I find out how you're put together . . .all about it. Then we can paint."

Steve looked at Lacey again. But now her eyes were shining with laughter, half at his embarrassment, half at Pike's outrageousness. "You are beautiful." She touched his hand. "I think it's a wonderful idea."

Pike grinned at her, then settled himself on the crate, raised the charcoal stick above the paper, and looked at Steve. Steve, with a sigh, set his glass on the floor and stood up. He pulled his T shirt over his head and tossed it to Lacey, who began folding it. He said, "It's going to be kind of boring for Lacey. We were going to walk on the beach today, maybe see a film."

"You can see a film tonight," Pike said.

"I won't be bored," Lacey promised. "I'll be happy watching. I love to look at you naked."

"Thanks, you're a big help." Steve turned his back on Pike and dropped his Levis. But before he could make himself face the blond man, he crouched and took a long pull from his glass. Then he stood straight. Pike began drawing right and away and he looked impassive, but Steve couldn't help feeling as if his genitals were the only visible part of him. He started to ask if he couldn't wear trunks, then decided it was too late, too late this morning, too late in this century. *Cool it,* he told himself, *cool it.*

"Where's Lacey?" Pike asked.

"I was right about boring her." Steve undressed mechanically. This was the fourth Sunday and he was no longer embarrassed. Today a Santana wind blew, hot, dry, tasting of desert. The temperature was over ninety. They might have been a hundred miles from the sea. It was no hardship to strip. "Today she admitted it. I dropped her off to watch Kim Novak and Jack Lemmon."

He walked to the sink and poured the wine and watered it and handed a glass to Pike who was squeezing ochre and raw sienna and naples yellow from tubes onto the square of galvanized iron he used for a palette. "I need white. You want to get it for me? In the chest. Use the flashlight."

The flashlight was a big, heavy, three-cell job. Its beam probed the clutter in the chest. A new tube of white lay there in its box. He shucked the box, put the flashlight down again, took the tube to Pike and stood drinking his wine, staring at the shadowy life-size figure on the tall, black board. "You going to finish today?"

"Maybe." Pike capped the tubes, dropped them into a cigar box on the floor and began dabbing with a flexible knife at the gobs of color. "I want to bring the left side of the figure up. I don't know how. Maybe I can do it today, maybe it'll take a long time. I'm not sure how to do it. I've got to find out. When it looks right, then we'll be finished." He gave Steve a quick grin, picked up his glass and, as he drank from it, studied the picture.

"It looks like me," Steve said.

"Yup. Now it's got to look like a painting." From a bouquet of long-handled brushes in a pottery jar, he chose one and dabbled its bristles in a rusty tin lid that held linseed oil. "Okay, let's get started."

Steve walked to the corner and took up the pose. The previous Sundays, Pike had done a lot of talking—about his car, about the art classes he taught at San Val State, and about the play Steve was writing. A couple of evenings he had come up to the big white room and listened to Steve read parts of it aloud. He said he dug it and to judge from his comments Steve believed he did. He criticized, but Steve didn't mind, because Pike was bright and knew what he was talking about.

But today, for twenty minutes, half an hour, he painted steadily, and wordless, scowling, mouth working tight and angry, blue shirt turning black with sweat. Now and then a car puttered past on the narrow street. Now and then gulls uttered high, pained cries, as if the air that was their element was burning them. From far off up the beach, the wind brought occasional snatches of wheezing melody from the old carousel on the amusement pier. Steve began to worry that he'd fall asleep standing there.

"Shit!" Pike said, and threw down the brush. "All right, break," he grumbled, "break, break, break." He got to his feet, and Steve eased his cramped muscles out of the set they had taken, and dropped onto the bed. Pike asked, "Do you mind?" and then didn't wait for an answer: he peeled off the soaked shirt and kicked off the ragged shorts he'd been wearing, abruptly turning from John the Baptist into Jesus, from rough and dirty to sleek and beautiful, like something off a varnished cross in the window of a Catholic gift shop.

He picked up the glasses, took them to the sink to refill them, the white strip across his ass, where the sun never reached, gleaming in the shadows at the back of the room. When he handed Steve his glass, he was shaking so that he almost sloshed the wine. He sat down beside Steve and Steve felt the heat pouring out of him, felt the bed tremble with his trembling.

"Man, you're shaking like you've got malaria. Are you sick?"

"I'm not sick," Pike snarled.

"Did I do something wrong?" Steve asked. "Did I make you screw up the picture?" He started to get up to look at it. Pike pulled him back.

"No. Sit down."

Steve looked at him. He started to form a question, but there was no need. The answer was in Pike's face, in the hand that burned Steve's thigh as if it would leave a white scar. "Ah, no," Steve breathed softly, and turned away from Pike's begging gaze. "No."

"For Christ's sake, why not?" Pike said. "Don't try to tell me you're not at least as queer as I am."

"I won't try to tell you anything, Pike," Steve said.

"My name is Jimmy," Pike said. "Don't go."

"I better," Steve said. "I better go sit in the show with my wife." He set down his wine and dragged his Levis off the end of the bed where he'd dropped them. "And baby," he said, and got to his feet.

Pike said, "Don't do this to me, Steve. Please. I've sat watching you, every perfect blue-black-brown naked part of you, three Sundays in a row, man, hour after hour. Fine. You're worth looking at. A lifetime. I meant it when I said you're beautiful. Understatement. So . . .I want you, Steve. I want you so bad I couldn't make a controlled stroke with that brush today if Huntington Hartford was paying me a million bucks. Steve, for Christ sake, is it asking so much? Is my having it going to turn it limp forever? Don't tell me you never screwed around with boys, baby. Don't tell me you hated it." He ran out of breath.

Steve stared down bleakly at him. "I didn't hate it."

Pike's look of desperation faded. His face relaxed. He knew better than to smile. But he realized at the same instant Steve did, that it was going to happen. With a sigh, Steve tossed his Levis away. He sat down facing Pike and took hold of his hard shoulders. He shook his head.

"But it won't be any good, Jimmy. You don't want me just once. You'll keep wanting it. And I—I've got Lacey, and we're all right. I'm not hard up."

"No, you want this too sometimes." Pike touched himself. "Don't tell me with a body like yours, you don't spend some pretty sweaty sessions in front of mirrors."

"Shut up," Steve said. But it was true. Now and then he would remember Smith Tyler's tall, coffee-with-cream body, the hard straight-up declaration of his sex, with a fierce, photographic brightness he couldn't wipe and didn't want to, but which made him almost cry out with yearning. To that yearning, the mirror acts were a kind of deflected answer. Lacey was wonderful, her mouth hungry, surprising, her little hands deft, inventive, all of her willing, giving, even eager, however often, however crazy the moments he chose to need her. And the fine, quick, inverse shapes and secrets of her, her small, childlike softness, so cool, so slender in the bone, delighted him. Thrust deep into her, her legs and arms clutching him, he sometimes walked around the night room carrying her, laughing, rejoicing in her littleness and lightness. But she was not Smith, nor could she ever be. She filled his

30

need. But need and want were perversely different things. And fear—he had feared this happening from the moment Pike had kissed him that first day—fear and want were often perversely alike.

"Shut up," he said again, and with his own mouth covered Jimmy Pike's. The blond beard was soft as a child's hair. Pike gave a low sob, shuddered, and clamped Steve hard against him. Mouths and bodies locked, they fell together back across the bed.

4

A RE YOU OUT OF IT on Zen or something?" Pike's hand rattled the thick cup in the thick saucer. The cafe was a hole in the wall a block down Fifth from the library—coffee maker, hamburger grill, counter with three stools, two very small tables, the proprietor a fat man in dark glasses. "Have you got some moral code or something?" Pike's blue gaze flicked at Steve's face, flicked away. His beautiful fingers shook a Gauloise from its pack and pushed the pack across the greasy formica toward Steve, who shook his head.

"I've got a moral code or something," Steve said.

"Sick." Pike lit the cigaret and blew the smoke away disgustedly. "No, young. Yeah, that's it—young. What in God's name do you think sex has got to do with morals, Steve? Does eating have to do with morals? Does breathing? Crapping?"

"Is that the level you put sex on, Pike?"

"My name is Jimmy, God damn it!" Tears came in the blue eyes and Steve stood up.

"Jimmy, why not forget reasons?" He crumpled the paper that had wrapped his hamburger, crumpled it into a tight ball in a hard fist.

"Because I don't know the reasons—that's why."

"They don't matter." Steve tossed the paper into a wire basket in the corner. Pike got up.

"They matter if you hate me."

"I don't hate you," Steve said patiently. He stepped out into the river of people on their way to lunch, coming back from lunch to work. Pike followed him.

"If you don't hate me, then why did you run, take off, not even leave a note? I come home Monday night, the place is empty, your car's gone."

"Because sex is my hangup, Jimmy. Bought me all kinds of nothing. Twice now. Anyway, I'm married, I get enough. Sure, I know it sounds square, but you just don't . . .cheat on somebody who loves you."

"You're sick!" Pike said it loudly this time. They were climbing the steps into library park. Pigeons flew up off the grass. An old wino in a long overcoat was washing his pink false teeth at the drinking fountain. He stared at them.

"Cool it," Steve said to Pike.

Pike whispered angrily, "It's not cheating to have a stud when all you've got is a chick. Man, you're heading for real trouble." He threw away his cigaret and poked Steve's chest. "Inside there." He made a motion at Steve's head and Steve ducked away. "Inside there. Try to be dead when you're alive—you've got real trouble."

"Look, Jimmy, I'm sorry, but this is no good. The way I did it was the only way. I want you. That was why I had to split the scene. It was so great . . ." Steve took a deep breath and blew the air out and stared off at the towering library walls. "Already, in a couple of hours, by the time I had to get up and leave that funky bed of yours and go get Lacey from the theatre . . .I was . . .in love with you. I couldn't stay, Jimmy. She's had enough bad breaks. I couldn't do it to her."

Pike turned pale under the suntan. His mouth dropped open. "In . . .love?"

"You heard me."

"Do you mind?" Pike turned away, sat down on the grass, clutched his knees in his arms, rested his head on his knees. Steve watched him for a minute, sorry as hell for him, sorry for himself too. Then he said gently:

"I've got to get back to work."

Pike raised his head. His back was to Steve. He didn't turn his head. He said, "Wait a minute. Sit down."

Steve stepped onto the grass beside him but didn't sit. Pike looked up, working at a smile. It was a pretty sad smile. "Do you know, I never expected anybody, I mean anybody I wanted, to say that to me. Not and mean it."

"I mean it," Steve said.

With two quick motions Pike was on his feet, gripping Steve's arms. "And so you ran away?"

"I should have changed jobs, too. The only answer is for us to stay away from each other, Jimmy. We'll both get over it."

33

"What have you got," Jimmy cried, "a strong character?"

"No. Weak. That's why I cut out."

Jimmy went on as if he hadn't heard. "Because I haven't. That's why I'm here. I can't stand it without you, Steve. You were right. One time wasn't enough. I've got to have you . . . like, forever."

"Ah, Jimmy . . . there are other boys."

"Not like you, Steve. Sure, trade, hustlers, faggots. Freaks, morons. The really bright ones will laugh at a dirty joke if you explain to them. All crotch and no brain. That's not what I'm talking about. You better believe me."

"I believe you," Steve said gently. "I understand. And, I guess, thanks. Sure, thanks."

"Oh, Christ!" Pike let go of Steve's arms.

"But it's too late for me, Jimmy. I'm committed. So forget me, huh? It's no good. I know it hurts, hurts me too. But we'll get over it."

Pike looked into Steve's eyes. Then he looked down at the grass. Then he looked up again. He opened his mouth to say something, then shut it without saying anything. He looked down at his sandals, dug with them at a dandelion in the grass, chopped at it with the heavy sole, stubbed the yellow button off its stem, ground it down systematically until it was a hurt smear. He looked at Steve's face once more, hopeless, big-eyed.

Steve turned and walked away from him.

The apartment they had found was above a set of shops in a blue stucco building on Fairfax Avenue. It was built around a courtyard where a big olive tree sheltered rusty wrought-iron furniture. Both shops that faced the street were rented—one by a bookseller, the other by a maker of sandals. The shops that faced the courtyard were empty, windows dusty, flyspecked FOR RENT signs curling in them. All but one. The sign on this one read BERNICE KATZMAN PHOTOGRAPHER. She owned the building.

When Steve came through the rusty iron gate now, she was trying to unlock the door to her shop, awkward with bags of groceries in both arms.

"Can I help, Mrs. Katzman?"

"Thanks." She handed him the bags, a short, stocky woman nearing forty, who wore rough woven skirts and big Navajo jewelry. She keyed the latch, pushed the door open. "The name will be Bernie to you. That *Mrs.* is strictly residual. I've been single

34

for twelve years, *Mr.* Archer."

"Steve," he grinned. "There you go."

She took the bags from him. "Thanks. How goes the play?"

"I keep hitting it back," he said.

"May the best man win," she laughed and went inside. But before he reached the top of the stairs she was out her door again and calling up to him. "Oh, Steve, I'm sorry. May I ask a favor?"

"Sure thing." He came back down.

"I had a sitting this afternoon." She glanced into the shop. "And apparently I overloaded the circuits again. When I'm working I forget the wiring in this old building just isn't up to six flood-lamps. Would you put in a fuse for me?"

"Pleasure," he said. "Where's the box?"

She led him through the studio, her living quarters at the back, into the kitchen where she handed him a fresh fuse from a drawer, a ring of keys, and took down from a hook by the back door a big, glistening, three cell flashlight. She pushed open the back screen and he stepped out. She pointed along the driveway.

"At the end of the building you turn right and you'll see stairs leading down. There's a little cellar." She laughed apologetically. "You probably think I'm crazy asking you when I could do it myself—perfectly able-bodied woman. But the fact is, I'm terrified. Once when I was down there, there was this enormous rat. . . ."

"Forget it," he grinned, and went and put in the fuse.

He climbed the steps again, then walked along the gallery, and when he opened the door to the apartment, Lacey was all over him before he could even speak. She was trembling and hot, and stuck kisses to his face, eyes and mouth as if she couldn't aim. "Steve, Steve . . ." Her little hands worked frantically at his belt. "Oh, darling Steve, oh, darling . . ." And she was kneeling in front of him, hugging his legs, face pressed against them, crying his name softly, muffledly, again and again. Startled, dumb, he stroked her cropped hair, looking down on her puzzled but all the same responding to the warm, enclosing softness of her mouth. "Hey, hey, hey, baby, Lacey . . ." He tried to bend and stop her, but her grip on his butt only tightened and she shrugged his hands away and went on, rough and determined, with her love-making, hurting him but he was too much on fire to want her

35

to stop . . . until he gasped and spurted hot and sudden and bright, so that he felt his eyes roll up and he shut them and fell back panting, hands splayed against the wall, dry laughter gasping from his throat. "Hey, hey, hey . . ." "Ah, Steve, I love you, I love you, Steve." And she was sitting back on her heels and looking up at him and crying, and he let himself slide down against the wall till he sat on the floor and gathered her into his arms and held her, while the world went slowly dark outside.

When the world was light and Lacey was in the little kitchen and he could hear bacon frying and smell coffee, he rolled over onto his stomach and lazily let an arm dangle from the edge of the bed next to the wall. His hand touched something. He looked down.

A Gauloise package.

He blinked. As if it was detached, somebody else's, his hand picked up the pack and shook it delicately. It still held cigarets. He rolled onto his back and held the pack at arm's length above him, staring up at it the way a baby studies a rattle.

Lacey came in with his cup of coffee. He watched her set it down. Then their eyes met. Then she saw the blue package and her eyes widened and she looked at him again. He propped himself up on one elbow, sun through the tin venetian blinds laying strips of warmth across his naked shoulders. He laid the pack on the sheet and gave it a little tap, nudging it toward her.

"Pike's," he said.

She swallowed. "He came here," she said faintly.

"Did he do it to you? Is that why you acted like you did when I came home?"

"No, Steve, no."

"Then why didn't you tell me he'd been here?"

"Well, I was scared you'd be bugged, and you *are* bugged, Steve, and he didn't. He just . . ."

Steve threw back the sheet. He knew she would cringe, scared because she was lying. He didn't want to see her cringe and he didn't look at her when he stood up. He didn't look at her while he dressed.

"Steve?"

But he didn't want to talk to her either. She was lying. The pack was there on the floor on the wall side of the bed, and the way she'd acted when he came home was exactly as Lacey would act if she'd let Pike do it to her—the only kind of apology she'd be able to think of, if you could call what Lacey did in her head thinking. And, of course, coming here and doing it to Lacey was exactly what Pike would do—what nobody, including Pike himself, would have predicted. And Lacey could no more have prevented him than she could prevent Steve's mother, that time, from learning from her where Steve worked. She was weak.

He left her crying.

Salt whitened the glass of the phone booth beside the hamburger stand on the corner half a block from Pike's. Steve dropped a dime into the phone and dialed Pike's number. When he heard Pike pick up the phone, he said:

"I'm up at the carousel. I guess I have to talk to you."

"Is this Steve?"

"Who else? Listen, Jimmy—walk. Don't drive it, walk it. I want a little more time to think."

"Why don't you come here?"

"That goddam bed is too close there," Steve said. "Maybe, after we talk . . . Look, come on, Jimmy. Only walk, huh?"

Pike didn't answer right away. At last he said, "Okay, I'll walk. Only it'll probably be more like a run, because I need you, Steve. Christ, I need you!"

"Yeah," Steve said. "I'll be here."

He hung up and turned and looked through the misty glass along the street. After a minute Pike's door opened and he came out. He didn't shut the door, he didn't look back. He walked quickly to the end of the block and turned toward the beach. He would walk to the pier along the sand.

Steve yanked open the phone booth door and ran down the street to Pike's place. After the glare of the sun outside, he had to stand still a minute, panting, sweating, in the big room that smelled of turpentine and sour red wine and Turkish tobacco, until his eyes got used to the dimness. Then he went for the chest in the back corner.

He found what he wanted. The blowtorch. He had watched Pike use it. He and Lacey had been down here maybe four or five evenings while Pike welded sculptures together. Pike had explained about the torch. There were two nozzles. Steve chose the one with the fiercest flame, the hoarsest roar, the one that cut hottest and fastest. Hands shaking, he attached it to the gun. He draped the hose around his shoulders, jammed the torch into his waist band, and picked up the twin tanks of acetylene and oxygen and lugged them through the doorway into the garage, where Pike's silver-gray Jag stood proud and gleaming.

He set down the tanks, unwrapped himself from the hose, took the torch in his hand. He was scared of lighting the gas, but he knew how it was done and he did it. Then he put on the mask and gloves and adjusted the nozzle of the blowtorch to where the flame was long and intense, and he turned the flame on Pike's car, grinning till the muscles of his face ached, grinning as the flame bit into the perfect sleekness, melting the enamel, blackening and rainbowing the metal underneath.

When the first jagged slab, hacked from the left-hand door, slipped loose and gonged rocking at his feet, he laughed aloud. But he didn't pause. He had only thirty minutes at the outside till Pike figured he'd been tricked and came back. Steve went to work on the left front fender. Next came the hood, then the right front fender, then the right door. Finally he climbed up and knelt on the roof, laughing as the flame chewed. . . .

When it was all done, he killed the torch flame, dropping torch and hose, threw off the mask. Piece by piece, he half dragged, half carried the big torn chunks of metal out to the rusty back yard. The last slab stacked against the fence, he went back and stood looking for a minute at the raw, scarred, stinking skeleton that had been Pike's beloved Jag. Then he shut the door on it and left.

5

I N THE QUIET NIGHT BOOKSHOP, Ross Wheatley closed the manuscript and pushed it across the desk toward Steve. He took off his black-framed glasses and tucked them into his jacket pocket. He was a small, neat man, with receding gray hair. That he didn't always hear well gave him a worried, pained look much of the time. Now he smiled.

"It's fine," he said. "Messrs. Albee, Williams, Miller and Inge had better duck. Also Mr. Baldwin. Somebody large is coming."

"Thanks," Steve grinned.

"A friend of mine teaches Drama at Central College."

"You mentioned him. Name of Shepherd."

"Yes." Wheatley's worried look returned. "I hope it was all right—I gave him your play to read."

"Great," Steve said.

"That's his opinion of it." Wheatley leaned back in his leather swivel chair and locked his hands behind his head. "He'd like to talk it over with you. He teaches evenings. If you'd care to, when I close up here, we'll swing by the campus and pick him up and all go to the house for a drink or two and what I expect you'll find a profitable conversation."

"Thanks," Steve said. "I'd like that."

He had been afraid of coming back here after giving Wheatley the play to read a week ago. He liked the bookseller and thought Wheatley liked him, and he didn't want that to change. The man had become important to him. So had the shop which, like its owner, was compact and tidy—carefully chosen books straight on the dark, varnished shelves and tables, good prints against the cream-colored walls, comfortable chairs in the corners, lit by handsome lamps.

When he wasn't talking with Wheatley—when other customers interfered or the bookseller had letters to write or bills to figure—Steve had spent hours in those chairs, reading. The shop was a refuge. It was cool while the apartment upstairs was sweltering. It was quiet, with only the whisper of baroque or chamber or symphony music from an fm radio while upstairs Lacey ran the stations with the forty top tunes, ran them loud while he tried to write. It was orderly and clean, while Lacey let the dishes stack up in the sink, the stove go greasy, the bed unmade, herself go day after day in the same soiled, rumpled shift.

When he couldn't stand any more of it, he came down here. It was no answer. But Pike, the memory of Pike, got in the way of any answer. His lean, gold-skinned presence refused to fade. It was always between them. If she acted scared of him it was because she was thinking about Pike. If she sulked and glowered at him and banged the plate of canned hash down on the table in front of him, it was because she resented what he'd done to Pike. If she was hot and wanting with him, it was because she imagined in the dark that she was grappling to her Pike's blond nakedness. His mother had been right. She'd never been able to snag a white boyfriend. Now, regardless of the bizarre reason, she'd found she could make it with a white boy and was sorry she'd settled for a Negro.

"Lacey, when are you going to take this stuff to the laundromat? I've got to have clean clothes to wear to work."

"Steve, I don't like to go there. They look at me funny. They whisper."

"What do you mean, whisper? Whisper what?"

"Oh, you know . . ." Tears in her eyes.

"I don't know. What?"

"*Schwartzer.*" It was a Jewish neighborhood. They meant Negro. " 'She's married to a *schwartzer.*' "

If she was married to Pike, they wouldn't whisper. At first he'd had nightmares of guilt about the blowtorch and the Jag. Now he brooded grimly for hours in the shadows of the green steel stacks of the library, wheeling his truck, shelving books, on what more terrible thing he could have done to Pike. And he decided there was nothing. You poke holes in what I love, I poke holes in what you love. That was the the best he could manage. Except to kill. But you couldn't kill the memory of a man you had got hung up on and who had betrayed you and was your wife's hang-up as a result. A memory had to fade. *Fade, Pike,* he chanted fiercely in his mind, *fade, man, fade. . . .* But Pike obeyed the incantation only when Steve was either deeply immersed in writing his play, or when he was down here in Ross Wheatley's bookshop.

Yet Wheatley's apartment, high in the brush-covered mountains above Mulholland Drive, constrained him. It exaggerated the bookshop's orderliness and taste. It went too far. It was sterile—handsome but sterile, aseptic. White walls, slate blue curtains, carpeting the color of terra cotta, cream naugahide upholstery—all were perfect, as in a color photograph for a department store ad.

He sat stiffly in the handsome Danish chair, clutching a stubby crystal glass filled with expensive bourbon over ice cubes, and sweated with uneasiness. Why? Of course—it was like the houses he had grown up in, showcases, declarations to the world that Negroes too could be hygienic—tasteful, smart, expensive as whites. But prompted by conviction? No—defensive, apologetic. But what had Wheatley to defend against? He didn't have to apologize for being the wrong color. What did he have to apologize for?

Steve glanced at him and saw that the bookseller was looking at him. Then he realized that Bob Shepherd had stopped leafing over the playscript in his lap and had raised his big, handsome head and was talking to him, Steve. His voice was rumbling, musical, masculine. His grin showed large white teeth, strong and even.

"You're pretty savage with the Doctor character here," he said. "Your father? You must admire him very much."

Steve didn't return his grin. "Analysis time, is it? Maybe I'd better lie down on the couch?"

Shepherd's face sobered. "Sorry. Just a thought that struck me, that's all."

Steve shook his head. "Don't patronize me, man."

Shepherd looked unhappily at Wheatley.

"Now, Steve, I'm sure you don't think I brought you here to be patronized."

"Look," Shepherd interrupted. "I want to do your play at L.A. Central. We've already done *Take a Giant Step, Purley Victorious, Raisin in the Sun . . .*"

"And there aren't that many black plays and you've got a lot of black students," Steve finished for him. Afro-American U.—that was what they called L.A. Central.

"We can do white plays," Shepherd said defensively. "We could do only white plays. With Negro casts. What's the matter, Archer?"

"Steve," Steve said.

"What have I done to make you so angry?"

"I'm an angry young man," Steve said flatly, and drank from his glass.

"Well, suppose I put it this way," Shepherd sighed. "Your play is good. If you were as white as the moon, I'd still want to do it. May I?"

"Why not?" Steve shrugged indifferently.

"Oh, really, Steve!" Wheatley's laugh was a small, irritable explosion. "You're being over-sensitive."

"Over-sensitive?" Steve stood up. "What's that? Can you define it? Under-sensitive I can define fine." He swung his stare to Shepherd. "It cuts and kills. But how there could be in this world over-sensitivity, too much sensitivity—that I don't see. If somebody's got it someplace, they've got the most precious thing there is. I hope I can find them pretty soon."

He turned away from them, walked to the big floor-to-ceiling window that looked down past dark, shaggy eucalypts to the broad stretch of twinkling lights that carpeted the San Fernando valley.

Shepherd cleared his throat. "I think I understand you, Steve." Reflected in the dark plateglass, Steve saw him rise, walk toward him, stop two paces away. "I blundered and I'm sorry. Write it down to the teaching habit, occupational hazard. But believe me, it wasn't prompted by your color. And you're very wrong—I'm sure you know this—to equate insensitivity with whiteness. Now, if we're going to get along, work together, do this play—and I very much want to do it—I'd suggest you give me the benefit of the doubt."

"Because it's to our mutual advantage?" Steve asked harshly.

"Really, Steve," Wheatley said again.

Shepherd cut in, voice heavy and driving now, "Steve, there's a difference between healthy sensitivity and the painfulness of a bruise."

"You mean I'm black and blue all over?" Steve asked. But he couldn't sulk any longer. Hell, what did he want? The man had apologized and his excuse made sense. He wasn't hostile. That was all he'd wanted to be sure of. He turned and held out his hand. "Okay. I apologize."

Shepherd's handshake was bone-crushing. "Forget it." He put an arm over Steve's shoulders and steered him back toward the center of the room. "What do you say we take a page by page look at the script, now?"

Hours later, as Steve followed Wheatley down the dark, steep driveway to the carport under the apartment building, his head buzzed—with the good whiskey and with Shep's exciting talk of sets and lighting and blocking for his play. The warm night was rich with the sharp perfume of sage. Steve folded himself angularly into the bookseller's Austin-Healey, puzzled that the drama teacher wasn't with them. The little motor spluttered into life. They nosed out and up the drive. They would pick Shep up now, Steve thought. Instead they swung into the road and past the apartment. For a bright yellow second Steve saw through a small window Shep under the shower, eyes shut, face turned up, head and shoulders only. Then they were racing through the darkness down the curving road toward Cahuenga pass. Steve looked sharply at Wheatley's profile.

"Hey, does Shep live with you?"

Wheatley answered stiffly, "We share the apartment. Bookselling isn't especially lucrative, Steve, and neither is teaching. This way, we manage to live quite well, don't you think."

"It's a beautiful place." Steve let himself slide down on the seat, closed his eyes and pretended to sleep. He understood now the impersonality of the apartment: correctness, perfect middle-class respectability. A cover-up. *See how normal flits can be, just like the Joneses.* His parents all over again. He shivered.

"Cold?" Wheatley rolled up his window.

"Thanks," Steve said.

When he pushed the gate open, light was streaming into the patio from Bernie Katzman's studio. Music came out too—the Bartok concert for orchestra. Steve glanced through the window. Lacey was there. She looked like somebody else. Bernie had posed her in a chair and arranged a white lace *mantilla* so it framed her face and fell over her shoulders and covered the shabby shift. Her little hands lay relaxed, palms up, in her lap. Small spotlights shone down on her and made shadows and highlights where shadows and highlights should be so that Lacey could look beautiful.

Steve stepped through the open doorway.

Lacey saw him but she didn't change her expression, which was pensive and wistful and innocent. Bernie didn't see or hear him. She was intent on the camera. Steve kept still where he was until the shutter made its buzz and click.

Then he said, "Hi."

"Why, hi, Steve," Bernie said. "This little wife of yours has bones, did you know that—beautiful bones?"

"Sure," Steve said, "beautiful everything." He tried a smile on Lacey but she didn't respond. She unwrapped the *mantilla.*

"Guess I have to go," she told Bernie.

"Oh, stay till the record's over." Bernie turned to Steve. She was without her customary thick lipstick now, her dark hair was rumpled, there was excitement, exhilaration in the way she moved, in the loudness of her voice. Her square, handsome face was flushed. "You'll have a nightcap, won't you, Steve?"

The drive home, the half-sleep he'd managed, had lost him some of the buzz he'd acquired at Wheatley's. "Okay," he said, "thanks." And to her inquiring eyebrows, "Bourbon, on the rocks."

"Ah, you manly brute, you!" She gave him a broad wink. "We ladies have been drinking grasshoppers."

"It figures." Lacey's choice. Bernie was a Scotch drinker. He'd glimpsed empties of White Horse in her trash barrels. And Lacey loved candied drinks. Bernie went out and he said to Lacey, "They're going to do my play at L.A. Central."

"That's nice," she said. "Where have you been?"

"Up at Wheatley's house. Friend of his is the drama man at Central. We went over the script."

"It was nice of you to tell me where you were going. Have you got a cigaret?"

He tossed her the pack. "I didn't think you gave a damn where I was as long as I was someplace else."

She lit the cigaret and gave him a stare for an answer. Bernie came in with a tray that had on it two spindly little glasses filled with green foam and a squat amber-filled glass for Steve. Bartok went on making invisible geometry in the warm air. Out on Fairfax cars passed with the swish of tires. Far off a siren cried. . . .

"You hate that kind of music," Steve said to Lacey's back as they climbed the steps to the apartment.

"I never heard that one," Lacey said. "I like it."

The apartment was dark. That meant she had come out before sunset, been down thee with Bernie all evening, since right after he'd gone to the bookshop. She turned to him in the dark, took his arms and put them around her and gave him a kiss that tasted of mint, of grasshopper.

"Steve?" she begged in the smallest of little-girl voices, and began to unbutton his shirt.

He thought, *Dear God! Bernie, too? Not Bernie too?* And then, because he didn't know anything else to do for this particular kind of pain, he began to laugh.

6

H E SLUMPED LOW on a seat in the front row of the dark, empty auditorium and stared up into the white glare of the stage. At its center stood a table with legs of sleek metal tubing. Seated at it, back to the auditorium, was Bob Shepherd, coat off, collar loosened, pencil hovering over the script open before him. Downstage crouched Murray Fine, the student director, bony, stoop-shouldered, bearded. Upstage, facing them, a dozen Negro boys and girls stood, sat on chairs, sat on the floor, scripts in their hands.

They read. Fine interrupted them sometimes, sometimes Shepherd, sometimes their two voices together, Fine's cracked and highpitched, Shepherd's rumbling, so that they sounded like a duet from *Wozzek*. The actors without lines in this scene tended to punch each other surreptitiously, to scuffle, whisper, giggle. Two of them necked. Steve paid them no attention. His attention was on the words—read, misread, it made little difference.

He was filled with wonder. These same words he had fought out at the portable typewriter in his room at home, in the apartment next to Hoxie's, the place at Pike's, the hot rooms above Wheatley's bookstore—silent words, words on paper, strings of black marks. Now voices banged them naked off the clean new walls of this public place, brought them to life, and the true, forgotten speakers with them, his father, his mother, his grandma, and yes, himself—somebody else up there on the stage, Carlo White, a boy younger, smaller than himself, big-eyed, and with a voice like melting chocolate. . . .

"Time," Shepherd said. "Twenty minutes."

Dazed, Steve pushed himself slowly to his feet, stretched, and turned to look at the clock face, dim at the back of the auditorium. 8:20. They had started at seven, would break up at ten. Fine huddled with Shepherd at the table. Steve waited, watching, until Shep stood up and with the student director began pacing around among the actors' chairs, arguing, blocking out action. They were absorbed and might not even take a break. He wanted a cigaret and coffee. He trailed up the aisle.

The coffee he bought was scalding. He carried it cautiously, edging between bodies, heading across the broad, noisy room toward the patio. Almost nobody sat out there at night. He, Shep, Fine and sometimes a few of the cast favored a table in a far corner, a big plank table from which each night they had to brush the curled, brown, fallen leaves of an overhanging live oak. The doors to the patio were glass. Through them he saw Carlo White at the table, laughing, a girl on each side, his arms around both of them. Then somebody stood between Steve and the doors. His eyes refocused. Smith Tyler grinned and held out his hand.

"Steve Archer. Hi."

"My Christ. Hi, Smith."

He shook the hand. Then they stood, awkward, tongue-tied, smiling stupidly into each other's eyes, while students pushed and crowded past them. Somebody jogged Steve's elbow. The hot coffee sloshed on his hand. He hardly felt it. He was back in the funky little bedroom at Smith's mother's house, the little kids yapping and squalling outside in the dirt yard, the tattered shade down, schoolbooks and clothes dumped on the dusty, paintless floor, himself naked, clasping the smooth, hot, slender nakedness of this *cafe-au-lait* boy, tongue seeking deep in the sweet mouth, both of them trembling on the bed, scared of being caught, even with the chair propped under the knob of the rickety door. . . . He shook his head, moistened his lips. Los Angeles was a big town. He hadn't expected ever to meet Smith Tyler again. . . .

"What?"

"I said, what you doin' here?"

"I wrote a play," Steve said. "Drama department's doing it. You going to school here?"

"Nights. Days I'm a clerk—records department. If you want any grades faked up, just let me know." Smith frowned. "Hey, I thought you were going to Stanford. When your old man—your father—broke us up that time, he said—"

Steve grimaced. "Later he said something else. I knocked up a chick. I'm married, Smith. How about that?"

"Yeah, how about that?" Smith repeated it mechanically, but the light went out of his eyes. Then it came back, and a smile came with it. "Hi, baby."

A white boy came up. The sun had silvered his hair on top. His skin was the color of clover honey. A child's face, pretty, unmarked. He was small but perfect—except for his hands, that were too big—square, strong, yes ugly, though scrubbed very clean. "Hi." His blue eyes took in Steve, head to foot. "Who's this?"

"Steve. Old buddy of mine," Smith said.

"Oh?" Then the smotth face flushed a little and impudence came into the smile. "Oh! *That* Steve." He held out his hand. Steve took it. As he'd expected, the grip was strong. "I'm Coy Randol," the boy said. "Smith's told me about you."

Smith bragged, "We've been together eight weeks."

"Great," Steve said. "What are you drinking?"

"Gin," the blond boy said, "But not here. Here we drink coffee." He looked at Smith.

"I'll fetch it," Smith walked off.

Steve turned toward the nearest long table. The blond boy followed him. "I can only stay a minute," he said. "I'm from across the street—Galilee College. I just duck out at break time to see Smith."

"That's a religious school," Steve said.

"I can't help it. I still go there."

They sat on the bench. The table was crowded and their legs touched. The table top was gray formica stained with coffee rings, mustard, grease. Somebody had left a crumpled paper napkin. Steve used it to wipe the place in front of them.

"A minister in my home town sends me."

Steve grinned into his cup. "Sends you? Crazy, man!" He drank.

"Pays my tuition," the blond boy said, "you know."

"I know." Steve watched his own hands as he lit a cigaret. "But I don't know why."

"Doesn't know I'm gay."

"You said it." Steve stared across the room. "I didn't. Does he know you drink gin?"

"No. Why don't you look at me when you talk to me?"

Steve glanced at him and quickly away again. Inside his head he said: *Because I want to take the clothes off you right here and eat you alive.* He said, "I'm shy."

The blond boy laughed. Smith came with the coffee and they sat and drank and smoked and talked. Coy Randol talked. About the little orchard town he came from, about how this minister had found him when the kid was only six, how he had been a boy preacher at revival meetings all over the Imperial Valley and once at Aimee's temple in L.A. Many times he'd been on radio stations with call letters full of X's, and on tiny TV stations that had only evangelists and amateur country music groups. The minister had decided the kid would make another Billy Graham if he had an education. So here he was in Los Angeles at Galilee College.

"And study?" Smith said. "This boy a studyin' fool."

"It took me a long time to get there. My career . . ." he made a face " . . . held me back. Have to make the most of it now. I'm already twenty-two."

"You're kidding," Steve said. "Look, I have to split." He got up. "Good running into you, Smith," he told the coffee-colored boy, who was staring at his crotch, "Good meeting you," to the blond boy, who was not.

"Later," Smith said faintly.

"Yeah," Steve said, "later."

He crossed the parking lot that was dark and empty. This was usual. It was past eleven. The play was three weeks into rehearsal now. They kept staying later, working harder, repeating, changing, building. What had started out as three acts was now two with only a single intermission. Tonight he and Shep and Fine had stayed alone, planning cuts because the play was still timing out too long. He was tired. He tossed the ragged script onto the seat, got behind the wheel, slammed the car door and turned the ignition key. The engine wouldn't start. This wasn't too much of a surprise. The car was twelve years old. He tried the key again. Starter noise but no action.

"Shit!"

He pushbuttoned the glove compartment. Blue Chip stamps showered out. It was where Lacey stored them. She always asked for them, planned to get a TV, planned to get sheets—but she never pasted them into books. They got as far as the glove compartment and there they stayed. Steve found the flashlight, a black, rubber-coated two-cell job like a robot's erection. He got out of the car, opened the hood and shone the light on the motor. It failed to show him anything. He knew nothing about cars anyway, so what the hell did he expect to see? He slammed the hood, turned, and saw, far off across the lot, the headlights of a car swinging in at the entrance. The car bore toward him, the lights holding him in their glare. He blinked. The car veered and halted—Shep's Sunbeam.

"Something wrong?"

Steve stared. "Yeah. How'd you know?" The faculty parking lot was on the other side of the campus.

Shep clambered out. It was a ridiculously small car for such a big man. When he drove it, he wore a little flat leather cap on his theatrical hair. "I didn't know," he said. "I just realized I'd forgotten my clip-board, all my notes. I swung in here and saw you."

"It's a frigging miracle," Steve said. "Can you drive me home? Buses don't run too often this time of night. If you give me your key, I'll trot over and get the clip-board for you. Is it on the table on stage?"

"We'll walk over together. Then I'll drive you home."

Shep put an arm over Steve's shoulders and steered him back across the lot. The gesture didn't bother Steve. With Shep it was habitual. He stood six five. Steve at five eleven was like a kid to him. It wasn't uncomfortable to walk this way. Shep used the gesture all the time. If he sat next to an actor puzzled over a speech, around the shoulders went Shep's big, comforting arm. You expected it of him, the way you expected the rumble of his voice.

It didn't rumble now. They walked wordlessly along the deserted campus paths where the lamplight made romantic circles on the lawns, cast romantic shadows from the towering old acacia trees. Shep keyed the stage door, found the lightswitch inside. Beyond the tall straight falls of wing curtains the bare stage glared. Steve went and fetched the clip-board. Shep turned out the light. Then, instead of hitting the noisy crossbar that would unlatch the stage door and let them out, he took Steve in his arms and kissed him. Steve was surprised and let it happen for a minute before he turned his face away.

"What did you do to my car?" he asked.

Shep's hands slid down his back, gripped his butt. "Loosened the distributor head," he said softly. "It's a basic trick, easy. . . ." One hand slid around front, began gently kneading. "Steve, I just can't go on resisting. Being with you all the time. . . . I'm only human, as the grade B films say."

"So am I." Steve's voice wobbled. "Look, Shep, it's wrong. I've got Lacey, you've got Ross." He grabbed Shep's wrist. "What we've got isn't what makes problems." Shep pulled Steve tight against him. He was very powerful. His heart was banging hard. "It's what we haven't got." His mouth closed over Steve's again, hungrily, tongue probing deep.

It was no good struggling. He was outclassed. He let himself go limp instead, just hanging there indifferent for a minute, until Shep got the message, pulled his mouth away, loosed his grip. The backstage blackness was total. He couldn't see Shep's face and that was probably a good thing.

"I'm sorry," he said gently. "Come on. Show me how to tighten a loose distributor head."

And he pushed open the door.

Three boys with shaggy hair and tight little suits and highbutton shoes, of all things, sang and beat plastic guitars and glittering drums on a tall corner platform in a room dim with weak colored spotlights and cigaret smoke. The place was called The Bug You. It was in a store building on Cherokee Avenue near Hollywood Boulevard and it was for underage kids and served only soft drinks. Except that vodka sometimes got into 7-Up bottles and whisky into Cokes. You could also get pot there. And snort. And smack.

Steve stood just inside the front door, wincing at the racket, peering around. The place was jammed and jumping. The kids were very young and pathetically square. He couldn't figure Carlo White, with an I.Q. of 180, liking these joints. But as the police closed them and new ones opened, Carlo went from one to the next. Never a night at home. He was here in a back corner, mouth glued to that of a little plump girl in a blond beehive wig that was coming apart. As Steve came up, she was struggling a little but not meaning it. Steve sat down. He reached across the little table and tugged Carlo's shoulder and Carlo turned, sore, popping his eyes. Then his expression softened into a grin.

"Steve, baby!" he said. He stopped smiling. "What's the matter? You look like Charley Funeral Director. What you doing here? Thought you hated these little hells."

"I couldn't find Fine," Steve said, "and something's happened." He had to yell to be heard. He looked at the girl. She was sulking. The light above the table was lavender. It turned her green.

51

Where Carlo's kiss had taken off her lipstick, her mouth looked dead. "Can we go somewhere and talk?"

"Aw, man . . ." Carlo looked at the girl. "Listen, I . . ."

"I know," Steve said, getting up. "You've got it made. But you make out every night, Carlo. This is important."

"Okay," Carlo said. He turned to the girl and told her something, easing his hand along her thigh, that was clad in tight, shiny capris. She made a face, but he got up. "Come on," he said to Steve, "five minutes. She's ready, Steve. She doesn't want to wait."

There was a cluster of kids around the door of the place and straggling along the sidewalk, enjoying free of charge the racket of the shag-haired performers through a loudspeaker over the door. Steve led Carlo away from the noise, down the street past the darkened bookshops, radio repair place, the hardware store, to the parking lot that was wide and quiet.

Carlo looked at his watch. "So what's on fire?"

Steve told him what he happened with Shep.

"So did he fix it?"

"He put up the hood as if he'd like to tear it off, and he fixed the thing. But he was bugged as hell, Carlo. I never saw anybody so sore. He wouldn't even look at me. I tried to say something to him, but he wouldn't answer. He just got into his car, slammed the door and tore out of there. Like, I hate to be a fink. So he's gay, that's his business. But when he gets up there tomorrow night and says the whole thing's off and sends everybody home—hell, you and Fine have put so much work and time and hope into this thing—I just wanted you to know I'm sorry. It's my fault and—"

Carlo was staring at him. "You mean he told you he's going to cancel the play because you wouldn't have sex with him?"

"No, he didn't *tell* me that, but . . ."

"No," Carlo said, "exactly. Man, Steve, honey, you really surprise me, sometimes. Sometimes you're such a swinger, and sometimes you act like they've been keeping you in a light-proof, sound-proof box all this time."

"What do you mean?"

"Man . . ." Carlo shook his head and his smile was pained, patient, patronizing. "I read for the part, remember? Twenty cats read for the part. And I got the part. Remember?"

Steve nodded, puzzled.

"Now, I don't want to injure your pride, baby, but do you think you're the only one Shep made passes at?"

"You don't mean the old casting-couch routine?"

"Call it that. He made a pass at me, Steve, and I can't go that route, you know, but I still got the part. Shit, man, he makes passes at a lot of dudes. Now and then he makes out. But he's not going to drop your play because you turned him off, man. Hell, if he only used the boys that lay for him, we'd never put on a play around here." He laughed and punched Steve's shoulder. "Sorry if it hurts your feelings to find out you're not the only cat that ever tempted Bob Shepherd off his pedestal, but you're not, man, that's all."

Steve smiled at him wanly. He had been badly worried, sick with panic. It would take him a while to shake that. "So I'm an idiot," he said.

"Forget it. When you get to be my age, you'll know all the answers." Carlo was two years younger than Steve. He looked at his watch again. "Listen, I've got to get back to Lilly Ann." He turned, lifted his hand, and trotted off up the block toward the blare of folk rock from The Bug You.

Steve stared bleakly after him, thinking: *I'm an idiot, but I'm not the only one, and not the biggest one. Because if Carlo knows this and there are other boys—how many?—who know it too, then sooner or later Shep is going to be in bad trouble. Every time he does this, he lays his whole life, his work, his future, on the line. Some time he'll pick a boy who'll tell on him....*

7

"SO, YOU DID DECIDE to come home, ha?"

The patio was dark. The voice came at him out of the shadow of the olive tree. Bernie. At first he saw only the red coal of her cigaret. She was sitting on the wrought-iron bench. She rose and came toward him, dressed in her white jump suit, a firm, square little ghost.

He said, "When I was a kid, that's how my mother used to greet me. Of course," sarcastically, "with a thick nigger accent." Then angrily, "What the hell do you mean: 'So you did decide to come home, ha?' What is this? Where's Lacey?"

"Lacey is inside, asleep," Bernie said.

"Inside where?"

"My apartment. Anyway, what difference does it make to you? You're gone all day and half the night. You don't give a damn about her."

Steve squinted. "Look, I don't know why the hell I should even be talking to you. Where do you come in? No, wait. I get the message. You *do* give a damn about her—right?"

"She's a scared, pregnant kid," Bernie said. "A young girl, not even a woman yet. All alone up there at night—she doesn't understand your treating her this way."

"I guess she didn't tell you about Pike."

"She told me she was raped, yes."

"You're a big girl, Bernie. Didn't anybody ever tell you? Rape is impossible."

"It's funny," Bernie mused, "how wrong you can be about people. I liked you at first, thought you were a nice kid."

"Maybe I was," Steve said. "What am I now?"

"A little bastard."

"Look, Bernie, I work for a living, remember? And I've got a play rehearsing. I can't be those places and here, too."

"Did you ever once offer to take her to a rehearsal?"

"She wouldn't want to go. She never wanted anything to do with that play. Christ, she's jealous of the goddam play. She makes out with Pike, she makes out with you, but I put words on paper and she's jealous. Of words."

"Makes . . . out . . . with me?" Bernie's tone menaced.

"Oh, come on, Bernie. Did you think you were kidding somebody? What the hell else would you want with her?"

Bernie said, "You're really a very corrupt person, aren't you, Steve? You're really empty." She fumbled a cigaret between her lips. The flame of the butane lighter trembled when she lit it. "Your generation makes me shudder."

"Why?" Steve asked. "Because we look at what's there? We don't soften the focus? We don't add romantic violins to the sound track?"

She stared at him, her face a vague, pale square in the darkness, her mouth a lipsticked slash. She shook her head. "You break my heart," she whispered.

"I don't," he said, "but Lacey will."

"You don't know the first thing about her," Bernie flared. "You don't understand her at all. You're too ego-centered to understand anybody else. It's a male occupational disease."

"Yes? Well, I want to understand her now." He swung off, headed for Bernie's door.

"Where are you going?"

"I think I've got a right to see my wife, don't you?"

"She doesn't want to see you. She's through with you."

"Is she? All right, let her tell me."

He struck the door latch with his fist and walked in. Bernie hurried after him, panting. She'd been drinking. He could smell the Scotch. The studio was dark, and he ran into a floodlight standard that toppled with a crash. He pushed open the door to Bernie's living quarters. On the far side of the sitting room the door was slightly open, beyond it lamplight. He pushed the door wide so that it slammed back against the wall. There was only one bed. Lacey sat up in it and stared at him, frightened, wide-eyed. She was wearing some kind of fluffy pink thing. She looked terribly clean.

"Is what she says true?" he asked.

55

She bit her lip, looked at Bernie for a minute, then looked at him again and nodded. Her voice was small. "It's true, Steve." For a second she was defiant. "She's good to me. She's kind and sweet." But then her mouth trembled and she started crying. "What do you care?" she wailed. "You don't love me any more. You hate me. You never come home, never talk to me. . . ."

Disgusted, he turned to Bernie, who stood in the doorway, white and ravaged looking, but stubborn, her eyes unyielding. "Okay," he said, "okay. You want her, you can have her. Only, there's a baby coming, and that's mine—mine, Bernie, understand? I'll be back for him. Because I'm damned if I'm going to let him be raised by any bull dyke."

She took two short steps toward him and her hand slashed hard across his face. He stumbled back, by reflex touching his cheek. It was wet. He looked at his fingers. Blood. Her ring had cut him. He stared at her and she stared at him. Neither of them said a word. What more was there to say? He pushed past her and walked out of the place and shut the door.

It rained. November was no month for rain in Los Angeles, but it rained. The dry ground soaked it up. Then it wasn't dry anymore and couldn't soak up any more, and still it rained, heavy and warm, and the sound of it was very wet. Steve lay in the dark on the super-springy little bed of the room he'd rented near the campus and listened to the rain. It was late. He should sleep. But he couldn't sleep, hadn't slept more than a few troubled hours since walking out of Bernie's.

He was tired, bone tired from the long days on his feet at the library, long nights of final rehearsals. The play would open this weekend. Carlo had of course been right: Shep had made no such announcement as Steve had feared, was friendly and easy with Steve as if nothing had happened. The banner was up across the front of the auditorium building—THE TRUE FORGOTTEN SPEAKERS—limp and weeping in the rain. On the bulletin boards around the campus and in the streaming windows of the bookshops and cafes across the street the posters had appeared. His title, his name. It was in the papers too. And on the radio. And it was going to be all right. Fine. It was tight, close-coupled, played sharp and fast.

It was a great break. Everything had worked for him. Shep was smart. Murray Fine was smart. They knew what to cut, how to clarify, intensify, tidy his sometimes too sprawling, too cluttered, too blurred scenes. And Carlo was good. So were the other actors. He was lucky. It all had a good feel about it. They were all tense, but with the kind of excitement that isn't anxious but eager. It would be all right, better than all right. He should be happy, laughing at everything, should sack out every night with a grin all over his face.

The reactions at the library had been funny. Before, he'd been just another colored boy pushing a cart of books through the dim stacks. But when he'd brought three posters to work, found tacks in a drawer of the horseshoe-shaped desk in the Department, and put the posters up on the cork bulletin boards, there'd been a change.

Miss Williams, gangly, boyish, striding into the big room, had halted and with head poked forward like a chicken about to attack a scrap of lettuce, had read the poster through her thick lenses. Then, coat draped over her shoulders, big handbag swinging, she'd come to him where he was shelving dramatic criticism.

"Stephen, am I correct? You've written a play?"

"Yes, ma'am."

"Why, that's wonderful. I had no idea we had an incipient Sophocles in our midst."

"I always leave my crown of laurels home," he said.

"You must wear it," she laughed. Then she grew sober, her eyes like blue fish swimming back of her glasses. "Stephen, have you ever thought of Library School? It seems such a waste for a boy of your gifts to be simply paging."

He grinned—now as then. How predictable people were. It was the best thing she could think of to say: You're bright—therefore you ought to become a librarian. Not—you're going to be a famous playwright soon; you won't have to shelve books forty hours a week at a dollar sixty-five an hour. No. Being a famous playwright lay outside the realm of the possible in Miss Williams' world. But, since you were a smart colored boy, you *could* be a librarian.

"That your play? You the Stephen Archer?" Mr. Roebuck asked him, the bald librarian. Cold cat. Steve had made the mistake of smiling and saying good morning to him once. He'd looked away. He never spoke to Steve, even in a business way—just handed him slips with the Dewey numbers of books he wanted, or the names and dates of magazines. He wasn't the department head—

57

Miss Williams was that. But it was he, not Miss Williams, who ate lunch upstairs in the staff cafeteria with the Chief Librarian and his lieutenants. He was going to make the top with politics.

Steve told him, "I'm the one," and moved past.

Roebuck cocked a friendly eyebrow. "You proud or sorry?"

"This is a pretty lengthy conversation, isn't it?" Steve asked him. "Sure you won't be embarrassed explaining to your bigshot friends why you talked all this time with a page, Mr. Roebuck? And a nigger page, at that?"

He walked away happy. The play was doing him good.

"Oooh! Steve, baby, you didn't tell me you wrote no play." It was Bea Jackson, a little impish black girl who was a page in Reference and who also had never given him time before. Everybody liked Bea. How could you help it? Steve could help it. "Honey, Ah'm gonna see that play if Ah don' nevah see no othah." Her diction and grammar were perfect when she talked to whites, her manner demure, correct. "Why, Steve, you gonna be gettin' rich, baby. Bet they makes a movie out of it." She had big eyes with long, soft lashes. She looked up at him through the lashes now, pressing against him, stroking his arm.

"You wanna ride in mah Rolls Royce, chicky," he Jim-Crowed back at her, "the line form on the right. Only I gotta fuck Miss Williams and Mr. Roebuck and evah so many nice white folks first, child. Ah may be just too pooped to get around to any little darkie girls aftah that. . . ."

Yes, he should be happy, laughing at everything, should sack out every night with a grin all over his face. Instead he lay and listened to the rain. It did his crying for him. He couldn't manage it—not after the first night. He just lay and hurt. Now and then, when some memory cut too deep, he would turn with a moan and bury his face in the pillow. Why it should hurt so, he didn't know. Leaving Lacey was the first intelligent thing he'd done since he met her. Bernie's interference was lucky for him, freed him from the burden of his own stupid mistake. He ought to be grateful to her instead of hating the thought of her. He tried.

And, because the memories kept filling his head, he also tried to understand all that had happened, from the very beginning. He supposed it had started because he wanted to show his father he wasn't queer. His father's scorn for him after the Smith Tyler episode had been scalding. Maybe that was Steve's reason for taking up with the skinny white girl on the bus home from Terra

Rosa High. If it was, he hadn't known it then. He'd just let it happen—the going to her folks' empty little slap-up house, afternoon after afternoon, until they were kissing and feeling each other up while they listened to records or looked at TV, and then, finally, one day, hotly making it on that flimsy Sears couch, on the cool, waxed floor, in Lacey's little bed. That would show his father!

But where was the logic of proving something to somebody you wanted to keep it secret from? Wasn't Steve half out of his skull with fear his father would find out? The man's threats weren't idle. Steve knew him well. What he said he would do he would do. Steve grinned painfully in the dark at the illogicality of what he, Steve, had done, and why. Yet, granting anybody could be so perverse, so convoluted, then the next development had to be that he must make a slip, get Lacey pregnant—so that he would have to go and confess to his father. But he'd been extra careful *not* to get her knocked up—hadn't he?

He pawed out at the little nicked bedside stand for cigarets and lit one. And love? What about love? That too he had traced through this last week of sleepless nights. He had felt great want and need of Lacey, maybe only as an echo of her intense need of him. She had been the aggressor all along. Had he maybe been flattered—as his mother had suggested? Yes, probably. But he'd also been an opportunist. When his cock said go, he went—as his father had more than suggested.

But he did feel tender toward Lacey—she was so fragile and so simple. He had got to thinking her pretty too, very soon after they began making it, her wisp of a smile with the neat little white teeth, her body slim as a young child's, and so pale and trembling. . . . But the love, the actual love—that hadn't come, he realized now, until her words that had hit him in the stomach, sunk him, her words that she had his baby inside her.

Why? Because it proved what a stud he was—to his father, to himself? No, he didn't think so, not really. Really, the love that came in a rush at that moment, was for the baby. He felt it even stronger now—a tugging in his chest. He could leave Lacey, but he couldn't leave the baby. He had told Bernie, meaning it, *I'll be back for him*. Him. Yes. It was always in his mind a boy child. That it could be a girl hadn't once occurred to him. He told himself now that, of course, it could be—better than a fifty percent chance, weren't those the statistics? But he didn't believe it.

And what about that? He was queer. That was one thing certain among all those nightmare uncertainties. It was boys he saw, at the library, on the street, on the campus, boys who focused his mind on sex, roused him—never girls. Not even Lacey, until after she'd made him. So what about his want of this boy child? When he was a child himself, a lonely little kid, he had fantasied a child himself, a baby brother. He never came. Was that what all of this was about, this whole mess with Lacey? By the time you're seven years old you are what you will be forever—wasn't that what the books said?

Steve shrugged, grimaced, snuffed out the cigaret and lay back on the bed, his mind tired from working through all of it again. He let his hand stray down his nakedness. *Do it yourself time,* he thought wryly. Maybe it would make him sleep.

8

O N OPENING NIGHT, he stayed backstage, leaning against the
cage of heavy woven wire that enclosed the lighting panel
Inside the cage, Andrew Harbison, head of the Stagecraft Department, gaunt, grayhaired, ran through a last-minute light
rehearsal with his two student assistants. Their copy of the script
was cued with heavy markings in colored pencil. Thumbing it,
they pulled and pushed levers that caused the lights beyond the
canvas flat backs to brighten and grow dim, change color, spot
now this, now that area of the set. Last of all, they lowered from
the high shadows above the ranks of colored lights over the stage,
a big, gleaming metal dome in which a fierce bulb burned, that
would shine down on the surgery table in the last scene. They
raised it again.

In the bleak semi-darkness back of the set, Shep moved large
and dim, conferring with Murray Fine, with Jack Kilroy, the
red-haired stage manager, and with Jean Agajian, the fat, good-
humored costume girl. Up the narrow cement steps from the
dressing rooms drifted the voices of the actors—Carlo White's
rich laughter, the booming bass of the lean, jet-black boy they'd
found to play the Doctor-father role—Ap Griffin. There were
highpitched giggles.

Steve wished he could laugh. He couldn't. He shivered, his
body covered with cold sweat. For the third time in an hour he
went downstairs to the shiny men's washroom to urinate. In the
mirror over the handbasins his face looked strange to him. He felt
as if he was staring into the eyes of a condemned man. Why? Why
the sense of doom? It was ridiculous, but he couldn't shake it. He
told himself he wished he was a thousand miles away. Yet when he
heard movement in the hall outside the door, he panicked, afraid

61

he'd miss the curtain. He left the men's room and took the stairs two at a time.

But backstage all was still preparing. The clock over the lighting panel read 8:25. A few more minutes. Trembling, weak in the knees, he walked onstage and eased the stiff new curtains open a crack. The auditorium lights were still glaring. About two-thirds of the seats were filled. The aisles were crowded. At the head of the aisles, the doors were open and people stood in them, shedding raincoats, waiting for the busy ushers.

In the crowd he saw faces he knew—Ross Wheatley from the bookstore; Miss Williams from the library; Miss Hogan, his journalism teacher at Terra Rosa High, who had given him a lot of encouragement with his writing; Smith Tyler with another Negro flit. Where was the blond boy, Coy Randol? There, away toward the back, hair shining like a renaissance angel's. He looked for Lacey and Bernie. No sign. But there was Jimmy Pike. His mouth twisted in a sour grin.

The grin froze. There were three more faces he knew. His father, his mother, his grandmother. He let go of the curtains and turned away. This he hadn't expected. For a second it stunned him. Then it filled him with rage and despair. What were they doing here? They were supposed to be finished with him. They'd tossed him out, hadn't they? Well, then, why had they come? To share his little glory. *My son, the playwright.* He exploded into savage laughter. Christ, what a shock they were in for! He laughed till it doubled him over, till he had to clutch his middle against the pain of it. He laughed like being sick.

"Steve?" A hand touched his arm. He straightened, gasping, blinking, trying to control the bitter mirth that shook him. He saw Kay Foss, the prompter, a tall girl with long, taffy-colored hair. She looked alarmed. "What's the matter, Steve? Come on. Curtain time." He let her take his hand and lead him into the wings. He was weak from laughter. It made him stumble. But he couldn't stop it. "Steve, what's wrong with you, honey?" she asked, bewilderedly. "Look, I've got to get to my place. Somebody?" She blinked around at the scurrying figures in the half-darkness offstage. "Steve's hysterical."

"Go along," he gasped, pawing at his face, trying to straighten it, to wipe away the tears. "I'll be okay."

"First night nerves, huh?" She smiled uncertainly.

"Yeah, yeah . . ." and he began to laugh again.

"Kay, where the hell are you?" came Shep's voice.

"All set, Mr. Shepherd."

"Curtain!" Shep said.

And in a minute, the grin that had been more like a snarl, twisting Steve's face, left it. His fists, that had been clenched so tightly the nails bit into the palms, relaxed, hung easy at his sides, wise hands, accomplished hands. Inside him sunshine broke. He began to smile, and it was a good smile, warm and like a child's, but better than a child's. He saw with new eyes, heard with new ears his true, forgotten speakers, as if there hadn't been weeks of rehearsals, repetitions, interruptions, cuts, rewrites—as if, instead, horrifying and funny by turns, the play was life itself. From the huge, hollow, rain-damp-woollen darkness beyond the dazzling box that was the stage came the laughter and breathless quiet of the audience—each reaction where he had meant it to come. Sixty minutes later, when the curtain came down, the applause rushed up with the roar of an oilwell fire.

"They're with it, baby!" Carlo grabbed him and hugged him hard. "You've got a smash, lover! Man, I hope they've got movie scouts out there. I'm tired of being black and white. I wanta be Technicolor!" He clattered off down the stairs to change clothes for act two.

Mrs. Hayes Brown, the heavy, whitehaired old woman they'd got for the part of Grandma, told him in her sweet, husky voice, "Young Stephen Archer, you know . . .you've written a beautiful play." She hadn't said word one to him till now. She was forty years a professional—regal, unapproachable. Now her eyes filled with tears. She tugged at his shoulder and, when he bent, gave him a grandmotherly kiss on the cheek.

In the fifteen minutes of this one intermission Steve got kissed a lot—by Rubye Frye, the buxom copper-colored girl who played the Doctor's wife, by Jerri Baumgartner, the cast's one white girl, and by a couple of the boys as well. But not, this time, by Shep.

"It's going great, isn't it?" he asked the big man.

"So far," Shep grudged, peering over his glasses. The script he held was damp with the sweat of his hands. "But I'm afraid of a good first act opening night. Everybody gets overconfident and the rest falls apart."

"Not tonight," Murray Fine grinned. His eyes shone. He scrubbed his beard excitedly. "Tonight everything's good, feels good,

63

smells good, tastes good. Nothing can go wrong with this."

And nothing did. The final half of the play was grimmer than the first. There were fewer laughs. But there was emotion, there was tension. Would they pick up on it? Back against the wire mesh of the lighting panel cage, Steve sweated through the key scene with Grandma, the argument over her son's insistence that she take a shiny new apartment, her stubborn determination to keep her shacky little house. And when Mrs. Hayes Brown, terrible and pathetic in her old woman's anger, thrust Ap Griffin out and slammed the door on him and wept, Steve swallowed gratefully, for from the vast dark that hid the audience he heard the tearful blowing of noses. They were with it still. They grew hushed, expectant, afraid in the last, tense scene, when the black doctor in his snowy surgical gown grimly lectured the white girl, shivering in her slip, as he purposefully drew on rubber gloves, ready to abort her of his son's illegitimate child in order to save his own political career. And when the boy burst in the stop the thing, the relief of the audience swept over the stage like a physical tide. Two heartbeats later, when the curtain came down and the applause roared up even wilder than before, Steve had to stop his mouth with both hands to keep from cheering.

But Carlo cheered. With a whoop, he grabbed Jerri, and in an ecstasy waltzed her around the surgery table in its sinister bore of light, whirling her so her feet never touched the floor. She clung to him and laughed, head flung back, yellow hair flying. Ap, tall and awkward in his surgeon's gown and cap, followed them around, grinning, jigging, pawing at them. It was like a scene from an old Marx Brothers movie.

Shep yelled, "Carlo! Curtain call!"

Mrs. Hayes Brown, Rubye Frye and the others came on smiling from the wings. They formed a ragged line, holding hands. The curtain rose. The applause that it had muffled slammed against them. They bowed and bowed. Kay Foss brushed past Steve. She carried a big bouquet of roses for Jerri, who hugged her when she took them. Tears ran down her face. To make her laugh, Carlo broke a rose off the bunch, clamped it in his teeth and started a flamenco dance. The curtain came down, went up, came down, went up. There was more than clapping now. They were shouting. Someone gave Steve a jolting shove between the shoulder blades.

He swung around, scowling. "Hey, man!"

It was Shep. "Don't you hear them? They're yelling for the author. That's you, you silly flit." He grabbed Steve's shoulders and thrust him onto the stage. The others took hold of him and passed him from hand to hand until he stood in the middle of the apron with the huge darkness roaring at him like an amiable dragon. He nodded at them awkwardly, grinned, swallowed hard, said, "Thank you, thank you, thank you," a few times, and fled offstage, followed by friendly laughter.

The curtain came down, went up again for Shep and Murray to bow, then came down and stayed down.

9

"SHEP SAID,Mother? Stephen Archer."

The woman in the beautiful doorway was tall, gaunt, handsome. Her long face, under the sleekly groomed gray hair, broke into a smile. Intelligence and humor lit her magnificent brown eyes. Her hand was dry and bony but its grim was firm. Steve fell in love with her voice—deep, husky, the speech cultivated.

"Stephen. Your play is splendid. We'll make time to talk about it later.As soon as everyone's here." She deftly passed him back to Shep. "Lead him to the champagne, Bobby." One more fine, warm smile for Steve, then she was greeting Jerri Baumgartner and her parents. Same smile.

The room Shep led him into was handsome as the woman who owned it. Spanish California, thick white walls, low arched windows and doorways, glossy pegged floors, tremendous corner fireplace, adobe style. There were deep, comfortable chairs and couches. On a sideboard waited platters of sliced ham, roast beef, smoked turkey, bowls of creamy dip, mounds of potato- and corn-chips. Big fiberglass tubs of chopped ice held bottled soft drinks. But the champagne wasn't just a figure of speech.

"Was you mother an actress?"

"Long ago." With a nod to the white-jacketed caterer, Shep pulled a bottle from a silver bucket and, wrapping it in a fresh bar towel, unwired the cork. "She married oil, gave birth to little Bobby, and left the stage. But she never really quit acting. Performances daily. Watch her tonight."

"It'll be a pleasure," Steve grinned. "She is something else, man!"

Shep smiled. The cork banged out of the bottle. The neck smoked and sudsed. The caterer handed them chilled glasses. Shep filled them and tilted the bottle back into the ice-rattly bucket. With the rim of his own glass, he touched Steve's.

"To a fine future for a fine playwright."

Steve laughed. "Whoever he may be." He drank, blinking at the bubbles. "Hey, this stuff has got it all over Pepsi Cola."

"We won't tell Joan Crawford," Shep said.

"Naw. Don't want to hurt her feelings."

Jerri and her parents came through the archway and stood looking lost. Shep said, "Excuse me," and strode across the wide room toward them, booming, "Welcome, welcome. . . ."

Steve stood sipping champagne, watching the arrivals. The women mostly climbed the big, sweeping staircase to leave their coats somewhere overhead. Kay Foss came down in a boxy dress of yellow satin with a big orange bow below the breast line, Rubye Frye in flaming cerise with pearls in her hair, Mrs. Hayes Brown in stately black with an antique cameo brooch. There was a spooky little girl in thick glasses with Murray Fine. Steve grinned. Murray was one of those cats who looked naked without a picket sign. Now, in place of that, he flourished a long, slim cigar. Instead of Levis and a sweatshirt, he wore a tight little Madison Avenue suit, strictly wrong with the beard.

The girl Carlo brought was a milk chocolate Easter bunny in a strawberry wig. She looked scared. So did Ap Griffin's tall, black parents, and the parents of the two youngest girls in the cast—shy, uncomfortable, in their Sunday best, as if they'd wandered onto a movie set and didn't know how to get off. But Mrs. Shepherd herded them warmly, graciously, to the buffet, saw that their plates and glasses were filled, and left them smiling. Jean Agajian brought a fat, butter-colored man who smiled all the time and didn't speak much English—an uncle from Iran. Jack Kilroy's much-bragged-about Jesuit brother turned out to look like Raggedy Ann dressed up as a priest.

Naturally, as soon as Carlo and his girl had eaten and tossed off a couple glasses of champagne, Carlo found the sound system. The music came out clean, large and swinging. And before the party was an hour old, the area of sleek floor Mrs. Shepherd had cleared for dancing was crowded with shoulder-shaking, hip-swiveling color.

Watching, Steve felt lonely.

Mrs. Shepherd said, "Let's chat a little, shall we? Bring your glass. Come along."

He followed her upstairs out of the noise. The second floor was low-ceilinged, raftered. The door to the bedroom nearest the stairs stood open. Inside he glimpsed strewn on the canopied poster bed women's coats and handbags. Mrs. Shepherd led him to the far end of the hall. The door was like the others, redwood planks, black handforged iron fittings. It opened on a handsome lamplit sitting room. Quiet. French windows showed a balcony crowded with plants. She drew the curtains over them and dropped into a big beautiful rubbed plush wing chair. She shut her eyes for a moment.

"I'm not the girl I used to be," she said with a small, weary sigh. "Sit down, Stephen. I wanted to get away from the tumult and the shouting for a few minutes. I hope you don't mind."

Steve shook his head and smiled.

"Plus which, I've worn new shoes, and that was foolish." She bent forward and pulled off the shoes—slate blue to match the Grecian style dress she wore, with small buckles of coiled gold like the clips at her shoulders. She rubbed her feet and flashed him a pained smile. "Forgive this touch of informality. They're simply killing me."

"I know what you mean," Steve said.

"I have an old pair of blues. The trouble is, they're not quite the right shade. And they have definitely seen better days. But I simply cannot hobble about in these one moment longer."

She rose and limped across the room, opened a door, clicked a light switch. Sipping from his glass, Steve heard her click the switch rapidly on and off, on and off. "Oh, damn," she said.

"Can I help?" Steve went to her.

It was a dressing room.

"The light bulb's burnt out. And the shoes I want are in that closet, along with several dozen other pairs. I couldn't possibly find them in the dark. Be a dear boy and step outside—"

"And bulb snatch?" Steve suggested.

"No, there's no need to burn your fingers. There's a flashlight. In the linen closet—next door down the hall."

"I'll get it."

It lay on the middle shelf in a fine smell of soap and sachet, a shiny, three-cell torch. He took it to her, she found the shoes she wanted, he returned the flashlight.

After that they sat for fifteen minutes while she talked about the play. She said good things.

"A lot of it was Shep's doing, you know," he said. "He and Murray. I gave them the sow's ear. They came up with the silk purse."

"No. Thank you. I'm very proud of Bobby for this. But he didn't make the play, Stephen. That's not where his talents lie. You made it, and whatever technical improvements you can thank others for, it's your vision that's the finest thing about it. You see very deeply into people. It's astonishing in anyone so young. I only hope . . ." She let her voice trail off, then shook her head in a brisk, regretful way. "No. It's no use saying to you: 'Never give up your insistence upon the truth—if you keep that you'll always do fine work.' It's unrealistic. Not in the world of the theatre. Today."

"I'll try," Steve said.

"Not too hard," she said. "You'll only break your heart."

She had the shoes on now. They returned downstairs. She went to scatter graces among the non-dancers on the sofas and chairs. He stood alone again by the buffet.

"Hello?"

He turned. It was the blond kid, Coy Randol.

"Well, hi," he said. He felt like smiling and he smiled. "Where did you come from?"

"I know this is a cast party and I don't belong here, but I had to tell you how much I liked your play, and I didn't know if I'd ever get another chance."

"No. That's all right," Steve said. "In fact, it's great. I'm glad you came. How about some champagne?"

"Mmmm! Bubbly!" The words came from a big girl with a round, mama-doll face, wide lavender eyes, black balloon wig. Steve hadn't seen her till she spoke. God knew, she was noticeable enough, but he guessed he'd never see much of anybody else when Coy Randol was around. She wore stiff, heavy, purple satin, full of tucks and flounces, stitched too tight at the waist. "I'm Marvel Sweeny. Introduce me, Jess."

The blond boy grinned. "You've already done it, Goof. Steve Archer, Marvel. Our Marv!" He gave her thick middle a squeeze. The girl wore too much powder. It had caked on her lardy shoulders. "My best girl," Coy said.

Beauty and the beast, Steve thought.

"Your play is beautiful," Marvel gushed, "swinging, too much!" She clutched Steve's hand. Hers was like a damp silk pillow. Soiled

69

lace showed at the low-cut neck of her dress.

"Thanks."

Steve looked at the caterer, who produced two glasses and filled them with fizzy yellow liquid. They drank, oohing and ahing and giggling. Like high school girls. Only Marvel was too old for that, wasn't she? Hard to tell. She might be any age from eighteen to thirty-five. He didn't care. He didn't like her. Instant loathing. He was sore at Coy for bringing her.

"Where's Smith?" he asked him.

"Oh, Smith . . ." The boy twisted his perfect mouth. "That didn't work. We split up. Weeks ago."

"Smith was so jealous." Marvel drained her glass and held it out to the caterer again, with a big, painted smile. "I mean—you never saw such green eyes in a black boy."

"Did he have something to be jealous about?"

"Me. Little old me." Marvel's grape-juice eyes closed and opened slowly. "Isn't that silly?"

Across the room Shep was motioning to Steve.

"Ridiculous," he told Marvel. "Excuse me." He walked off. Coy Randol followed him, pulled his sleeve.

"What's wrong? You're bugged."

"What did you bring Barbie Doll for? Why didn't you come by yourself?"

"I'm broke. She paid for the tickets to your play. She's got a car. I haven't. She drove me."

"I don't like her. I like you, but I don't like her."

"You will," Coy said.

"I'm not going to waste time trying."

10

T HE MAN SHEP WANTED STEVE TO MEET was gray—skin, hair, eyes. His name was Babe Blaustein and he was an agent. His clothes were London tailored. Whoever cut his hair did it by appointment and not for two dollars. His shoes were British handmade. He was short. His smile was nice but a little tired, as if it had been used a lot. When he shook hands he timed it just right. His voice was gentle, the accent Broadway.

"It's a good play," he said. "Tough subject. But I'd like to option it. Oh . . . meet Jack Freeman, Jayhawk Productions."

Freeman was tall and bald, with a golden mustache. His skin had a leathery, ship's officer look. He was probably fifty-five or sixty, but he was in good, hard shape, flat-stomached. He wore nubby Scots tweeds.

"We might want to film it." His sea-blue eyes scanned the dancers. "Maybe we'll use the kid. What's his name? Carlo. I don't know, though. His eyes stick out. Don't know if you can photograph him."

"With today's cameras," Blaustein said, "you can photograph anybody. You know who'll want this play?"

"Do you want to eat?" Freeman asked.

Shep smiled at him, gestured. "The buffet's at your disposal, gentlemen."

"Come on, Archer." Blaustein took Steve's elbow and walked. He told Freeman, "Who would want this play is that kid who made *Lilies of the Field* for U.A."

"Ralph Nelson. He's overseas—halfway through shooting that Mitchum thing. Then he's got a deal for Japan."

"In other words," Blaustein said, "*you* want it."

They laughed. Steve wasn't exactly able to follow. He watched the men pick at the slices of roast beef and turkey, touch their glasses without really drinking, dip corn chips into the ravaged bowls and nibble. He listened to their talk and looked puzzledly at Shep but got no answers there. Shep's face was painted neutral.

Freeman was saying harshly, "Controversy you can get in the newspapers. Abortion is nasty. Negro villains are out. Negro heroes knocking up white girls you can't show in the South. In the North either."

"You can win a prize at Berlin or Venice with that kind of courage," Blaustein said.

"Overseas money means you have to shoot your next picture in one of those cockamamie French studios. Worse—Italian. It's not enough trouble trying to produce a picture with people who understand your language?"

"One of those festival prizes behind you, you can pick up business one hundred percent in the States. Five hundred. *Lilies* did. And an Oscar."

"That was before Watts. The riots hurt the subject."

Blaustein winked at Steve. "They don't want to pay your price."

Steve smiled feebly. "What *is* my price?"

"Fifty thousand dollars," Blaustein said.

Freeman laughed. "For a one-shot high school play by some kid nobody ever heard of?" He set down his plate and wrapped Steve in a bear hug, rocking him. "I'm sorry, sweetheart. Please don't hate me. This is business." He let Steve go and peered anxiously into his face. "You all right?"

Steve nodded dumbly. The man wore a great cologne.

Blaustein said, "You want to wait till it's a Broadway smash? Then it'll cost you five hundred grand."

"In that case, maybe *I* want to wait," Steve laughed.

Shep scowled and shook his head.

Blaustein smiled at Steve. "That's all right, kid. Talk up. I'm not kidding about Broadway. It's a cinch. Tomorrow morning I'll phone a few people—Dave Merrick, Fred Coe, Feuer and Martin. They'll be racing each other by jet to catch your show tomorrow night. Martin Gable and Hank Margolis—they'd love this play. Kid, you'll be in the Ethel Barrymore by March."

"It's melodrama," Freeman said. "Corn."

"And the public hates melodrama and corn?" Blaustein asked. "Since when? As far as that goes, since when does Jack Freeman hate melodrama and corn? Since when does Jayhawk Productions hate it?"

"Now, if it was comedy . . ."

"It is comedy. You heard the laughs. It's loaded with comedy. It's human, Jack, deeply human. They laugh, they cry. Like Lorraine Hansberry."

He took from his pocket a flat, red cardboard box, opened it, held it out to Steve. Inside lay spindly, brown cigarets. "Go ahead, try one. John Huston started me on these. Made by a guy named Sherman in New York. Great, natural—like health foods. No lousy chemicals."

Steve took one, so did Freeman and Shep. Blaustein took one for himself, shut the box, slid it away. He lit all the cigarets with a dented Zippo that waved its flame like a flag. Blaustein tossed the lighter proudly in his palm. "Twenty-five years I had this. Best bloody lighter ever made." He dropped it into his pocket and turned to Freeman.

"I can pick up a lot of loot for this kid on television. Come to think of it, that's the only idea. Break it into a series. It's a natural. Problems, drama? The everyday life of a Negro family in this country today—who else has got problems? It can't miss."

"You like sailing?" Freeman asked Steve.

"I never tried it," Steve said.

"How'd you like to come out with me and my wife and kids tomorrow? Sail around Catalina. Stay out a day or two. Nothing like it in this world. You'll love it."

"You let him get you out there," Blaustein warned, "and he'll take your play away from you for the price of a crumby ship's biscuit. Don't go. This play can make a mint for you, Archer. Just let us handle it. Give me a six month option. We can do the Broadway bit, I'm positive of that. Then the television bit. Who needs motion pictures? You'll be so fat they can run the whole space program off your income taxes."

"Dream, dream, dream," Jack Freeman intoned in a flat, raspy baritone, against the unrelenting uproar of the music.

Steve turned to Shep. "Oh, God," he said, "what do I do now?"

Shep put an arm around Blaustein's shoulders. "Babe is one of my oldest friends," he said. "He knows the business end of the theater. That's why I asked him to come see your play. I thought it would be wise to have him handle it, if he was willing. He seems willing." The big man grinned at Freeman. "And since I know Babe and Mr. Freeman are old friends, I don't think I'd take their wrangling too seriously. I suspect you'll end up with a Jayhawk Production."

73

"Come to the office tomorrow morning," Blaustein said. "I'll have an option contract ready for you to sign at eleven o'clock."

"I'm sending a car for him tomorrow morning early," Freeman said. "No, come to think of it, I'll pick him up in person. We're going down to the sea in ships."

Steve didn't hear Blaustein's answer.

He saw his father.

Abel Allen Archer, M.D., stood tall and ominous in the archway on the other side of the broad, noisy room. With him was a short, light-skinned Negro with a pencil-line mustache and an attache case. Mrs. Shepherd stood beside them, looking anxious. His father's eyes met Steve's. He said something to the man with the attache case, and they started across the room. Steve went to meet them, the sense of doom on him again, that he'd felt in the washroom hours ago. He stood in their way.

"What do you want?" It sounded young, feeble.

"Don't speak to me." His father didn't look at him or break his stride. "I have nothing to say to you."

They pushed past, leaving Steve standing with his hands out, mouth open, chest empty. They confronted Shep.

"Robert Shepherd?" The man with the attache case did the talking. "My name is Bixel, D. J. Bixel. I'm an attorney. I represent Dr. Archer here—Stephen Archer's father."

"Steve's father?" Shep smiled. "I'm pleased to meet you." He held out his big hand.

Archer said, "I have no desire to shake hands with you. We have a legal matter to discuss. Shall we discuss it here?" He glanced coldly at Blaustein and Freeman, who were watching, expressionless.

"A legal matter?" Shep gave a small, bewildered laugh. He glanced at his watch. "At this time of night? Here? What kind of a legal matter, for heaven's sake?"

"If you do have an office we could step into," Bixel said, "I think it would be preferable. It's a matter of some privacy."

"Why, I—" Shep shrugged and repeated his small laugh. "Good Lord, all right. My den's down the hall. Babe, Mr. Freeman—excuse me?"

"We'll run along," Blaustein said.

"Don't go," Shep said. "This can be taken care of in a minute, I'm sure, whatever it is."

"Nah, we'll split," Blaustein said. "Time for my pills, my black mask and ear plugs. Steve? I'll see you in the morning about that contract?"

Bixel had started with Archer toward the hallway. Now he turned. "What's that about a contract?"

Blaustein narrowed his eyes, questioning. "I'm an agent. I'm going to handle Steve's play."

Bixel looked at Archer, who nodded. The attorney told Blaustein, "Perhaps you'd better stay too. And you, sir?" To Freeman. "Have you some interest in this play?"

Freeman frowned. "I'm a picture producer. Yeah, I might be interested in it. I might be."

Abel Allen Archer made a sound like a groan.

Bixel said, "Well, I think it would be advisable for both of you gentlemen to join us."

"Oh, now, look here—" Shep protested.

"It's all right," Blaustein said. "Let's see what it's all about. Game, Jack?"

"Why not?" Freeman said. "I love hardboiled lawyers. I read myself to sleep with Perry Mason. Tonight I can save my eyes. . . ."

Shep's den had a sloping ceiling with hand-hewn beams. On a long, black, forged iron chain, a Tiffany dome of colored glass hung low over a big, round coffee table. The furniture was deep leather. Bookshelves lined one wall, filled with bound volumes of Theatre Arts, plays, books about the stage. Over an antique desk, elegantly framed and matted, hung an old poster, richly colored. Maude Adams in *Peter Pan*. *The boy,* Steve thought wryly, *who never grew up.* For Shep it figured.

When they came in, a man was on his hands and knees on the floor. Jean Agajian's fat, saffron uncle. He was caressing the deep silken nap of the oriental rug that was the color of plums. He scrambled to his feet. His smile was childlike and ecstatic. "Beeyooteefool carrpatt!" he laughed. Then, when nobody smiled, he said, "Axcuse, axcuse," and with hurt eyes sidled out of the room, giving the rug a last, longing glance before he shut the door.

"All right," Shep said, "sit down. Let's get this over with. What's on your mind?"

Bixel laid his case on the coffee table. The snaps clicked. He opened the lid, took out a paper and handed it to Shep. It was folded. Shep unfolded it drearily and looked at it. "What is it?"

"It's a restraining order," Bixel said, "signed by Judge Herter. That's where we've been, the reason we're so late getting here."

"Restraining order?" Shep squinted at him.

"Requiring you to cease and desist from the presentation of a dramatic composition entitled *The True Forgotten Speakers,* written by one Stephen Archer, a minor."

The Tiffany dome lit the top of the table brightly enough, shone on the gloss of Bixel's case, reflected dazzlingly off the paper that Shep threw down with a laugh. Outside the circle, however, the faces of the seated men were mottled with the harsh broken reds, blues, greens of the stained glass.

"A minor?"

"Exactly. Stephen Archer is nineteen years old."

"Well, nineteen is hardly twelve," Shep said.

"Until a youth in this state is twenty-one," Bixel said, "his actions are within the province and control of his lawful guardians. In this case, his parents."

"All right, suppose that's so?"

"It is so," Bixel said, "and I'm frankly shocked that you didn't take the precaution of consulting Dr. Archer before you went ahead. Didn't it occur to you this play constitutes an invasion of privacy?"

"Worse than that," Archer said. "Slander."

"Libel," Bixel corrected him.

"Call it what you want to," Archer snarled. "It's a vicious mixture of distortions and outright lies."

Bixel's hand came into the circle of light and touched the doctor's knee. "Let me handle it. It's late. Arguments and lost tempers only waste time. We have the law."

Shep said, "The play is a work of art. It rings with truth. It's human. It's real."

Bixel said drily, "That's precisely the trouble, Mr. Shepherd. It's too real. It holds Dr. Archer, his wife and mother, up to public ridicule and contempt. It's actionable. I so inform you here and now. If need be, I can inform the College authorities tomorrow morning."

"Oh, come on, now," Shep said, "aren't you being a shade melodramatic? Isn't this something of a tempest in—"

"If it was you and your family," Archer said, "paraded in public, naked, all your private affairs exposed, you wouldn't think so. You wouldn't tolerate it. Neither will I."

"Look, Doctor . . ." Shep leaned forward into the light so it glowed on his handsome hair. "Your son is a gifted playwright. Life is the heart's blood of any first-rate writing."

"This is too close to life," Bixel said. "There are actual speeches, actual situations. You'd lose in court, Mr. Shepherd."

"Court, court?" Shep's laugh was a snort of impatience. "Who's going to court, for heaven's sake? You can't be serious. Look— what is it that's objected to here? We'll change the offensive lines. But I can't see that the public is any threat. Playgoers don't think of what they see on the stage as being reality. It's drama, fiction. Who in the world are you worried about, doctor? What harm can a story—a made-up story about some anonymous, fictional family—do you?"

"I'm a public man, Mr. Shepherd. I'll be entering politics next spring, running for Assemblyman. At present I'm a physician. As a physician, my ethics are besmirched in this—this crapulous play. Changing a few lines wouldn't help. The whole character of the so-called doctor is a libel on me. Of course the public will know this monster is supposed to represent me. Did anyone doubt James Baldwin was writing about his father in *Go Tell It On The Mountain*? Well, I'm not some illiterate, half-mad preacher. My son is still my son, and until he's twenty-one, I'll be the one to rule this monster is supposed to represent me. You had no right to put on this play without my express consent."

Bixel said smoothly, "Of course, if the play were harmless, Dr. Archer wouldn't have interfered. But the play is anything but harmless."

"It's harmless now," Archer said flatly. "That paper kills it."

"Tickets have been sold to performances tomorrow night and next weekend," Shep said.

"Refund the money."

"People will want an explanation. Especially when they see the reviews in tomorrow's papers."

"There'll be no reviews," Bixel said. "We've already spoken to the papers. Nor will there be any further announcements in the calendar sections. It's all over, Mr. Shepherd."

"What if I tell the public the truth?" Shep looked at Archer. "Won't that hurt you far more than just letting the play go quietly on?"

Steve cried, "No, Shep! I don't want to hurt him."

His father gave a contemptuous bark of laughter. But he didn't look at Steve. He looked at Bixel and jerked his head at Shep. "Bixel, that's a threat."

"I'm sure you didn't mean to say that, Mr. Shepherd," the lawyer said softly. "A statement like that suggests you intended harm from the beginning. Is that so?"

"Oh, Lord," Shep sighed, "deliver me from lawyers. No, of course I never meant Dr. Archer any harm."

"I thought not," Bixel purred.

Jack Freeman cleared his throat. "Doctor," he said, "suppose I told you that tomorrow morning I plan to present your son with a check for twenty-five thousand dollars for his play. To film it."

Blaustein said, "Offer him a percentage, Jack."

"All right," Freeman said, "twenty-five thousand plus a percentage of the box office receipts. He's a minor. That would be your money to control."

It was crude. Steve felt sick.

"Good God!" His father rose, towering in wrath like a *Green Pastures* Jeremiah. "My honor and my future are for sale—is that what you think? This boy has tried to destroy me. Do you think I'd permit such a picture to be made? And crawl off and hide my head somewhere and live off his charity? What kind of men are you? Come on, Bixel. This place turns my stomach." He marched to the door and yanked it open.

Bixel closed his attache case and stood up. His smile was ghastly in the jigsaw of colored light. "It's all quite clear, then? It's all settled?"

Shep threw Steve a look of cold fury. "It's all settled," he said. But it wasn't all settled. When Bixel had shut the door, he turned on Steve, voice choked with rage. "You little bastard! Steve, how could you do this? All those weeks of work, all that sweat and grief. All those people—" He swung his arm, despairing, toward the door beyond which music played and there was laughter. "Dear God, you knew this man. He's your own father. You're not stupid. You knew what you'd done, what you'd written. You knew how he'd react. Why no word of warning? To get your play staged one solitary time with this kind of aftermath? That doesn't make sense. Or—" Something changed in his face and slowly he stood up. He leaned above the dome of cracked colors. "Or was it hate? I'm Whitey, is that it? And this was a great way to shaft Whitey. Yes, yes . . ." He nodded his big head with a twisted smile. "I remember. I remember all your little graces the night we met.

78

You were boiling over with hostility. You showed me. I should have taken the warning. But then you went cool, didn't you. Real cool cat. What a put-on! The put-on of the century. Stop smiling, God damn it!"

He wasn't smiling. He didn't know what was the matter with his face, but he wasn't smiling. And he couldn't listen to any more. He went to catch his father.

11

H E WOKE INTO DARKNESS out of some kind of horror. He was covered with sweat. The rain had stopped. Night air breathed across him and he shivered and reached out for sheet and blankets. Instead his hand touched life, naked skin. "Lacey?" he said hoarsely. But it wasn't Lacey. From the ribs that moved gently with the easy breathing of sleep, his hand slid down to a hard, flat little belly. No, it wasn't Lacey. Anyway, Lacey wasn't his any more—that much he remembered. He propped himself on an elbow and leaned across the pale figure to peer at the shadowy face. For a second, somewhere deep inside him, joy tried to put out leaves and flowers. He half smiled. It was Coy Randol. How? He sat up and stared at the room. It was bare, white. Madras curtains stirred at three tall windows. Not his room. Must be Coy's. So how had he got here? Where from?

There was a taxi. Something about a taxi. He'd been sick. They had to stop the taxi going around corners and curves and up hill and down hill. They had to stop it so he could get out and throw up. Rain. Big, dark yard, lots of trees, big old dark house looming up. The grateful cool of the drenched grass against his face. Lying there sick, crying, with the rain coming down all over him, wanting to die. The voice of the taxi driver: *Okay, Mack.* Hands lifting him, his own legs trying to work, mouth trying to work. Apologize. More dizzy swinging through the empty dark in the taxi, somebody holding him, his head rolling against the seat back. Then stairs, narrow cement stairs between trimmed hedges—lots of stairs, endless, climbing, stumbling. Somebody taking the clothes off him and, yes, this room, this bed. He'd been drunk. How?

There'd been a bar, a gay bar. Loud jukebox. A skin-and-bones boy dancing naked, a motheaten fur piece at his scrawny throat, picture hat with big cloth roses shaking. *I enjoy being a girl.* . . . Boy who looked like he worked in a bank, business suit, white shirt, necktie, rattling *maracas*, eyes shut, shoulders moving in a dream of sex. . . . Silver-haired man following Steve into the cramped little washroom. *I'm a great admirer of the beauty of your race.* Standing close beside him, craning to see. . . . But most of the time at a table in a corner with a big glass pitcher of draft beer and Coy listening to him, smiling at him, while Steve talked and talked, Coy looking more like an angel than ever because behind him, framing him, was a stained glass window.

Stained glass. The Tiffany dome in Shep's den. Now he remembered. The memory came at him with a roar, like a dark car running him down in a deserted nightmare street. With a cry, he turned and grabbed the sleeping boy. "Help me," he begged, "help me." The boy stirred, murmured, and gently pulled Steve's face against his chest, stroked his head, caressed his back. "It's okay." He kissed his forehead. "It's all over now." Steve shuddered and held him tight. Epitaph, he thought bitterly. Short and to the point. All over now. Family, marriage, friendship, talent, promise—all in one common grave. Numbly, blindly, his mouth sought, found, clung to the sweet mouth of this stranger kid. Rescuer. How, why? What difference did it make? Coy wasn't in that grave. Against his belly now he felt the eager upthrust of the boy's sex, and his own sex stirred. He reached down and took both together in his hand. Grateful. *Something*, a wry voice commented inside his head, *to hold on to.* . . .

When he woke again, daylight was in the room, red-orange from the thin curtains, sunwarm. He lay there with Coy curled against him, smooth, softly snoring, and he smiled. His sleep this second time had been deep and without dreams. And long—that he knew without his watch. It might be noon, he didn't care. He'd asked for this Saturday off because of the play. His mouth tightened. What play? He turned sharply from that, turned to the good things he and Coy had done here hours ago now in the dark. Good, but frantic, like food taken in great need, great hunger. No time to taste, to savor. But unforgettable. Oh, the best. Gently he slid his arm from under Coy's head, carefully disentangled his legs from the blond boy's and stretched, quivering, feeling his body come to life. He sat up, swung his feet to the floor and went to find the bathroom. Shutting the door so as not to wake the sleeper, he pissed loudly and happily, like a young horse. He grinned at himself in the mirror as he headed back for the bedroom.

Coy sat rigid in the rumpled bed, staring at the place Steve had vacated.

"Hey!" Steve said.

Coy looked up. "Oh, there you are. I—" He licked his lips and gave a scared little smile. "I was afraid you'd gone."

"Gone?" Steve laughed. "Where the hell would I go?" Then suddenly the laughter drained out of him. He said again, "Where the hell would I go?" but this time his voice broke, and he flung himself onto the bed, pulled the boy hard against him, and cried. He cried like a little kid, lost and afraid. "Ah, Jesus, I'm sorry," he choked. "Only hold me, baby, don't let me go. Love me, Coy— love me."

He flinched out of sleep. Something had hit the bed at his feet. Something alive. He sat up, back against the wall, blinking, heart banging, shaking his head. "Wha—?"

"Wake up, wake up!" It was a little kid with orange hair. About six years old. She was on her knees between Steve and Coy, banging their naked legs with her fists. In a little red coverall suit, she looked like something out of a Disney hell. The voice was shrill. "Wake up, wake up! Bloody Mary time!"

A little girl. Steve grabbed for the sheet to cover himself. No use. The kid was pinning it down. He rolled onto his stomach. Now Coy was awake. But he apparently wasn't concerned about the fact that he was naked. He sat up with a sleepy grin.

"Oh, shut up, Bunny. Shut up. Too loud, baby." He reached out and gathered the wriggling brat into his arms. "Sorry," he said over her shoulder to Steve. "She thinks she's an alarm clock."

"I don't get it," Steve said. "Who is she?"

The miniature turned him a scornful face. "Don't you know who I am? I know who you are. You're Steve, and you're Jess's new lover. But you're blacker than Smith, and you don't have such a big penis, eye-ther." She flung herself out of Coy's arms, bounced off the edge of the bed, and ran out of the room.

"Huh?" Steve gaped at Coy. "Am I awake?"

Coy laughed. Then his eyes moved from Steve's to something beyond. Steve turned.

"Hi." Marvel Sweeny stood in the doorway, smiling. She wore

an armless, bellbottom overall suit, green, printed with insane blue flowers. Her hair looked as if it had been combed with an eggbeater. Her face was shiny—not like clean but like very lightly greased. "You're awake, all right. And about time too. It's three o'clock. P.M." She held two tall glasses. "Marys, Bloody, a pair," she said. "Bunny wanted to serve them, but I—"

"No," Coy said. "She pours them on people. Ruins sheets."

Marvel stood over Steve, holding out the glasses. "Doesn't look like you've done these sheets much good, yourselves."

"Maybe not them," Coy smiled, "but us, yes." He reached across Steve and took his glass.

Marvel pulled the other glass back when Steve reached up for it. "You going to drink this lying on your face?"

Steve nodded at his clothes scattered across the floor. "Not if you hand me my pants," he said.

"What for? Heavens, when I arrived you were both lying here mother naked on your backs. And even if I hadn't looked, Bunny's given me a full report on how you're hung."

"Yeah," Steve grunted. "Sorry to let down the side." He sat up grimly and took the glass.

"Oh, don't pay any attention to Bunny's odious comparisons," Marvel said. "You're an intellectual. You're not supposed to be hung like a truck."

"Thanks," Steve said and drank fast and choked.

"Too much Worcestershire?" Marvel asked.

Steve couldn't speak but he shook his head, and Marvel walked out, saying:

"If you're going to shower, shower. Frankly, you both smell more than a trifle seminal, shall we say? Breakfast in ten minutes."

"Shit!" Steve slammed the glass down on the bedside table and turned on Coy. "Shit!"

"Don't." Coy put his hands on Steve's shoulders and kissed him. "Look . . . it'll be all right."

"Nothing will be all right while she's around. You got rid of her last night. Somehow. Get rid of her now. Permanently."

"Ah, Steve, you can't do that to somebody who's come out of the goodness of her heart to fix your breakfast."

"She didn't come to fix our breakfast," Steve said. "She came to stare at our cocks. She's sick, Coy. Can't you see that? Chicks who hang around faggots all the time—there's something wrong with them. She's got this kid, so where's her husband? Is that what she's broiling out there in the kitchen?"

Coy said, "He's a merchant seaman. He's gone a lot. She gets lonely. And she doesn't like women, and the only men a girl can hang around safely in a situation like that are—well—people like me."

"Well, let her pick somebody like you, then. Only not you. *I* pick you."

"I . . ." Coy looked down into the empty glass in his hands. For a moment he rolled it thoughtfully, mouth tight. Then he looked up. There were tears in his eyes, but he made himself smile at Steve. "I'll get rid of her. You—pick me?"

"Hell, what do you think? They have operations to separate Siamese twins. Do you think they could do it the other way around? If they could, that's what I want for you and me."

Coy stared solemnly into his eyes. "Sure?"

For an answer, Steve took him in his arms and kissed him as if he was trying to diagnose his appendix. Coy gave a little moan and his arms went around Steve and he clung. Their hearts thudded against each other. Coy's glass rolled off the bed and smashed on the floor. He pulled away, shaking his head.

"That sure enough for you?" Steve panted. "Or shall I—?" He started to bend low over the boy.

"Steve, it's sure enough. We can't begin again now. Showers, breakfast—remember?"

"Damn her soul," Steve said.

"Steve, she's been my friend for a long time. You wouldn't make me throw her down completely. Not if you love me."

"Okay, okay, okay." Steve rolled away from him, looked at the floor, sat up and put his feet off the bed edge, away from the broken glass. "Not completely." He turned his head to say it to the blond kid's face: "Only I don't want to see her, for Christ sake, when I open my eyes in the goddam morning." He stood up. "Once a week, Coy—at the very most." He went and took hold of the bedroom door and swung it. "And we're getting a lock for this."

12

T HE STREET WHERE STEVE had his room was lined by big old houses, frame, stucco, that needed paint. Porches, bay windows, cupolas. Fifty, sixty years ago they'd been expensive family places, prideful. But generations of students had worn them out. Palms with thick trunks and tin rat guards towered in front of them. Magnolias lined the curb, old ones, their dark leaves glossy after the long wet spell. Under one of them, the faded red paint of Steve's car gleamed dully from the wash the rain had given it.

"This is the place," he told Marvel.

She braked her Volkswagen. He didn't want to give her time to park. From the back seat he prodded Coy and the blond kid got out. Steve followed, shaking off Bunny, who had been playing a game with him all the way from Silverlake, poking her sharp little fingers at his eyes to see him blink, then collapsing helpless with laughter.

"Now, seriously, shouldn't I wait and help haul some of your goods and chattels back?" Marvel asked.

"Hell, no. I told you, there isn't much. My car will handle it." He slapped its dented fender.

"A real winner," she said.

"It'll get us there."

"All right. I know when I'm not wanted," Marvel said. "Do I get a goodbye kiss?"

Coy started to lean into the car. Steve yanked him back and slammed the door. "Dig you later," he yelled at Marvel, waved his arm, and dragged Coy after him toward the house. "That's something else that's got to go," he said. "From now on, I get the kisses. Me and only me. Right?"

"Right," Coy laughed. "Only I think my arm is coming out of its socket. She's gone. You can let go."

"Sorry."

The front hall of the house was dim and smelled damp. Its carpet was mud tracked. A pay telephone was fastened to the wall on the right, wreathed with a scrawl of penciled numbers. Beyond it rose a stairway with heavy banisters, many times painted, chipped, scarred. They bypassed it. Steve's room was at the end of the lower hall on the left. He halted. Its door was open. He pushed it.

Shep sat inside on the bed, hunched forward, elbows on knees, big hands hanging, cigaret forgotten in the fingers. The air was stale with smoke. He looked up. Pain flickered in his face. He jammed the cigaret out in the ashtray that was stuffed with butts, and stood up.

"Steve, I apologize." He didn't come forward. He just stood there, abject. "I'm sorry I blew up at you last night. Terribly sorry. I was sorry two minutes after it happened. I hunted for you, but you'd gone. As soon as I could, I came here. You weren't here, so I waited."

"All night? All day? Jesus, Shep, it's nearly five o'clock in the afternoon."

Shep gave a wry, woeful laugh. "I got here at two-thirty in the morning. I had to phone Dean Burleigh first. I had to think of something to tell the cast and crew, something that wouldn't bring your father into it."

"What did you say?"

"That the play was too controversial—Negro boy, white girl, illegitimacy, abortion. That the College authorities had seen the performance and ordered us to close. The Dean was scared to death of it—everybody involved knew that. So they believed me. I thought they would. It's that kind of world."

"Yeah . . . so what did the Dean say?"

" 'I told you so,' " Shep grunted. "He thinks we were lucky to get out of it so easily. He's relieved."

"You . . . won't lose your job or anything."

"I won't lose my job," Shep said, "but I expect from now on to be directing *Chicken Every Sunday.*"

"Yeah . . . Brave Burleigh." Steve moved into the room and Shep saw Coy.

"Who's this?"

"Coy Randol. When I caught up with my father last night, he was just climbing into Bixel's car. I grabbed his arm and tried to tell him it was a stupid, kid mistake, that I hadn't meant to hurt him or anybody. He pushed me on my ass in the mud. Maybe I deserved it. Maybe I deserved your blowing up at me. But I didn't want to live much. Coy picked me up. Out of the mud. I'm alive."

Shep shook Coy's hand. "You saved something worth saving." He tried for a smile and missed. He looked exhausted.

Steve told Coy, "Listen, baby, there's a place up at the corner of Santa Monica that sells coffee to go. Here's the car keys. Get the big cups." He looked at Shep. "Sugar? Cream? You've got to be hungry. Hamburger?"

"Thanks. Just the coffee. Black. I'll appreciate it." This time he managed the smile. He dug into his pocket. "Let me buy it."

"I've got it," Steve said.

But Coy was already on his way. When his footsteps had crossed the porch and faded, Shep looked at Steve.

"I should have done the saving," he said. "Should have been calm enough and wise enough."

Steve looked at the palms of his hands, then laid them together flat and raised them to his mouth, not meaning the Hindu blessing, not meaning anything, maybe. He looked at Shep. "You couldn't," he said, "not shook the way you were. It all happened so fast. But Coy was outside of it. He hadn't come unglued."

"I love you, Steve," Shep said. "That should have overridden whatever happened. It always should."

"I'm sorry," Steve said. "Christ, I've been good for you, haven't I?" He dropped his hands and gave a crooked smile. "Next time you see a black boy wearing the sign BIG TALENT, cross to the other side of the street."

"No. The blame is mine, Steve. I'm a grown man and I saw what you'd done when I read your play. You remember I told you the night we met at Ross's that you were rough on your father. I didn't know your background. But the play had to be autobiography. It was too right to have come from anything but life."

"Yeah," Steve laughed sadly, "and I cut you down."

"You did," Shep nodded, "but it wasn't that that made me ignore the warnings I gave myself. Granted, it never occurred to me you weren't twenty-one. I still think I'd have gone ahead as I did because of the quality of the play. And the quality of the boy who wrote it."

"To you it's a work of art," Steve said, "and to me. But to my father it's just libel. And that's what counts. Christ . . . he was so far from me when I wrote it! He'd turned his back, I'd turned mine. I mean, this isn't him, Shep." He picked up the ragged script off the desk and shook it. "He's not in here. The doctor in here is somebody made up, fictional."

"Your father must be a fine doctor, Steve. He doesn't take chances. Not the slightest. I think if the play had gone on, it wouldn't have hurt him. But there was a chance it would—just a chance. And he wasn't going to take that chance. He has a strong sense of self-preservation."

"You bet," Steve said bitterly. He sighed and dropped into the room's only chair, a bulgy overstuffed with a faded slipcover. "I'm sorry about your friend Blaustein and that movie producer. Really a waste of time for them. Will they forgive you?"

Shep smiled wryly. "They still want to see you. But with a different play. And not till you're twenty-one."

"Slight postponement." Steve nodded. "Look, Shep, all you did . . . so it folded up. I mean, what there was was so great. I'll never forget it." He reached out to paw the keys of his portable typewriter on the desk. "If I ever work up nerve enough to write another play, it'll be hell of a lot better, a hell of a lot more ready, because of what you taught me. I'm grateful. I mean it."

"Thanks," Shep said.

"And that party!" Steve made himself grin. "Was that ever something else, man!"

"Yes . . ." Shep sat down heavily on the bed again and pinched a cigaret from his jacket pocket. "But with a sad ending." He set the cigaret in his mouth and lit it. "Twice sad. We had a robbery."

"What?" Steve blinked at him.

"When the girls went upstairs to get their coats and purses, there wasn't a nickel left. Somebody cleaned them right out. It didn't amount to much—mad money, cab fare, that sort of thing. I gave it back out of my pocket. Maybe thirty dollars in all. I really only feel badly about Mrs. Hayes Brown's brooch."

Steve remembered it, a big cameo. "How could they steal that? She was wearing it."

"The clasp came loose," Shep said, "in the middle of things. My mother took it and put it in Mrs. H. B.'s handbag for her. They stole it, all right."

"But who?" Steve cried. "None of our kids would do a thing like that."

"Hi." Coy stood in the doorway, clutching a big paper sack. "Three coffees, as ordered."

There wasn't much to pack. It wasn't much of a place to leave. He hadn't been here long. The stringy-haired landlady, Mrs. Polk, wearing a crisp, daisy-printed apron over a greasy housedress, led them to the tumbledown stable at the back of the lot, where they found empty cartons. His books and papers went into some of these, his sweaters and wash clothes into others. Suits, jackets, good shirts they carried out and laid on the back seat of the car. The typewriter in its case. The radio too. He'd brought it from the apartment at Bernie's, wryly figuring Lacey had Bartok now and wouldn't need the top 40 tunes anymore. It was dark by the time they'd finished and stood in the room looking to see what he'd forgotten. Nothing. He might never have been here. He shivered. Was he going to leave the world like that? Yesterday he thought he'd written his name on it big. Applause, Broadway, interview in the New York *Times,* movie contract, Academy Award, sleek new house in Malibu, Lincoln Continental, jet to Europe, the Isles of Greece. Fame, immortality. Yesterday. Today? He turned and pulled Coy tight against him and held him for a long time. Then he muttered, "Come on, let's get out of here."

They stopped at a neon-embroidered drive-in on Vermont Avenue to eat. Hamburgers, malts. When they'd finished and Steve was lighting a cigaret, Coy dropped money on the tray among the crumpled napkins. The dumpy-rumped girl in slacks unhitched the tray. Steve started the engine. "I thought you were broke," he said. "You paid for the coffee before, now this. You don't have to keep me, you know. I've got a job. We talked about that, remember?"

"I remember." Coy didn't look at him. "But I'm not that broke. Are we going to argue about a dollar and eight-six cents?"

"We're not going to argue about anything." Steve nosed the red car out into the Saturday night traffic. "Only we agreed to split everything fifty-fifty. Right? So let's keep the agreement. Okay?"

"Okay. Now let's go home. I want to love you . . ."

But first they had to unload the car. It took time and sweat to haul the stuff up the long stairs. When they came panting, legs aching, with the third load, a man was standing on the terrace. Paunchy, fiftyish, he wore baggy denims, a baggy dark blue sweatshirt. His face, in the glare of light from a wrought-iron standard at the top of the stairs, was round and red, with a tracery of little broken veins. He wore a glossy hairpiece. He peered down at them where they climbed in shadow.

"Coy? Smith?"

"Hi, Brubie," Coy said. "It's not Smith."

"Oh, dear." The man bridled like a matron at a flower show who has mistaken a geranium for a carnation. "I *am* sorry."

"This is Steve Archer," Coy said. "He's my new room mate. Steve—Brubie. Mr. Brubaker. He lives upstairs. Owns the building. It's him we pay the rent to."

Steve was carrying a box of socks, T-shirts and shorts. He set it down beside the ivy-covered terrace rail and held out his hand. Brubaker shook it. His smoky false teeth smiled but his little eyes were wary. "It's a pleasure. Do you go to school with Coy?"

"No," Steve said. "I work. At the downtown Public Library."

"Oh? Have you been there long?"

"Six months," Steve said.

"Ah." Brubaker relaxed. "You must enjoy your work." They had stacked the cartons of books beside the front door. He nodded at them. "I see you're quite a reader."

"He writes, too," Coy said. "Plays."

"Really? I love the theatre." But Brubaker had lost interest, now that he figured to get his rent all right. His eyes wandered. Somewhere a bottle waited. "Well, I'll let you get on with your settling in. So nice to have you. Come up tomorrow for a drink. . . ."

He shuffled away into the dark.

They carried the cartons inside. They looked shabby in the handsome, long, white room. Steve bent wearily to begin taking the stuff out of them to put away.

"No," Coy said. Steve straightened. The boy kissed him. "You can do it tomorrow while I'm at church."

"Church?" Steve looked at him sideways. "You're putting me on."

"I teach Sunday School from nine till eleven. Service is from eleven till one. Then I go back at seven for Christian Endeavor. Part of being a good Galilee College student." He turned toward the hallway, pulling the cherry red velour shirt off over his head. "Come on. Let's do it in the shower. I love that."

13

A NOISE WOKE STEVE, a querulous, highpitched whine. It wasn't
yet daylight. Through the curtains the windows were gray
indefinite oblongs. He reached out for Coy. Not there. And what
was the noise? He scowled. Then he knew—a blender. In the
kitchen. The dark fragrance of coffee reached him, good smells
of cooking. He rolled groggily out of bed, pained at how early it
was.

It had been a wild night. What they did in the shower, the light
gleaming off the white tiles, off their soap-slick nakedness, he had
thought he'd never go for. You could get hurt doing that. But he
hadn't been hurt, nor Coy either. It had been good—crazy,
laughing good. And it had been only the beginning. They'd made
out again on the clean white bed. And later—middle of the night.
So what was all the rise and shine about?

He used the bathroom, then staggered into the kitchen, naked,
blinking, still 90 percent asleep. The kitchen was a bright room,
new paint, glittering new stove and refrigerator, yellow linoleum
dazzlingly waxed, cottage curtains of crisp yellow gingham. Coy
looked bright and new too, in a blue happy coat with a big, white
Japanese symbol in a circle on its back. Christ, he had beautiful
legs!

Steve walked up behind him and put his arms around him.
"Good morning." He kissed the nape of his neck. It tasted nice.
He began to lick it and let his hands explore. The kid was naked
under the happy coat. Steve reached inside. The boy shivered,
gave a soft laugh, slid away from him.

"Breakfast time," he said. "Drink your orange juice."

He held out a foaming glass. It was great stuff. The whole
breakfast was great—link sausages wrapped in big, fluffy flap-
jacks with belts of bacon, golden-yolked eggs cooked and turned

gently in deep butter, toast made from crunchy, stone-ground bread, English marmalade, and coffee that tasted the way coffee always looked in the color layouts of *Good Housekeeping*.

"Man! Where did you learn to cook like that? Down at the ranch?"

"Down at the ranch," Coy laughed grimly, "you work so hard and you get so hungry you don't care what the food tastes like. And that's how they cook it."

Steve watched Coy's hands again, as they reached for toast and buttered it. It was hard work that had shaped them square and ugly, then, hard work while the kid was still growing.

"No," Coy went on. "When I was sixteen I did a series of broadcasts all summer long for a TV station in the Central Valley. And the people who owned the station, Mr. and Mrs. Wallace—I lived at their house. It was beautiful. I mean, before then I never dreamed people could live like that. I'd never seen a movie then—our church is against movies. But now I know it was like a movie. Big, low-roofed redwood ranch house just . . . out there on rolling green hills with oak trees. I mean, just out there. They didn't have to raise anything. They were rich. They had horses to ride. Swimming pool. Hot there in summer, but they had air conditioning. So quiet you couldn't hear it. Big beautiful rooms. . . ."

His blue eyes were wide and staring far away. Now he blinked them and smiled at Steve.

"So . . . it was Mrs. Wallace taught me to cook. It was her hobby. She even did a cooking program on the station. Didn't have to. Just loved to teach people to cook."

"Let's hear it for Mrs. Wallace," Steve said. "Only if you cook like this all the time you're going to end up with one big, fat lover."

"Not if you keep loving the way you did last night," Coy said. "You'll more likely turn out to be skin and bones."

Then they were both sitting there gazing into each other's eyes across the table, Coy holding the last corner of his piece of toast, Steve with his coffee cup at his mouth, his heart beginning to thud. He swallowed, set down the cup, pushed back his chair. But Coy was up more quickly. There was a buttercup clock on the wall. He nodded at it. The hands pointed to eight.

"Have to get ready for church."

"Ah, come *on!*" Steve reached for him. "Don't give me that jazz."

"It's not 'that jazz.' " Coy dodged, laughing.

But Steve caught the end of the white cloth tie at his waist. He yanked it and the happy coat fell open. It was plain to see church wasn't on Coy's mind any more than it was on his own. He clamped his nakedness against him. Both their hearts raced. But Coy struggled, turned his mouth away from Steve's.

"No. There's not time, Steve. Please."

"You're serious?"

"I have to get there before nine. I've got to bathe and shave and dress. And then, unless you drive me, I won't make it."

Baffled, Steve shrugged and let him go. Coy bent, kissed him lightly where it mattered, and headed for the shower. Steve rummaged from the cartons in the living room a pair of clean white Levis and a T-shirt, put them on and returned to the kitchen. He poured himself another cup of coffee, lit a cigaret, and sat there with one eyebrow raised, shaking his head. This had to be the world's wildest send up.

But, ten minutes later, when he heard Coy come out of the bathroom, and ambled in to lean against the doorframe and watch him dress, it began to look as if the kid meant it. After he had strung around his neck on a thin chain a little silver and blue enamel medal with the initials C.E. intertwined—for Christian Endeavor—he put on a corny white shirt and a terrible green stripy silk tie. From the closet he brought out a stiff blue serge suit and got into it. It looked like something from a Walker Evans photograph—dustbowl finery, circa 1935. The kid owned hip threads. That was a sharp little Mod suit he'd worn to Shep's— vest, shawl collar, two rows of brass buttons. So what was this? Coy sat on the bed to put on shoes. Brown shoes, yellow brown. Shades of *Elmer Gantry*. Unbelievable.

"What are you grinning at?"

Steve wiped his smile. "Nothing. You ready?"

"One second." Coy reached into the closet again. A hat, a little gray straw, right off Woolworth's 59-cent counter. He set it straight on his bright hair. "Now, my Bible." He walked past Steve into the living room. Built-in bookshelves flanked the fireplace, fresh white and empty except for a stereo rig, a few record albums, and the Bible that had a floppy leather cover, rosy gilt page edges, and a lot of varicolored ribbons hanging out of it. Coy picked it up and stood staring solemnly at Steve, who couldn't help it now—he had to laugh.

"Beautiful," he said.

Coy looked down at himself doubtfully, then up at Steve again.

"Something wrong?"

"No man. Too right," Steve said. "We at Western Costume are proud and humble."

Coy laughed then.

But he still went to church.

Steve let him off at the corner. He didn't need to be told Coy's co-religionists would never trust him again if he showed up in a car with a Negro. But his curiosity made him drive around the block and past the church. It stood, scaly white in the cool morning sunlight, on Applewood just south of Santa Monica. Its builder had maybe once seen a California mission, but when it came time to draw up the plans for this church, he couldn't remember exactly what it had looked like. The black wooden signboard said in gold gothic letters, *Third Evangelical Pentecostal Church of Jesus.* Two old pepper trees were dying on a front lawn that had bald patches. Under the trees, little kids in stiff Sunday suits and cheap print dresses tried to play tag without seeming to—hurrying, stiff-legged. Each of them, even the smallest, carried a big, black Bible. There was Coy with his. He stood on the church steps and talked to a freckled, fat, towheaded girl and two skinny boys with glasses and pimples. They smiled gawkily at something he said. Steve drove on.

After Steve got him home, Coy shed the Tom Joad clothes and kicked into tight, blue, wide-wale corduroy bells. It was warm now. There was no wind. He didn't bother with a shirt. He pushed his bare feet into blue and white rubber go-aheads. As he started to leave the bedroom, Steve barred the doorway with an arm.

"It's been nice having you for a friend," he said, "but now I'm afraid I'm going to have to eat you up."

"Thanks." Coy gave him a brisk kiss, then ducked under his arm and ran for the kitchen. "What we're going to eat right now is lunch. I'm famished. Hey, thanks for washing the dishes. Come watch me make the salad." Steve came. "Next Sunday you can do it while I'm gone."

His big hands tore up lettuce into a wooden bowl. He sliced tomatoes, peeled and cubed avocados, handling everything with love. The dressing was the tricky part—olive oil, vinegars, herbs, carefully measured and shaken. He recited the names and proportions and made Steve write them down. When he put the salad into the refrigerator to chill, he brought out ice cubes and vodka. "Martini time."

"I thought you told me once you liked gin."

"On Sundays, vodka. I have to go back to church, remember?" Steve groaned.

The mixing was a mad scientist routine. Coy used for it a tall pitcher of green, bubble-flecked Mexican glass, crammed with ice cubes. He bent to a lower cupboard for Vermouth. Steve blinked. There must have been thirty bottles of different kinds of liquor down there. Coy poured vodka into a big glass jigger and emptied it over the ice. Six times. Then Vermouth.

"Craftily," Steve said, "Dr. X measured out the secret ingredients."

"Do not jest, Igor," Coy muttered, "you will cause me to ruin the formula. Ah . . . there!" He capped the vodka, corked the Vermouth, found in a drawer a long, glass rod for stirring, and pushed the pitcher toward Steve. He dropped the Transylvania accent. "A hundred turns," he said gravely, "no more, no less."

"Mrs. Wallace teach you that, too?"

"Oh, Lordy, no. They're very religious. Never let a bottle in the house. Not even cooking sherry. No . . . when I grew up enough to know I was thirsty, I bought a bartender's guide."

Steve grinned and began moving the ice around, watching Coy butter on both sides yellow, creamy-looking slices of bread, then cut thick, square slabs of ham, and rich, orange cheese, sandwich these between the bread slices, and finally lay them in glossy black iron skillets over circles of low, blue flame. He lidded the pans, rinsed and dried his hands at the sink, then, smiling, reached for the pitcher. Chilled glasses out of the freezer. Olives. Twists of lemon peel.

They carried the drinks into the living room where winter sunlight poured in through the French windows. Coy put a Montovani record on the stereo. The couch had clean lines. It was upholstered in nubby, expensive beige. Coy sat at one end, legs tucked under him like a girl. Steve dropped down next to him. There was a low, plain, rectangular coffee table, Danish teak. Steve stretched his legs across it, barefoot. He looked at Coy, eyebrows raised.

"Okay?"

"It's your table as much as mine," Coy smiled.

Steve tasted the drink. Perfect. The good life. He sighed, leaned back comfortably, laid his hand in the blond boy's lap, gently kneading.

"Nice." Coy stroked his head. "But I'll have to turn those sandwiches in a minute. Then in two more minutes they'll be ready to eat. Your books look nice there."

They did. They helped the room, gave it a little color. He guessed the proximity to Montovani wouldn't turn them to sugar. Anyway, their presence made him begin to feel like maybe he belonged here. Which led him to a question. He took his hand away and lit a cigaret.

"Listen," he said, "I don't want to get out of line, but I know a little about your kind of religion. My grandmother goes for it. And, I mean, baby . . . drinking is out. And sex is out. Especially our kind. Right?"

Coy nodded, glass at his mouth, eyes amused.

"Well . . . so . . ." Steve shrugged worriedly. "What if one of them walked in here? Like now. Or last night when we were fucking up a storm?"

"One of them?"

"Yeah. Say your folks."

Coy shook his head, swallowed the last of his drink, set the glass down. "They never leave Dead Oak. Anyway, don't worry. I'm their little Jesus boy. It would never enter their heads to check up on me."

"Well, how about the preacher?"

"Here? At Third Evangelical?"

"No, the one who pays your way."

"Sister Myra Lusk. No. I go to her, she doesn't come to me. She's busy. Church to run, radio programs, mail-order healing lessons. Anyway, she's like my family. She thinks I'm a saint. You couldn't tell any of them down there any different." He stood up. "Come on. Time for seconds."

Steve followed him into the kitchen where he turned the sandwiches. Their undersides were toasted golden brown now. Cheese bubbled out deliciously at their edges. They smelled great. Coy replaced the lids of the skillets, then filled the glasses again. He went on:

"That's how I can have this place. The other kids at Galilee must live in dormitories—six unwashed backwoods adolescents to a room. Not two seconds of privacy in twenty-four hours." He set the green pitcher back in the refrigerator and brought out the salad. He poured the dressing over it and used wooden forks to toss it, then heaped portions in two smaller wooden bowls. "I put up with it for one year." He pulled on a quilted mitten and took yellow plates from the warming oven. "Then I told Sister Myra if I was coming back, I had to have a place of my own. *Voilà!* Of course, it's grander than what she pays for. She doesn't know it's a full-sized apartment, thinks it's a room or something. Doesn't know I share it."

"Especially not with a Negro boy," Steve said. "Especially not a queer Negro boy. If she found out... What if they tell her, somebody at the College?"

"They won't." Coy took from a drawer two bamboo place mats, two blue linen napkins. He walked out to lay them on the blond, square, dropleaf table at the near end of the long white room. "They don't know, and they're not going to knock themselves out to learn. You have to remember, I'm a kind of celebrity." Coming back into the kitchen, he gave a quick grimace. "I've been on what they worshipfully call the Tee Vee a lot. That's good for enrollment." From another drawer he took Danish stainless steel knives and forks. "Also it explains—to their so-called minds—why I don't socialize with the other students much." From the other room, he went on, "But I'm careful, just the same. Very careful. Never miss a class, get good grades, even run a junior evangelist's class. I show up at *Third Evangelical* every Sunday—no matter how hung over, teach like mad, sing, carry on."

"Yeah," Steve said. "Only aren't you going to split down the middle one of these days? Isn't it a pretty schizoid way to live?"

Coy spatulaed the sandwiches out of the pans onto the warm plates, sliced them from corner to corner, looked at Steve. "No," he said. "This is real. That's not." He carried the plates to the table, came back for the salads. "Want to bring our drinks?"

Steve brought them and they sat down. It was a nice place to be. Montovani kept spinning out meaningless sweetness. The French windows at this end of the room looked out on a flagged patio sheltered by the umbrella leaves of a big castor plant. At its edge the hill climbed steeply, deep in green ivy. Steve touched the sandwich. Too hot. He began to work on the salad. But he was troubled.

"Look," he said. "Sure, you've got it made now. But how about when school's out and there's no more loot from Sister Myra?"

"By then I'll have my degree. I'll be ordained."

"So? Any preachers you know live this well?"

Coy grinned. "Remember Brother Olin Swett—ran a television program here years ago? Faith healer?"

"Sure. Every night for hours. Grandma watched."

"Steve, I was on his program once. Stayed at his house." The kid's eyes sparkled. "I mean—twenty rooms! An estate, acres and acres in Laurel Canyon. Gold plumbing fixtures, a bar like the Biltmore. That man never drew a sober breath. Cadillacs and caviar. Live liked a king. A queen, I should say."

"Gay?"

"As a flying snake. I was eleven, and he couldn't keep his hands off me."

Then Steve remembered and felt cold. The story had been in the papers—how Brother Olin Swett died. The father of a fourteen-year-old boy had caught them in a motel room and shot the evangelist full of holes. Steve studied Coy.

"It doesn't shake you," he wondered, "the idea of making a racket out of it?"

"Religion?" Coy asked. "Oh, Steve, it won't be me. They made a racket out of it a long time ago."

14

L A PAZ VALLEY WAS A SCOOP OF GREEN hemmed in by stony, brush-covered mountains. Steve drove into it through a narrow, crooked pass between sheer rock walls that shut out the sun and made it cold. He was shivering and the car radiator was boiling when he came out of the pass and the valley lay below him, picture postcard pretty in the afternoon winter sunshine.

In its center was a big oval of grazing land, jewel-green. Rainbirds slung lazy, looping crystal arcs over sections of it. In other sections, white-faced beef steers browsed. Like an immense horseshoe of deeper green, orchards belted this meadow land, climbing the foothills in orderly rows. Wind was turning the leaves, making them shine.

Steve drove down into the town. Dead Oak. It had a few live oaks and many fine, big, shaggy old eucalypts. They threw their moving shadows on a pink stucco motel, a yellow filling station, an old wooden building that was a combination food, dry goods and hardware store, a painty little clapboard cottage with a flag and the sign U.S. POST OFFICE, and a raw redwood and glass hamburger stand identified in neon as OPAL'S EATS.

Steve swung the car in at the filling station that had loops of green tinsel and tin bells and wreaths hanging off it. Christmas was a week away. Coy had to spend the vacation with his family. Steve had driven him down the coast as far as Oceanside. There Coy had boarded a bus for Escondido, where his father would meet him. Coy meant him to think he'd come all the way from L.A. by Greyhound. And Steve was supposed to turn around and go straight back to L.A. He couldn't. He had to see this place first.

He climbed out of the car, lifted the hood and stared at the rusty radiator cap. A potbellied man in Levis and a cowboy shirt came around the station corner. There was gray stubble on his face, a grimy Stetson on his head. He smiled, walked over and, using a blue bandana to protect his hand, unscrewed the cap. He smelled of horse. When the steam gushed out he shook his head amiably.

"Wish I could figure out some way to harness all the steam I let out of radiators here of cars that come over that pass. Drive a dynamo."

Steve grinned. "It's an old car."

"The new ones do it too. And seize up with vapor lock. That's worse. Block the pass in summer—not that it's all that busy. It ain't. And it's a good thing too. Well . . . let her sit there and cool out a while, then we'll start her up and put in some fresh *agua*." He nodded at the rust-streaked red and white enamel box beside the station door. "You want a coke?"

"No, thanks. But would it be all right for me to use your men's room?"

"That's what it's here for."

"I meant—" In L.A. he wouldn't have asked. But this was another world and he was a little nervous.

"I know what you meant," the man said kindly. "It's around back."

Steve found it. When he came out, the man was pumping gas into the tank of a big, brand-new Buick station wagon. On its side, in crisp, professional lettering, were the words: *Jesus Christ—the Same Yesterday, Today and Tomorrow.* A middle-aged woman sat at the wheel. He couldn't see much of her face because the car was pointed away from him, but her hair was like a brass helmet. She had the radio on. The car had a tall aerial and it brought in the signals loud and clear—gospel songs.

Steve turned quickly and walked off along the edge of the road. There was the hamburger stand. It reminded him he hadn't eaten since breakfast. Now his watch said four o'clock. The front of OPAL'S EATS was beams and glass. All the glass was sprayed with frosty white for Christmas and on a couple of panes were painted red and green holly leaves and berries. There was a counter with shiny napkin containers and yellow and red plastic squeeze bottles of mustard and catsup. There were two screened service windows.

Steve stood at one. He could make out somebody inside in a white apron, leaning a hip against the edge of the black short-order grill. A woman. She was reading a magazine. Steve cleared his throat. Did she look up? He couldn't be sure. It was bright out here, dim in there.

He said, "Excuse me. I'd like a hamburger, please."

The woman put down the magazine, came to the screen and looked at him. She was skinny. There were knobs at the corners of her jaws, squint lines at her eyes. Her mouth opened and shut like scissors. "You might like it," she said, "but you're not a-gonna get it here." She slid a plywood panel across the opening. CLOSED it said. She stood glaring at him over it.

"Merry Christmas," he said.

He walked back to the filling station.

The Buick was driving off. On its rear end the lettering read *Jesus Heals*. The man who ran the station was standing with a bottle of Windex in one hand and a rumpled paper towel in the other, watching Steve come back.

"Say," he said, "I'm sorry you went there. I never seen you go, otherwise I'd have stopped you. Opal's all right in most ways, but there's one thing she's death on."

"Coons," Steve said.

The man got red in the face and he opened and shut his mouth and there was pain in his eyes.

"Don't blame yourself," Steve said. "Who was the battle ax in the Buick?"

"What? Oh . . . Sister Myra Lusk. Lady preacher. Runs a sort of church up at the other end of the valley."

"I've heard of her."

"Have you? Well, I suppose that's natural. She's on the radio a lot, the TV. That's where she's comin' from now—station in Diego. On the go night and day. Guess she does some people some good. But she's gonna kill herself if she don't slow down. She's no chicken, and she's had one little stroke already." Staring off down the empty road, the man shook his head. Then he looked at Steve. "Listen, you just let me ankle up to Opal's. I'll order whatever you want, pretend it's for me, and bring it back to you."

"Thanks. That's very kind," Steve said, "but I'm not hungry any more. Suppose we can put water in the car now? And I better have some gas, too. Check the oil?"

"Why, sure, sure," the man said. "But I'd be more than happy. I mean, I'm so goldarned ashamed of Opal."

"Forget it," Steve told him.

He followed the long two-lane strip of asphalt road that curved between the groves. The orange, grapefruit, lemon trees, the limes, were round, monotonous. *Sunkist,* the roadside signs said, *Blue Goose.* The avocados were different—sprawling, drooping trees that filled their groves with green light, green shadows. *Calavo,* the sign said. The signs were mass-produced, bright enamel on tin. Anonymous. But the growers' names were on RFD boxes. He was reaching the far end of the valley when he saw *Randol.*

He stepped on the brakes and backed a little. There was a rickety rail gate. Beyond that a dirt road, weedy and rutted, ran back about one hundred yards to a white, one-story frame house. The roof was patched in two different shades of green asbestos shingling. The screen door was of raw wood. Washing flapped off sagging wire lines at the side of the house. In the bare front yard chickens pecked. A cat, or maybe a little dog, slept in the shadow of a dusty, battered pickup truck.

It all figured.

Sister Myra Lusk's station wagon was parked beside the pickup. And that figured too. After all, she owned the kid, didn't she? His mouth twitched. Did she? A few yards back, he'd passed an open-sided shed with a corrugated iron roof that sheltered a few broken crates. There was room to park there. He backed the car.

The sun was dropping behind the mountains. It began to turn cold right away. But he kept sitting there, staring at the Randols' gate. A long time. Then he saw red sunset dust rising above the squatty trees. In a minute, Coy came to the gate. Steve's heart jumped, but the kid didn't see him. He unfastened the gate and swung it open. Sister Myra bucked her Buick into the road and slammed on the brakes, making the big car rock. She was one of those people who never learn to drive. Coy closed and fastened the gate, walked the length of the station wagon, opened the door and started to get in.

He turned his head.

And for a fraction of a second he held still. It was too near dark. Steve couldn't make out his expression. But he was sure he'd seen the car and it had shaken him. Steve grinned. Coy slammed the station wagon door, Sister Myra raced the motor, the tires squealed. The car tore off down the road. Steve was still grinning when he couldn't see it any more. But it was a bitter grin.

"I wondered when you'd be here."

The woman in the office of the pink motel was forty, but she obviously starved herself and worked hard on her makeup. She wore tight striped capris. The tangerine-colored blouse had a standup, roll-back collar. It opened nearly to her navel. She had on a lot of fake jade beads, earrings, bracelets, rings. A good wig, ash-blond. She hoped she looked fifteen. Steve didn't know how to take her greeting. He didn't shut the door.

"You wondered, or you were afraid?" he asked. "I can sleep curled up on the back seat of my car. I just thought a bed might be nicer."

"Come in. A bed is always nicer." She made a Mona Lisa smile that dug little wrinkles beside her mouth. She fluttered her false eyelashes. She'd smeared green stuff on her upper lids and powdered it with something that twinkled. "Sign here, Mr. . . .?"

"Archer." Steve wrote it on the card along with the Kean Terrace address. "You mean you saw me across at the filling station earlier?"

"And at Opal's, that bitch."

"When you eat at Opal's," Steve said, "you leave a little hungry. But they tell me that's good for the digestion." He slid the card across the counter.

"Ten even," she said.

He gave her the money. From the drawer she dropped it into she took a key. When she laid it in his hand, she let her own hand lie there for a minute. Mostly bone, the nails long and painted tangerine to match the blouse. "Cabin six," she said. "Rear corner. It's the quietest one, farthest from the road."

"You mean there's traffic?"

"Sunday morning there is. Five hundred hillbillies will stream past here headed for Sister Myra's salvation factory at the other end of the valley." There was a pink Christmas tree with pink balls standing at the end of the counter. She picked up a pack of green cigarets from beside it and lit one. Angrily. Blinking like Bette Davis. "Sister Myra!" she snorted. "That bitch."

"Look," Steve said, "I've driven all the way around this valley. I can't find a place to eat. Do you have a dining room?"

"I want one. It would do marvelously here. But I won't open it without a bar. I know that business. You have to have a bar."

"So have a bar," Steve said.

"Oh, honey. Pardon me, but you are naive. I mean, you come

over that pass and you're back in another century. Carrie Nation, the Demon Rum, the whole bit. No, Sister Myra's got this place by the throat. Why, even Charlie, at the store over there, can't sell liquor. Not even wine. Not even beer. Anybody in La Paz Valley depraved enough to drink—and there are a few embattled souls—smuggles in his supplies from outside." Her mouth twisted grimly and she stubbed the cigaret out in a glass ashtray. Then she remembered that frowning makes you look your age and she smiled. She patted his hand. "Don't fret. I've got a couple lovely big steaks in the icebox. We'll devour them together. And while they're broiling . . ."

She leaned over the counter. A yellowing laminated plastic sign hung there. WELCOME. She flipped it on its brass chain. The other side said FOR SERVICE RING BELL. She gave Steve a big, bridgework smile.

" . . . I am going to have a double martooni. Care to join me?" She opened the counter gate.

"Far out," Steve said. "Thanks very much."

"I just wish," she said, leading him out of the office, "it was warm enough for us to eat out by the pool. I'd love to have the whole valley see it. It'd make them so God damned mad."

The martini went down the way that remark had—like broken glass. While she mixed it, he sat in the small living room back of the office, in a chintz sofa, with his feet on a braided rug, and looked at the only piece of printed matter in sight, a furniture catalog that lay on a spooled maple coffee table. But when he tasted the drink, he got up and stepped into the kitchen for a look at the gin bottle. He had never heard of the brand.

He didn't let it make any difference. He had a second. Because his stomach was empty, it made him drunk very fast. That was all right. That was the way he wanted it. Presumably she wanted it that way too because she got drunk almost as fast. To make it easier to get cozy with a jig? She did get cozy. Her name was Laurette. His name was Steve. They did what she'd predicted to the steaks—devoured them. Also lettuce and tomatoes with roquefort dressing.

"Sorry I don't have man-type groceries. No p'tatoes and gravy. I'm a slimming girl."

He looked at her solemnly and lisped, "I couldn't stand it any more *mas*-culine than this."

She narrowed her eyes for a second, then opened them wide, threw back her head and whooped with laughter. "My God, my God! Thass funny. Fun-*nee*! Boy, you are priceless." Wagging her head and chuckling, she got up and zig-zagged to the stove for coffee.

While they drank it, she talked about the bar and grill she wanted to build. She owned the lot in back. She already had the plans. She tottered up a ladder stool, took the blueprints down out of a cupboard, unrolled them on the table. They didn't show him much. But there were also drawings of what the place would look like. Stone, glass, polished beams. Off the bar a lounge with hi fi, television, even books. A curved dining room to seat fifty. A conference-ballroom equipped for projecting movies.

"Customers?" Steve asked.

"The ones that stay on the other side of the pass now. Fruit buyers, that type. But tourists, too. Why not? This is a pretty valley. People like an unspoiled place. Mountains are great for riding. Heck Morris and I ride. He owns the service station. He'd love to get more horses, have a rental stable. But that bitch Myra—she's got us stymied every way we turn." Sourly she rolled the plans up. Then she remembered frowning is bad for the face. She smiled. "Now, that's enough about Laurette. Let's talk about Steve. What are you doing here in Shangri-La, Steverino?"

"I came to look at Sister Myra."

"You're kidding!" Laurette made a face. Lopsided, but a face. "I took you to be a man of taste and culture."

"Research," Steve said. "I'm writing a book."

"Oh-ho-ho! Well, let me tell you something to put in your book, Mr. Writer." She wavered to her feet. "Come on. Brandy time. Let's go get comf'table."

They sat on the chintz sofa. Closely. The brandy was worse than the gin, but to keep from sobering up, he drank it. Wincing. She drank hers talking, while her hand crawled up and down his leg and in and out of his shirt like a drugged crab. Sister Myra had this simple little ranch kid she'd turned into a monster. It was quite a story. Laurette wound it up looking at Steve from under half-lowered lids, sucking in her cheeks, and nodding as if she couldn't find the switch to turn her head off.

" . . . And if that old hypocrite doesn't sleep with little Jesse Coy Randol, I don't know human nature. And I know human nature. I been in the hotel-motel business all my life. She sleeps with that kid. Young enough to be her grandson. He's down here right now for Christmas. She'll have him with her there at church tomorrow. You watch them. You tell me they don't sleep together. . . ."

Steve said thickly, "Laurette, if you say sleep one more time, Laurette, I'm gonna fall 'sleep myself."

Then he saw that she had beaten him to it.

15

W HEN HE FOUND THE DOOR numbered 6, he pushed the key
around the lock for a while before it finally went in. The
little room had boxed up and held the sun's warmth from hours
ago. Since it was a cold night this wasn't bad. But the air reeked of
perfume from a spraycan of room freshener and that was going
to make him throw up. He didn't bother to switch on the light. He
left the door open and opened the window next to it. There were
two more windows in the corner. The second of them stuck a
little.

While he was arguing with it, somebody put arms around him
from behind.

He moaned, "Aw, listen, Laurette. . . ."

"Laurette!" Hands gripped his shoulders, turned him around.
It was Coy. The neon out by the road flashed and his hair glowed
in the dark. "Has that old drunk been trying to make you?"

"You guessed," Steve slurred. "But at least she fed me. More
than anybody else here in Equality Valley would do." Not true.
There'd been the filling station operator. But Steve wanted Coy to
feel sorry for him. Guilty.

"Aw, Steve." Coy led him gently to the bed and, when he
dropped down onto its edge, bent to take off his shoes for him.
"Steve, I warned you not to come. I said you'd only be miserable."
He stood and peeled off Steve's suit jacket. "Why couldn't you just
go back to L.A.?"

"I'll go. I'll go." Steve fumbled with the buttons of his shirt.
"Have to go. Work Monday. But I'll be miserable there too. This's
a bad setup, Coy. World I can't be part of. You need a white boy."

"I don't need anybody but you." Coy brushed Steve's hands
aside and unbuttoned his shirt. He sat beside him and ran his

107

hand over Steve's chest. "That's partly why I asked you not to come here. Don't you understand? I can't do or be what I'm supposed to, knowing you're around."

"Didn't mean for you to know," Steve mumbled. "Shouldn't have parked out there by your folks' gate. But I was . . . sad at being cut out. Sore. Maybe on account of Opal. I wanted to be there in your house with you. . . ." He had to stop because if he didn't he'd start a crying jag.

"Don't . . . don't." Coy drew the shirt off down his arms, flagged it away into shadow, kissed Steve's shoulder. "I told you, this isn't real, Steve. You're what's real. This is all fake. Don't be jealous of it. Between it and you, there's just no contest. That's why I've come tonight."

"Yeah. And I was dying, scared you wouldn't. But it's crazy risky. You could blow the whole bit, baby. How'd you get here? How'd you find me, anyway?"

"In our pickup truck." Coy unfastened Steve's slacks. "I looked for your car. It had to be here. It was here."

"But your folks. Sister Myra. What about them? They've got to be wondering where you are."

"No." Coy's teeth glinted in the half dark. He stood and put his hands under Steve's arms. "Come on, let's get the pants off, get you into bed. Sister Myra thinks I'm home asleep. My folks think I drove back to her place for something I forgot. They never bother me there, no matter how late I stay."

"How late do you stay? Do you sleep with her? Laurette says you sleep with her."

"Oh, please. Laurette's just bugged because she tried to get into my pants when she used to let the valley kids swim here at her pool. Naturally, she never got anywhere. Come on. Up! You're too much man for this girl to lift."

Steve stood, swaying. The slacks fell. When he pulled his feet out of them, Coy draped them over a chair back. Steve said, "Look, what if Laurette or somebody sees the truck?"

"They won't. It's parked way up among the trees. I came in here the back way. Nobody saw me." He jerked the candlewick spread off the bed, folded back the sheets, and covered Steve's mouth with his own. He drew back. "Wow! Are you ever the drunk one!"

"Sorry. Wanted to be stoned if you didn't show, sober if you did. Couldn't see how to have it both ways." He dropped back onto the bed and stretched out. "Lousy booze," he muttered. "God, what lousy booze."

"Sleep it off." Coy laughed softly and pulled the covers over him. "I'll wake you in a couple hours." In the vague pulse of the neon lights through the window, Steve saw him pull the T-shirt off over his head and drop his Levis. Steve smiled. That was all he'd worn. Except his little medal. He slid between the sheets carefully, as if Steve was already asleep. . . .

Next morning, when he came out of the shower, head aching, stomach grinding, he didn't know what he was going to do—if he lived. He wanted to go up to Sister Myra's church and watch. But he had to eat. He couldn't impose on Laurette again. And the only alternative was to drive over the pass, find a place that would serve him, then drive back. By that time it would be too late. He stumbled toward the bed. Maybe he wouldn't live. Maybe he'd just lie down and die.

Then he saw the tray on the bedside table. Pottery carafe of steaming coffee. Cup. Utensils in a napkin. Plate covered by a dome of spun aluminum. He lifted this. A hot breakfast roll, butter oozing into the jam and sugar frosting. Something else caught his eye—a little blue foil packet of Fizrin. Two waxed paper cups. He grinned feebly. In the bathroom he mixed the foamy stuff, drank it, shut his eyes and leaned against the basin, letting his unhappy head hang. After a minute he belched. Resoundingly. Three times. That was better.

He went back to the bed, sat down on it, drank the coffee, ate the roll. Maybe her motives were tarnished but Laurette had her points. Dressing, he checked himself in the maple-framed mirror. The gray-green corduroy suit had the press built in. That was why he'd picked it for this trip where he couldn't bring a change without making Coy suspicious. The shirt was moss green. He'd worn the collar open yesterday. It was high. He buttoned it now, took from his jacket pocket a hunter green tie, knotted it. Neat but not gaudy. He missed the shave, but nobody else would—he wasn't the bristly type.

He picked up the tray and carried it to the office. Awful as it was, the booze didn't appear to have damaged Laurette. She looked no worse than she had yesterday. Ruffled Spanish skirt this time, off the shoulder blouse of white eyelet lace, black wig, scarlet lipstick and beads to go with the hibiscus flowers printed on the skirt.

"*Buenos dias, Señorita,*" he grinned. "*Por el desayuno, muchas gracias. Lo salva me vida.*"

"You're kidding," she said. "I'd never have taken you for a Mexican. Sleep well? I mean . . . considering you were alone?" She eyed him archly.

"Considering that, very well." Little did she know. He reached for his wallet. "I owe you something for drinks, dinner, breakfast."

"Those were my pleasure," she said. "You look resplendent this morning."

"It's the tie. I'm on my way to catch Sister Myra's act." He glanced at his watch. "Christ, I'll be late." He turned for the door.

"Come back for lunch," she said.

"Thanks, but I can linger no longer in Mysterious Tibet."

"The High Lama will be disappointed," she said.

A side road that followed a dry wash full of boulders and deadwood led up a shallow canyon to the church. It was plain country style, stucco painted the color of sandstone. Its steeple pointed at the blue winter sky from a V-shaped slope of ground shaded by live oaks. Except for a patch of lawn in front of the building, the ground was tarmacked, parked solid with cars.

Steve was late. The only human in sight was a boy in a suit short at the wrists and ankles and tight at the armholes. He evidently had something to do with parking the cars. When Steve stopped his in the middle of the road and sat there for a minute, the boy came over and squinted in at him.

"Do you want Berea Church?" He couldn't believe it.

"What's the matter?" Steve said. "Doesn't Berea Church want me?"

"There's no more room to park."

"There's got to be room somewhere," Steve said. "This is God's great outdoors—remember?"

The boy sulked and backed off. "Up there." When he pointed, his jacket sleeve pulled back to his elbow.

Up there proved to be a rutty strip of raw ground that tilted steeply toward the barranca. A dozen cars were parked there already. Steve scraped past them and wedged his car between two boulders.

Singing came out of the church as he crossed the lawn. *Jesus,*

Jesus, Jesus—sweetest name I know . . . He'd never heard that one. He halted. Maybe this wasn't a good idea. He rubbed his fingers on his palms. Sweaty. If he turned around right now, he might save himself trouble. Be he couldn't leave here without seeing Sister in action. What the hell—this wasn't Alabama. He took a deep breath and climbed the three cement steps.

The outer doors stood open. There was a fifteen-foot Christmas tree in the vestibule. He walked around it and faced the double swing doors into the church. He hesitated, dry-mouthed. Then they began another song. *I was sinking, deep in sin, far from the peaceful shore. . . .* He knew that one, from the time when he was very small and went with Grandma to her church. That made him feel a little less alien. Then he heard Coy's voice. An amplifier and some tinny loudspeakers were distorting it, but it was Coy's voice, all right. He pushed open the doors.

Coy stood on the platform at a microphone. He wore the corny blue serge suit and he was waving his arms in time to the music, leading the singing. When he saw Steve his eyes widened and he forgot the words for a second. Steve gave him a grin. Behind Coy on the platform sat his father and mother and sister—gaunt man with a sunburned, furrowed face and huge, hairy hands; a faded, once-pretty woman; a pale, skinny girl. Steve recognized them from snapshots Coy had shown him. There was Sister Myra, smiling broadly, swinging her hymn book. Down in the crowd toward the front, Steve saw Opal.

And that was all he had time to see. A big man got in his way. Massive. He was dressed in a mattress ticking suit and had a slack Southern face, wisps of pale red hair combed across a freckled bald head. He breathed out wintergreen.

"You're in the wrong church."

"Isn't this Berea Church?" Steve asked.

People in the rear seats turned around and stared.

"There's a sign outside." The big man grabbed Steve's arm, whacked open the swing door, and dragged Steve out past the Christmas tree, down the three steps and across the lawn. He pointed at the sign. BEREA CHURCH. "Can you read that, boy?"

"Yassuh," Steve clowned.

The man didn't notice. "Does it say 'colored' anywhere on there? 'African,' maybe?"

"No, suh." Steve rolled his eyes.

"Then this *ain't* the church you're lookin' for."

"No, *suh!*"

"All right, then—on your way. We don't want no race trouble down here. This is a peaceful place and we aim to keep it that way."

He turned and lumbered back across the grass. Then a second man in mattress ticking, this one smaller and wearing rimless glasses, came bustling out the doors. He said something to the big man and then they both turned and stared at Steve, who started to walk away—fast.

"Wait!" The runty one came after him, jogtrotting. "Brother Archer?"

"Archer, yes," Steve said. "Brother I doubt."

"Oh, now, look. There's been a mistake. I mean . . ." He worked up a fidgety kind of smile. "Sister Myra passed me this note. She wants you to come inside and attend the service."

"What about Brother Lynch, there?" Steve nodded toward the big man who stood in the middle of the grass, trying to remember how to look amiable. "Does he want me?"

"Why, most surely. Just a misunderstandin' is all. We are—" He nearly choked on it. "We are all God's children."

"Especially sometimes," Steve said. "All right. Let's go."

Sister Myra didn't need the microphone. Her voice had brass and carry. She used it mostly to make noise about her good right arm. Jesus had healed it, the way He would heal anybody's good right anything if they only prayed and had faith. She whirled the arm around, reminding the congregation of how only last week she'd hardly been able to raise it this high. She made a bunchy bicep for them to admire. God had work for her to do. He'd only sent her that little stroke to remind her that arm belonged to Him, not her.

The hair was still a brass helmet. She wore a nylon flower print dress, brown and mauve, right off the sale rack at Sears El Centro. The body that filled it was lumpy and tough. But, from the back of the church, anyway, the face looked as if it had been borrowed from Carol Baker for the weekend. The effect was creepy.

So was the effect of Coy's little report on his months at Galilee College. He said sorrowfully that his listeners had probably read in the papers reports on student life at the big universities. Shocking. Longhair kids drinking whisky, gobbling barbiturate pills, smoking marijuana, printing filthy language on signs and marching up and down with them. But, worst of all, throwing naked parties where they wallowed in sordid orgies of unbridled SEX. He had the worshippers sitting on the edges of their seats, licking their lips, eager for more details. Then he switched to the pure and prayerful life of Galilee College, and they sat back, disappointed but covering it with little murmurs of "Praise the Lord" and "Amen."

Steve nearly broke up.

After that, they sang Christmas carols. When it seemed to him they'd about exhausted the list, he left. Not soon enough. By the time he'd hiked back up to his car and begun killing the motor trying to back it across the ruts and rocks to turn it around, the meeting broke up. The way out was blocked with cars crawling out of the parking lot below and onto the narrow dirt road. Trapped, he sat there with the handbrake on, the motor idling, trying not to notice the stares of people who didn't see a Negro often and didn't want to see one ever.

"Steve!" Coy put his hands on the window ledge.

"Baby, you knock me out." Steve grinned.

"I'm sorry about what happened, Steve. Why didn't you tell me you were coming?"

"Yeah, I should have, only I figured you'd make me promise not to. And this I had to see. Anyhow, you fixed it. What'd you tell Sister Myra?"

"You'll find out. Listen . . ." Coy was panting. The sun was high and warm right now. Sweat beaded his forehead. "I lost something last night. Must have dropped it when I pulled off my T-shirt."

"In the motel cabin? Oh, grand. What was it?"

"My C.E. medal. On a chain. Silver and blue enamel, round, about the size of a quarter. Remember it?"

"I remember. What about Laurette—will she remember?"

"No. She's never seen it. Get it for me, will you? Tell her it's yours."

"Shit," Steve said. "I didn't want to go back there."

Then he saw Sister Myra making for the car. In the bright sunlight the face paint didn't work as well as it had indoors. The walk wasn't so robust either. One foot dragged a little. One eyelid drooped, and when she tried for the big, genial platform smile now, only the left half worked.

"Mr. Archer . . ." Coy pulled open the car door. "I want you to meet Sister Myra Lusk."

Steve scrambled out. Her handshake hurt.

"Sorry about the little mixup there when you first came in," Sister Myra said. "If I'd been told you were coming, that wouldn't have happened." She gave Coy a look that was about ten percent reproof and ninety percent melting adoration. "Jesse Coy tells me you write for some pretty big magazines. Came to Galilee College one time. Now you're doing a piece on California evangelists. That right?"

Steve said, "Beautiful place you've got here."

"Oh, the sanctuary's only part of it," she said. "God's given us our own radio station. FM, six hours a day. Up yonder on the mountain. I took a course, got my license, run it myself. Then there's the mail order . . ."

She took them on a tour of what she called "the plant"—new rooms built off each side of the main church at the rear. The printshop had an offset press, a setup for photographing offset plates, stocks of paper and ink, a big, standup stapling machine. The office had new electric typewriters and an electric mimeograph. On a long table, shallow wire baskets held heaps of unopened envelopes.

"Here's where the girls sit and open the mail and count the dimes and dollars folks send in. Bless 'em."

Besides a wrapping counter with rolls of brown paper and corrugated board, the stockroom had shelves on all sides, sagging with printed pamphlets and tracts written by Sister Myra, mimeographed copies of her 26-lesson series on faith healing, Bibles, Sunday-school papers. She kept pushing copies into Steve's hands. On top at the moment was a glossy brochure about the radio station—*God's Voice From The Hills*.

Sister Myra looked blank. "Why, my book, Jess. *The Church In The Valley*. There's no copies here. Do you just want to scramble up in the loft and fetch me down say twenty?"

Coy and Steve got into the loft by a trapdoor up a ladder. It was hot and smelled of fresh pine sap. There was a lot of room up here under the pitched roof. All the stained glass in Berea Church was the color of rusty tin cans. The window at the end of this gable was made of it. It kept the place dark. The wiring conduits were in but they hadn't yet been connected to outlets: the ends of the different colored wires hung bandaged, like limp and useless fingers. So Steve held a big, shiny, three-cell flashlight that Sister Myra had put into his hand, while Coy lifted down from the unpainted shelves four bundles of books in brown paper.

Back in the office, Sister Myra signed a copy for Steve.

Laurette said, "Aw . . . I thought I was going to have a keepsake." She took the medal out of the counter cash drawer and dangled it by its chain.

Steve held out his hand.

She said, "Not till you tell me what it means."

He grinned and shook his head. "I don't know. I found it myself. It was a lucky day. I always wear it."

"Not last night." There was a flat sound to her voice, a flat look to her eyes. "You didn't have it on last night."

He remembered her hand crawling inside his shirt. "You're right. Sometimes I just keep it in my pocket. That's probably the reason it got dropped."

"It didn't get dropped," she said. "It was in the bed."

"Well, anyway, thanks for finding it."

"Lucky thing I did the room myself," she said. "If it had been one of the Mexican girls, she'd have kept it." She let it fall into his hand. Regretfully. Then she smiled. "Well, now you're here—how about lunch?"

"Sorry." He looked at his watch. "Sister Myra already kept me overtime."

"How did things go for you at morning worship?"

"They had me bound and gagged and covered with tar. They were just about to string me up to a tree and set me on fire, when Sister Myra got word I could give her some free publicity. She spoiled their fun. It was kind of sad to see their faces."

She laughed.

He dropped the medal into his pocket and left.

16

W HEN HE REACHED HOME FROM THE LIBRARY on Monday and tried to thumb the latch and found the door locked, he remembered he was alone, was going to be alone for two long weeks. At Christmas, of all times! He turned the lock with his key and pushed open the door. The white room was empty and cold. And dark.

If Coy was here, the lamps would be lit—big pottery lamps with streaky blue glazes and white cylindrical shades, that stood one at each end of the couch on little white and gilt Neapolitan tables from Akron's. The panelray would have the place warm. There would be good smells of supper cooking.

Steve would shower. When he came out, wearing the red terrycloth robe Coy had made him buy, the kid would hand him a martini, Manhattan, old fashioned. Always the best. Then, unless something cooked that needed close attention, they'd sit on the couch. If they happened to touch, nine times in ten they'd make out.

Whether they did or not, they'd listen to a record. Steve had got fed up with Montovani, Roger Williams, Percy Faith. He couldn't afford to, but he bought three albums—Bud Shank-Laurindo Almeda, Glenn Gould playing Bach, the Ravel string quartette. Not too hard on Coy, tolerable for himself.

Afterward, they'd eat. At first it had been different every time. Later Steve asked for things over again—sweetbreads with sauce almondaise, shrimp jumbalaya, beef Stroganoff, a creamy cheese pie that was to dream about. So . . . the candlelight idea was chi-chi. He didn't make an issue of it since it pleased Coy.

Then the kid would go into the little back bedroom where he had a desk, and study, while Steve washed the dishes, then read—

Samuel Beckett was his kick now: *Happy Days, All That Fall*—or listened to music or writer interviews or panel discussions on FM. He kept the sound level down so Coy wouldn't be bothered and the door could be open so Steve could look in at him, his head bent over his books, hair shining in the light of the lamp.

At ten, he'd quit studying. They'd have drinks—Scotch and soda for the kid, bonded Bourbon over ice for Steve. They might watch a 1930s gangster film on channel 28—no commercials. They might hit the bed right away for sex and sleep. Or they might put on jackets and walk down to Sunset for a beer. They never had more than two before they drifted back up Kean Terrace to bed. The little street was dark. Cars almost never passed. They could hold hands walking.

A good life.

He sighed, switched on the lamps, turned on the heat. After his shower, he got into corduroy Levis and a roomy, dark red flannel shirt. He looked at the stereo. The Ravel quartette lay on the turntable. He pushed the button, the tone arm moved into place, and violins, viola, cello began discussing the sadness of being young. He wandered into the kitchen to mix a Manhattan.

Eating was a lonely business. And even after he'd washed everything up and left the place shining, it still wasn't eight. Hours to kill. Empty hours. The music had quit. He stood aimless in the middle of the living room, hands hanging. What to do? He knew what he ought to do. He ought to write. When you were writing, you didn't miss anybody, didn't need anybody. But the idea made his stomach knot. Words on paper could stir up so much grief. He wasn't ready to go through that again—or put anybody else through it. Not yet.

He made a face. Excuses, excuses.

The typewriter stood on the floor beside Coy's desk. Steve crouched, opened the case, lifted out the machine. He set it in the circle of light cast by the tensor lamp on the desk. The desk was handsome—right out of a Dunbar ad in *The New Yorker*. So was the chair that went with it. Saddle seat in black leather. Good to sit in.

Yet he felt constrained. This was Coy's place. Sure, he'd told Steve to use it. But Steve had actually been in the room only once—to bring in the typewriter and the cardboard box that held his manuscripts, blank paper, carbons. It was Coy's desk. He'd preferred leaving it to Coy to put the stuff away. So that now, if he was going to write, he had to find it.

He opened a drawer.

Bills lay there, dozens of them, crisp and white, sealed in their window envelopes. He frowned for a second, then shut the drawer. He'd been raised in the strict understanding that other people's mail was their own business. He found the typing paper neatly boxed in a lower drawer, slipped out two sheets, rolled them into the Olympia. La Paz Valley was on his mind. Dead Oak. There was a play there.

But he couldn't concentrate. Those bills bothered him. Why were there so many, and why weren't they even opened? Hell, he gave Coy his paycheck every two weeks when he got it. He was supposed to be paying half the expenses. He pushed the typewriter aside, took the bills out of the drawer and laid them in the light.

The return addresses printed on the envelopes varied and repeated. Berg and Son Furniture. Supreme Appliances. Wizard Television and Electronics. Hafiz Carpets. Piccadilly Men's Attire. There were duplicates, triplicates. They dated back three months. He began ripping them open, laying them out.

It didn't take long to get the story.

On that stunning couch, the white carpets and drapes, the kingsize bed, the glossy chest of drawers, this desk, the television set, stove, refrigerator, even the dishes, glasses, kitchenware, to say nothing of the tape recorder that never got used—Coy had made the smallest possible down payments and paid nothing since. On his clothes he'd paid nothing ever. The best brands. Of course.

Steve tore open an envelope rubber-stamped with the name of the market at the foot of the hill on Sunset. He'd been there a few times with Coy. To reach it from here you took long flights of cement steps instead of sidewalks. It was a friendly place. The guy at the liquor counter was a genial Greek. The owner ran the cash register—a middle-aged woman with a farm-wife twang, who swapped recipes with Coy. Nice place. Jokes. Smiles.

The bill was ninety-seven dollars.

At the foot of it was written in ballpoint pen: *Please take care of this as soon as possible—Mrs. Terry.* The best food. The hamburger had to be sirloin. Fresh crab. Artichoke hearts. Tons of mushrooms. Gallons of sour cream. The best booze. Jack Daniels whisky, Bombay gin, Chivas Regal Scotch. Mexican beer, Dutch beer. You bet it was a good life. No wonder.

Nothing was paid for.

On a shaky wicker table in a corner where a big fern brooded fifty weeks of the year, his grandmother had set up a two-foot-high fir tree and decorated it with balls of surgical cotton and strings of popcorn and cranberries. The same as always. Its ten dim little red and green lights twinkled at him from across the room when she opened the front door.

"Hi, Grandma. Merry Christmas."

She blinked at him as if she didn't know him. Had he been wrong—was she not going to forgive him about the play? She was wearing her dimestore Bible-reading glasses. He dropped the soft parcel he was carrying, reached out and gently lifted the glasses off her flat nose.

"It's Steve," he said. "Remember?"

"Remember!" she said. "Remember!" Her wizened black face crinkled into a smile. Toothless. She owned dentures—the best. But she claimed they hurt her and she would wear them only to church. Tears shone in her eyes. She threw her bony little arms around him and hugged. "You did come. You did come, after all."

"Sure, I came." Her head reached only as high as his chest. He smoothed its sparse white hair and teased her: "You didn't think I'd pass up my Christmas cornbread, did you?"

"I did. He ain't comin', I says. Well . . ." She turned from him. "That don't make no never mind. You come on. I'll bake a batch right now. It don't take but half an hour."

"Aw, you don't have to, Grandma." He picked up the package from the porch floor and followed her inside. "I only came to bring you—"

But she was already on her way to the kitchen, her worn, old felt slippers flapping. "Don't talk silly. Course you wants your cornbread. I just foolish, is all. Thought you wasn't comin'. Says to myself, he think we all mad at him about that play. Come on out here and talk to Grandma."

He went into the gloomy green kitchen and sat on the familiar, much-mended wooden chair by the old dropleaf table whose paint had all been taken off by years of scrubbing. He watched her quick, excited movements, getting flour, baking powder, shortening, salt out of cupboards, milk and eggs from the old wooden icebox, sifting, mixing—watched as he'd watched every Christmas he could remember, smiling, mouth watering.

To his father and mother, cornbread was bad diet, Negro poverty food, symbol of a contemptible past. He'd only been allowed it on Grandma's insistence once a year—a generous chunk, right out of the baking pan, cut open steaming and drenched with sorghum. A treat. At that, Grandma had strict instructions never to call it cornpone in his hearing, though that was the natural word to her, and it was for a long time hard for her to remember corn*bread*.

He asked her, "You're not mad about the play?"

She set down the sifter and turned to look at him. "Where'd you find that old lady to take my part?"

"She's a professional actress, Grandma. Been in a lot of plays on the New York stage, movies, TV. She's very fine."

"That as may be. But what for did you have her talk like white folks? Cain't she talk like me?"

"She can, Grandma," Steve said. "But the men who were doing the play wouldn't let her. They were afraid some colored people wouldn't like it, would think the play was making fun of them."

"Makin' fun of 'em!" She snorted. "That the whole trouble right now. They all so worried what this one say and that one think. If they afraid of the truth, then they must be ashamed of it. But not shamed enough to change. And that no good." She shook her head, mouth pursed grimly, and turned and took up her mixing spoon. She beat the batter in the bowl grimly. "No good. The truth never did no harm—not to honest folks. Never will." She mixed up egg and milk together and poured them into the big bowl and went to stirring again. "That why I'm not mad about your play. Cept for how that old lady talk, it told the truth. Oh, I know . . ." She emptied the contents of the bowl, yellow and creamy, into a dented baking pan. "It was a lot of it just a made-up story. But the people was true." She bent, opened the creaking door of the black, old gas oven, and slid the pan inside. "No, I'm not mad. But your father, he didn't like it. Not one bit."

"He made that clear." Steve laughed sadly.

"He a fool." She shut the oven door, rinsed and dried her hands at the sink that was old and sagging and had chips out of its enamel. "He ought to be proud. I'm proud. From the time you was a little bitty thing, I always told you, tell the truth, Steve— didn't I? And you remembered, and I'm proud."

He felt like crying. He got up fast and went after the package in the parlor. Miss Williams at the library had helped him wrap it with paper and ribbons he'd bought on his lunchtime. He'd passed up the smart papers and found an old-fashioned design with poinsettias. With its big red bow, the package looked as if Christmas itself was bundled up inside. He laid it on the table.

Grandma was drying the mixing bowl. "What that?" She set the bowl down. "I'm too old for Christmas gifts."

"Then I'm too old for cornbread," Steve grinned. "Come on. Open it. I want to see if you're pleased."

"I'm pleased already," she said, and stood on tiptoe to kiss his chin. "I'm just pleased you didn't forget me." Her gnarled little fingers worked at the bow. "Oh, so pretty . . . you done it up so pretty." Then she had the paper laid back and was staring.

"Pick it up," he said. "Unfold it."

It was an old Spanish shawl, rich with color, and with a long, black, silken fringe. He'd found it in a jumble shop in Capistrano on the trip back from La Paz Valley. It had cost him too much, but he couldn't pass it up—not remembering how much his Grandma used to talk, with shining eyes, of such a shawl draped over a grand piano in a house where she'd worked when his father was a child. She thought it was the most beautiful thing she'd ever seen. His father could have bought her one, but he'd never have considered it. Too gaudy, typical ignorant darky taste. Steve grinned, watching Grandma's face light up as she unfolded it now.

"Oh, my goodness!" she breathed in soft wonder. "Oh, my goodness!" Then she gathered it against her shrunken breast and looked at him with tears streaming down her face. "Why child, where ever did you get this? It the loveliest thing I ever held in my hands. It beautiful, Steve. Just beautiful. I wanted one like this all my life long."

"I know. Come on, you don't want to cry all over it." He took it from her and while she brushed at the tears with her fingers, he draped it around her shoulders. She was so short that it dragged on the worn linoleum. He arranged it, stepped back, and she turned around shyly so he could admire it. "You'll be the envy of every lady at church."

"Oh!" She looked shocked. "I wouldn't dare wear it anywheres. Why, folks'd think I was crazy—a shriveled up old woman like me!" She laughed, took it off, held it out, gazing at it, her head tilted. "No, I'll just hang it where I can see it in the house." She hurried out. "I'll hang it over the back of the sofa."

He watched her fix it the way she wanted it. Then, when she went off into the bedroom, he moved to the sink and washed up the rest of the stuff she'd used to make the cornbread. When she came back, she was carrying two packages wrapped in white tissue paper.

"Oh, now, look . . . the cornbread is my present."

"That right," she nodded. "This ain't for you. It for your family."

"My . . . family?"

"Your wife and baby. There's a nice little sweater for your wife, kinda salmon color. Should look pretty on her. Lady at the church knitted it. I bought it off her. And there's a rattle for the baby. Don't know what all he got, but that what he'll like. And—and I wants you to bring him to see me." She'd obviously made a hard decision. She thrust out her chin. "And your wife, too. Lacey— that her name? I didn't treat her right before. Your play made me see that. I acted stiffnecked, like the Bible say. I wants to make it up to her. What the baby's name?"

Steve swallowed. "Grandma . . ." But he couldn't tell her what had happened. It would spoil the pleasure she was getting from this Christmas visit. "He's . . . not born yet." He smiled. "We don't even know if it's a he or a she."

"Don't?" The old woman frowned, cocked her head and counted on her fingers. "Why, it look to me like that baby got to be due."

"Yes, that's right," Steve said. "He's due."

17

I T WAS ABOUT THE SADDEST THING he'd ever done.
He walked down the green-tiled fifth floor corridor of Beth-El
Hospital behind an orderly in green overalls who was wheeling a
rubber-tired cart on which pans rattled. The sign NURSERY hung
above an alcove where there were chairs in pink and blue naugahide, clowns painted on the wall. At the back of the alcove a wide
window looked into a white room glowing with fluorescent light.

He walked to the window. In the room were rows of pink and
blue moulded plastic bassinets that held babies. New babies. Most
of them were asleep, eyes shut in bruised-looking little faces, but a
few were awake and making feeble undersea signals with clenched
fists, or jerkily kicking small legs under pinned-down pink and
blue blankets. It was an expensive hospital so not many of the
babies were Negro. Only one was half colored, half white.

He tapped on the glass. A pretty little nurse—her figure in the
starchy white uniform was pretty: most of her face was covered by
a white mask—turned and raised her eyebrows at him. She
seemed to be smiling. He couldn't smile, but he nodded and
pointed to the coffee-with-cream baby. She sidled between the
bassinets until she reached the right one. She turned and looked
at him again. He nodded again. It was a blue bassinet, so the baby
was a boy. Sadder and sadder. She bent over the bassinet and
slipped the baby out from under the blankets and brought it to
the window.

It wasn't much bigger than a three-dollar doll. It had on a little
T-shirt and diapers about nine sizes too big. It stared at him with
startled brown eyes. There was soft curly black down on its head.
The nurse jiggled it and it turned on a toothless grin. There were
double panes of glass in the window, but he imagined he heard it
laugh. A milky bubble appeared at its mouth. The nurse hiked

the baby on her shoulder and carried it back to its bassinet. It was a pretty baby, prettiest he'd ever seen.

Eyes blurring, he turned and walked away.

Why the hell had he come? Why had he sat last night in the empty apartment doggedly dialing hospital after hospital, asking whether Mrs. Stephen Archer had had her baby there? None of it made any sense to him now. He'd warned Bernie he'd be back for the baby, and for months he'd told himself how easy it would be when the time came. All he'd have to do was tell a judge the truth about Bernie and Lacey. Not fit. But would any judge think him more fit? And anyway, how in Christ's name could he look after a baby? Fantasy—that was all it had been. Stupid, adolescent fantasy. When was he going to grow up?

He punched the elevator button savagely.

In the next shaft, the Up elevator stopped. Its doors slid open. A rosy-cheeked intern in rumpled white stepped out, stethoscope dangling down his front, clipboard under his arm. Three smartly dressed matrons followed, chattering and laughing. Then came a white-haired couple carrying gaily wrapped gifts. And two little kids in yellow slickers, excited by the elevator ride and the fact that tomorrow would be Christmas.

And Bernie.

She wore a brown slouch hat with a pheasant feather, a wrap-around camel-hair coat, big leather bag slung off her shoulder on a wide strap. She swung in Steve's direction, saw him, and stopped dead. Her eyes widened. The color drained from her face, leaving it muddy and sagging. For a second he thought she was going to fall down. What in hell ailed her? She looked scared, and Bernie didn't scare. But it didn't last. She pulled herself together. Her voice came out hard.

"Have you been bothering Lacey? If you—"

"I only came to look at my son," he said.

Her eyes narrowed. She opened her mouth to say something.

The doors of the Down elevator opened. He got in. As the doors shut she was still standing in the same place, staring at him. He couldn't read the expression in her eyes.

Terry's Market was a long building of yellow stucco with arches that could be closed by green steel folding doors. They were closed when Steve swung the car off of Sunset onto the rain-glossy asphalt parking strip that fronted the place. But a couple of the doors had glass in them, and through this he could see lights inside and people moving around. Good. He'd been afraid they might close early on Christmas Eve, the way the library had. He turned up his jacket collar, left the car and ran, shoulders hunched, head down, through the gray drizzle, to the entrance.

Mrs. Terry, with a sprig of holly pinned to her dress, was kidding with a pair of bleached young men in girly transparent raincoats. He waited until they flounced off with their jingling sacks of Christmas cheer, squawking and giggling. One of them playfully slapped the other's rear as they went out. It made a wet, crashing sound.

"Mrs. Terry—remember me?"

She gave him a cheerful grin. "Why, sure. You're Steve, Jesse Randol's friend. Merry Christmas."

"Thanks." Steve gave her back the smile. It wasn't easy. He'd never felt less like smiling. "Same to you."

"How is that rascal, Jesse?"

"Fine. Went home to his folks for Christmas." Steve reached into his inside jacket pocket. He'd applied last week for a loan of one hundred dollars against his wages, from the credit union. It had been ready only today. He'd meant it to go for presents, mainly for Coy. He took the check from the pocket. Folded with it was Mrs. Terry's bill. Between racks of foil-sacked peanuts and bright candy bars on the counter he laid both pieces of paper.

"Why . . ." Unfolding them, she blinked through her bifocals. "My! This is a nice surprise."

"The bill was a surprise to me," he said. "I didn't know it existed till a couple days ago. Have you got a pen? I'll endorse the check."

"Yup." She handed him a long, black ballpoint. "It's a shock how fast they mount up."

Steve bent and signed the back of the check. He felt a pang, watching her slip it into the cash register drawer under the twenty-dollar bills. But when she'd rubber-stamped the bill PAID, put her initials on it and handed it to him together with three ones and another fine smile, he felt better.

"Sorry you had to wait so long," he said. "Thanks for being so patient."

"You're a very sweet boy," she said. "You have the nicest Christmas you can. You deserve it."

For a minute he paused outside the market, hands jammed into his pockets, the cold rain sifting down on him. The cars hissing carefully along Sunset had their lights on. But it wasn't late. He took a step toward his car, then halted. He didn't want to be alone. He turned, crossed the parking strip and walked up the block.

There were five bars in the neighborhood where no one went but homosexuals. In front of the one he chose, a little black hood awning with white fringe crossed the sidewalk to the curb. Steve pushed inside. Quiet. That was the best part about the place, that and its understated black and white decor. Nobody ever screamed, and there was no jukebox.

On weekends a man who looked like a tired, grayhaired twelve-year-old boy played a black and white baby grand—well. If he was just drunk enough and not too drunk you could ask him for "In a Mist" and he would play it just like Jess Stacy. He was there now, playing "The Little Drummer Boy" softly, and he nodded sadly at Steve, who nodded sadly back.

The place belonged to a big, blond Viking type named Norquist, and the Mexican kid he lived with, Jaime, who was beautiful and solemn-looking and told jokes. He told them with a thick accent and without cracking a smile, so that at first you didn't know what was happening. But the brittle people came from far away to get the new stories the way Jaime told them.

They came to get gossip from Norquist. His build was lean and tough. There was a mat of golden hair on his chest. His voice was heavy, speech slow. A man? Maybe, but inside lived a malicious fairy. Who was sleeping with whom? Who had been nabbed by the vice squad? Who had been robbed by a hustler, beaten up by juveniles? Who was seeing what psychologist, urologist, proctologist? Norquist knew and gave out the facts—impassive as a television newscaster, but enjoying the work.

Steve didn't like him and was glad Jaime was alone back of the bar now. He took the stool nearest the piano and ordered bonded whisky on the rocks and grinned sourly at himself for the extravagance. That would have to end. There were more bills to pay—almost two thousand dollars worth. But that was something else he wasn't going to think about now. Not tonight. "Have Yourself a Merry Little Christmas," the piano played. Sure. Sure he would. You bet. Jaime set down the drink in its squat glass.

"*Dónde está su amigo?*"

Steve told him in his lame textbook Spanish.

"*Siento mucho,*" Jaime said. "That's too bad. But he will be back.

126

Then it will stop raining."

Steve drank the drink carefully but quickly and ordered another. This one he worked on slowly, smoking, watching the place fill up. They brought in dampness. Men by themselves, the clothes they'd worn to work this morning wilted, faces drawn, eyes tired. The traffic was murder, they told Jaime. The streets were slippery. It was no good leaving the office party after one drink—not when you had to crawl ten miles to the next bottle. They ordered doubles. "Silver Bells," the piano played.

Then Pike came in.

Steve couldn't believe it. The beach was Pike's place. He taught in the valley. The route between was the San Diego freeway. Miles from here. Still, it was Christmas Eve. People went freak places at Christmas, once a year places. Who knew where Pike's relatives lived, if he had any? Besides, this was a gay bar. If you were queer, all gay bars were in your neighborhood.

Steve watched him slide onto a stool near the door. He looked thinner than he used to be. When he'd driven off to teach he'd worn easy clothes. What he had on now was generically office. Only the beard saved him. Brandy was what he drank and when he lit a cigaret the pack it came out of was still bright blue. So were his eyes. The piano began: *Chestnuts roasting on an open fire* . . . And the eyes turned and saw him.

Pike got off the stool and came back in his wet raincoat and holding the brandy in its bubble of glass. He stood behind Steve and Steve turned on the stool. Pike's hat was pushed back on his head. Raindrops sparkled in his beard.

"Hello," he said. "What are you doing here?"

"I'm on my way home from the hospital. I've been to see Lacey. The baby's born."

"Congratulations," Pike said. "Boy or girl?"

"Boy. And you? What are you doing here?"

"I stop here every day at this time. . . ."

It could be true: Steve and Coy never came till late.

"... On my way home from the agency. I'm in advertising now. Downtown. This is one stop. There's another one on Lincoln Boulevard. . . . Are you happy?"

"Jesus, this dialog is right out of *Brief Encounter*," Steve said. "What about your car?"

"It was insured," Pike said. "I've got another one."

"Okay." Steve turned back to his drink. "Goodbye, Jimmy."

"You know what I do?" Pike said behind him. "I still love you, Steve. If I could have you, you could cut up one of my cars every week."

"You're sick," Steve said into his glass.

"I was beginning to get well. Then I saw you at your play. My fault. My mistake. I wasn't going to make that mistake again. And now . . . you turn up here."

"Coincidence," Steve said.

"I don't believe in coincidences," Pike said. "I believe in fate. Lacey's in the hospital. You're going to be alone tonight. Let me come home with you, Steve. Please?"

Steve turned to face him and saw tears in his eyes.

"Jimmy, you raped my wife. Have you forgotten that little detail?"

"It wasn't like that. She asked me. She'd asked me before, at the beach. And . . . it was a way of having you. . . ."

"Okay. Whatever it was, it wrecked . . . damn near wrecked my marriage. You think I could love you? There? In the same bed where it happened, for Christ sake? Or any place, Jimmy, any place?"

Pike said, "You'll wear it out—this husband and father bit. You will. Then it'll be my turn. It's got to be."

"Don't count on it." Steve got off the stool. "I'm leaving. Don't look for me here any more, Jimmy. I'll remember not to come back."

When he reached the top of the long cement stairs, he saw lights in the apartment. He stopped on the puddled terrace and stood with the rain soaking into his shoes, and stared. Inside the windows was a Christmas tree. Black? The front door was unlocked. He pushed it and stepped in. The tree was really black, spray painted. It was hung with Mexican white sugar skulls the size of tennis balls.

"Merry Christmas, Steve!"

It was Marvel, of course. She came at him out of the kitchen, glass in her hand, arms open wide. *The hostess with the leastest,* Steve thought. But what could he do? Coy liked her and had kept her scarce the way he'd promised. And now she was meaning well again. He sighed grimly and was holding out his arms and giving her a big Louis Armstrong smile—when a man appeared in the kitchen door. Squat, about thirty, he had the fatty muscles of the failed high school athlete, a battered pink face, pale hair and eyebrows. He was holding a guitar.

"Who's this?" Steve stepped out of her reach around the coffee table.

"Why, it's Bunk. My li'l hubby. You know Bunk." She followed Steve, still eager to swarm all over him.

"We haven't met." Steve went to him quickly, hand out. "How are you, Bunk? Marv talks about you all the time." She never mentioned him.

"Pleasure." Bunk's voice was a gravelly tenor. His hand was like a dead but still warm slab of meat. Steve dropped it.

"Nice of you to come by. Drink?"

But Bunk, like Marvel, already had a drink.

"Let me fix you one," Marvel said, and then threw her arms around Steve's neck and gave him a messy, wet, gin kiss. She patted his cheek. "You have to catch up." She went happily to the counter and played with bottles.

Steve asked Bunk, "That doesn't ever bug you?"

"Not with a pansy," Bunk said. "That don't count, see? I mean, Marv knows about psychology and she explained it to me about . . . well . . ." His face went blotchy red. "You dig some other guy's ass the way a *man* digs chicks. That right? And, like, chicks turn you off. It don't figure, I admit, but Jess says that's how it works with him. And you're . . . well, like married to Jess, so . . ."

"Yeah," Steve said, "it don't figure, but it's true."

"Yeah." Bunk looked happy to be understood. "So I don't worry, Marv hangin' around pansies." Then for a minute his broken face turned mean. "Only there's some guys pass for queers that ain't. We get 'em at sea. They can make it with chicks, too. I find out there's anything like that, I'll bust the son of a bitch's head in."

"Don't be morbid," Marvel said. "It's Christmas Eve." She handed Steve a thick tumbler that held a toddy. It steamed. Apricot brandy. "We're here to cheer Steve up."

"Thanks," Steve said.

"Couldn't have you sitting here all alone and moping without Jess. We brang you a Nexmus tree."

"I noticed. Unusual."

"I decided mourning was the only motif for this year." She was wearing black, he noticed now—black leotards over her vast ass, black jersey with a round neckline and long sleeves, one of the little skulls hung around her neck. She'd also got Bunk into black—black Levis and a shrunken turtleneck jersey that left a line of suety belly showing. "I think black's the only color left for Christmas."

She was angling for him to in-joke with her. Tiredly he in-joked. "All my Christmases are black."

Bunk guffawed. Then he put his big foot on a step of the ladder stool and began plunking chords on the guitar. He hollered, "Come on, Bunny, baby!"

"No!" Marvel called. "Hold it, sweetie. Not here, Bunk. In the living room. Go on." She shooed them out of the kitchen and followed, snapping off the light. "All right," she told Bunk. "You're supposed to play here." She drew out one of the chairs from the luncheon table. He put his foot on that and rested the guitar across his knee. To Steve she said, "You sit on the couch. You're the queen and this is a command performance. I run the lights." She waved a big, shiny, three-cell flashlight. Then she drew the curtains across the French windows and switched off the lamps and the room was dark.

"Okay, Bunny, baby!" Bunk chorded an introduction. "You're on."

Marvel pointed the beam of the flashlight at the door to the hall and Bunny came out in a black velveteen frock, black top hat with a little skull fixed to the brim, black, skull-headed cane. She strutted the length of the room in time to the tune. In front of the black tree, in the harsh round spot thrown by the flashlight, she began rocking rhythmically from one foot to the other and singing in a loud kindergarten voice:

I'm dreaming of a Black Christmas,
Just like the ones we used to know,
Where, with faces haggard,
Little children staggered,
Robbing corpses in the snow . . .

There was a lot more of it. Steve burned his mouth trying to swallow the hot drink too fast and was grateful for the distraction. Finally Bunny wound up with a shrill Judy Garland quaver:

May your days be gloomy and bleak,
And may your death-struggles last a week!

"Perfect!" Marvel said. "Isn't that killing, Steve?" She turned on the lamps.

"Killing." That was one word for it. "Too great, Bunny. You're another Alan Sherman."

"Alan Sherman from Squaresville," Bunny said. And to Marvel, "Can I have my drink and go to bed? I'm beat."

"Aw, honey," Bunk said, "you promised to do your number for Archie and Phil."

"Oh, those two queens!" Bunny gave a noisy yawn and flung herself backward on the couch. "They just want to tape it so they can use it in one of their drag shows."

"Come on," Marvel said, "don't fink out now."

A minute after they'd gone, Steve found the flashlight. He ran it down the steps through the rain. Bunk hadn't got the VW started. He rolled down the window and Steve put the flashlight into his gloved hand. Then Steve ran back up the stairs, took the black tree with its skulls and pitched it off the terrace into the vacant lot next door.

18

T HE TREE IN THE APARTMENT Ross Wheatley and Bob Shepherd shared was white, sprayed with flocking and mica so that the long-leaf branches sagged. Very snowy. The ornaments were big silver balls, frosted on top. The tree stood against the floor-to-ceiling window, rainwashed blue sky beyond, the San Fernando Valley stretched out below in sparkling sunshine. Handsome.

The room wasn't so aseptic as the first time he'd been here because presents had been opened and gaudy wrapping paper lay around. The gifts themselves—bright shirts and socks, colorfully jacketed books, glossy record albums—stood under the tree. Steve stared at the setting and tried to let its cheerfulness sink in.

Ross Wheatley put an eggnog into his hand. "Why so mournful?"

"No suet for the chilly little birds," Steve said.

Shep laughed. "We're letting Hans Christian Andersen handle the avian poverty program this Christmas."

People kept coming. Faculty friends of Shep's, bookseller friends of Wheatley's. A leathery lesbian from the College art department, two middle-aged, bald and wistful men who sold arts and crafts in Topanga Canyon, a small, worried-looking man with a sudden, kid's laugh and a habit of drumming his fingers, who kept a shop full of old movie posters and magazines on Sunset Boulevard. His name was Eddie Lawrence. And there were maybe half a dozen others. They came, stood around amiably on the lovely rug, sat around on the fine furniture, drank eggnog and talked.

The talk was good—of books and films, music and theatre, painting and politics. And Shep and Ross kept Steve in the middle of it. At first this made him sore. He felt like a dwarf at the Spanish court. But he stepped on that reaction. Even if it was justified, he needed this kind of talk. He had starved for it for months now. This crowd kept it fairly shallow. Manners. Jokes. No controversy. Not on Christmas. But it did him good if only because it made him forget for a while his sadness about the baby, his panic about the bills.

He left at four, grateful they'd invited him.

The shop was called Poor Polly's. On the sidewalk in front, a wooden Indian ignored a spindly walnut melodeon and some shelves of tattered books. The window was crowded with chipped japanned boxes, ugly porcelain pitcher and basin sets, cast iron figurines, bad vases made into worse lamps. There were trays of secondhand jewelry.

Steve wandered inside. The walls were hung with age-blackened oil paintings that seemed to absorb what little light there was. He edged around marble-top commodes and General Grant tables piled with small, doubtful oriental rugs. He stumbled over a tufted red plush sofa. In the bellied glass of a tall cabinet that housed fu dogs and Staffordshire shepherdesses, he saw himself reflected tall and narrow against the shrunken sunbright doorway behind him—then saw another stick figure slide toward him.

"May I...? Oh, it's you! Hi!" He was a slender boy with glasses, lank brown hair, ladylike hands. He wore a brown cable-knit sweater, gray flannel slacks, crepe-soled suede shoes. Steve had seen him in the neighborhood bars with his fat, fiftyish lover. That must explain how these faggots existed. The bar owners bought camp antiques, the camp antique dealers bought drinks.

"Hi," Steve said. "You're my last hope."

"Really?" The boy had a beautiful mouth. he used it for a small ironic smile. "That sounds like an opening."

"To get a ring," Steve said. "I've tried all your competitors." There were six in these two blocks on Sunset. "No luck. What can you show me?"

"You throw lovely leads," the boy laughed. He walked away. "Here's what we have. Tarnished, but authentic."

"Authentic what?" Steve followed him.

There was a counter with a plate glass top. The boy lifted aside an American Indian feathered jacket and slid open the case. He reached inside and brought out a tray of rings stuck into purple satin slots. "Authentic junk," he said.

133

But Steve didn't hear him. Beside the space where the tray of rings had lain was another tray that held a jumble of earrings, gold lockets, enameled lapel watches, old coins and holy medals. Also brooches. And one was a big cameo. Steve stared.

"Something wrong?"

"May I see that other tray, please?" His throat was dry. When the boy set the stuff in front of him, his hand shook, picking up the brooch. It was Mrs. Hayes Brown's—the one stolen the night of Shep's cast party. He looked at the boy. "Where did you get this?"

"Why . . . I don't know. Do you like it?"

"Who does know?"

"Why, I . . . ." The boy's smooth face worked anxiously. "Maurice does all the buying." He turned and called. "Maurice." He accented the last syllable. "Can you come out here a second?"

The fat man came out, wearing a blue smock that had dribbles of paint down its front. In his hand was a tiny brush. "I'm sure it's a genuine Blakelock," he said. "I hope to God I'm not wrecking it. I'm nervous as a diva with the hiccups." He saw Steve. "Why, hello there!" Dimpled smile.

"Can you tell me where this came from?"

The fat man blinked at it. He smelled of linseed oil. There was a round smudge of umber between his brows, like a movie bullet hole. He twinkled.

"Why, certainly. Your little friend brought this in. Weeks ago. Said it was left to him by his grandmother. I gave him two dollars for it."

The small dangling tag said ten dollars.

"Will you take five? I'm pretty broke."

"Aw . . ." The fat man made a pink buttonhole of his mouth and tucked his top chin into the lower two. He fluttered his eyelids. "You're going to give it back to him, aren't you?" he crooned.

"It meant a lot to him," Steve said. "If I'd known, I wouldn't have let him sell it."

"You take it back for two." The fat man's moist hand closed Steve's fingers around the brooch and squeezed sentimentally. "I'm touched. I'm genuinely touched."

The bus terminal was empty except for a whitehaired Negro in loose blue coveralls, pushing paper cups and cigaret butts along the floor with a wide broom. And Coy. He stood by the tan ranks of rental lockers with his suitcases at his feet and when he saw Steve come in he smiled. Steve didn't smile back. He walked over and picked up the suitcases.

"Steve?" Coy said. "It's good to see you."

"Come on." Steve turned and walked off.

Outside, he headed for Spring Street.

"What's wrong?" Coy tried to stop him. "Aren't you glad I'm back?"

Steve shrugged his hands away. "Yes, I'm glad you're back. I wish I wasn't." He walked on.

Coy followed. "Where are we going? Where's the car?"

"There is no car. We're catching the Sunset bus."

"But you're bugged. Why? What did I do?"

"I'll tell you when we get home. . . ."

On the bus, the kid sat huddled in the corner of the seat, staring at him, big-eyed. But Steve ignored him and finally turned and sat for the rest of the trip looking out through the greasy window at the empty, sad, sunshiny streets. New Year's Day. Everything shut up tight. Desolate.

When they reached Kean Terrace, Coy carried the suitcases off the bus. But on the sidewalk, Steve took them away from him. They climbed the steep street, the long stairs, in silence. Inside the apartment, Steve set down the suitcases and shut the door. Coy stood and looked at him—wistful, wanting.

Steve slapped him. Hard.

Coy's face twisted. He stared. "Why?" he whispered. "Why, Steve?"

"I'm glad you asked that question." Steve took the brooch out of his jacket pocket and dropped it on the coffee table. "Ever see that before?"

The slap had left a red mark. "Oh," Coy said softly.

"Famous quotations," Steve said. "You swiped it at Shep's party. Why? What did you need it for?"

"I didn't. I just needed money till Sister Myra's check came. I'd done it before at parties. It's so easy. I'm sorry. If I'd known it was the place where you and I . . ." He held out his hands. "I didn't know, Steve."

Steve said sourly, "And that was the money you bought Shep's coffee with the next day, at my room. Christ, it's so ironical it's corny." He sighed. "Okay. So what about the brooch?"

The kid looked at the floor. "Marvel saw it when the old woman was wearing it. She said she wished she had one like it. So when I saw it in one of the purses, I took it for her. Afterward, I couldn't give it to her: you'd see her wearing it sometime. So I sold it. . . ." He looked up and there were tears in his eyes. "You shouldn't hit me. I love you, Steve."

"I love you too," Steve said. "That's why I hit you." He picked up the brooch. "You know how I happened to find this, happened to walk into that faggot junk shop yesterday?"

Mute headshake.

"To buy you a ring. For two weeks I'd been telling myself I wasn't going to get you any present. I was so pissed off about the bills. But—"

"Bills?" Blank bewilderment. "What bills, Steve?"

"Shit." Steve laughed helplessly. "You really don't know, do you? Baby—you owed Mrs. Terry at the market ninety-seven dollars. You can't do that to people. And the others—furniture, clothes. I can't get the figure out of my head. One thousand, eight hundred and seventy-nine dollars and thirty-four cents. That's the total, Coy. That's what we're in hock for, you irresponsible nut. Practically two thousand dollars."

"But, Steve, that's all time payment stuff. It's just a little bit every month."

"Sure. Only you don't pay it every month. Or ever."

"Steve, why do you worry about it? They're my bills."

"Then they're mine. Because you're mine. Right?"

Coy nodded, bit his lip, and began to cry.

"Don't cry," Steve said. "I'm sorry I hit you. Only listen to me now. I paid Mrs. Terry. I'd borrowed a hundred bucks from the credit union at the Library to buy you Christmas presents and I used it to pay her. Then I hocked my typewriter. I stuck a sign on my car and parked it in the student lot at Central College and a kid bought it. Sixty-five bucks. My mother sent me another twenty in a Christmas card. And I put in for another fifty at work and I got that Friday and I sent checks on everything but the desk. They don't cover the full three months arrears, but they'll probably be accepted. But that desk, baby. Two hundred dollars worth of desk you don't need. The desk has got to go back."

"Steve, there's no point in living if you don't live well. I've had the rest. Your father's a rich doctor. You don't know what it is to be poor."

"I'm willing to find out. Jesus, Coy, I'd sleep on the floor. I'd send the bed back. I'd send the chest back. We can keep our clothes in boxes. The couch we don't need. We've got the two basket chairs and they're from Akron's so I know they're paid for. We can get along without the television. And you never use that tape recorder."

"I need it for school. The TV too. There are religious programs sometimes and . . ."

"Well, the dining table, then. You don't need that for school. We can eat in the kitchen."

"No, Steve, please."

"Yeah, yeah. Okay. But the desk goes. Right?"

"All right." Unhappy, head hanging.

"Chicky, I don't want to make life bad for you. That's why I didn't just phone every one of those places and tell them to come get their stuff. I love you. I mean it." He went and took him in his arms, pulled his head against his shoulder. "But you have to use some sense, or it's always going to be like this. Somebody's always going to be hitting you, making you cry. You have to pay for things as you go. And with your own money. You can't keep crashing parties and stripping handbags, Coy. That'll catch up with you."

"Or with somebody," Coy mourned. "I'm sorry it had to be you."

"It had to be. You're my hangup." Steve smiled bleakly. "But I've only gotten us out of our bind temporarily. From now on, the installments have to be paid. We split them. Right?"

"Yes. And we have to get your typewriter back."

"Forget that. It brings me bad luck. The main thing is not to run up any more bills. What groceries and stuff we buy from now on, we pay for. Understand?" He lifted Coy's chin and the kid blinked and gave a quick little nod, sniffing, trying to smile. Steve finished, "And if we can't afford the best, we eat the cheapest. Sometimes, maybe, we don't even eat. We sure as hell can't drink."

"Oh, Steve!" Coy pulled away from him.

"We can't afford it. Booze costs a fortune."

Coy sulked like a little kid. "What *can* we afford?"

Steve grinned. Wickedly, he hoped. He held out his hands. "Come here and I'll show you."

19

THEY ATE. COY CLAIMED THEY'D starve. But he bought cheap because Steve made him. And he learned to cook cheap. Thick, fragrant messes of split peas with ham scraps, pinto beans with chili and stewing beef, lentils with curry and bits of Polish sausage—these would last them for days and taste better each time. The kid baked terrific bread. He could simmer a great spaghetti sauce. In his shining head he had recipes for half a dozen cost-nothing casseroles—tuna, sweet corn with pimientos, macaroni and cheese. He could make magic with rice. The cheapest hamburger, when he got done with it—Worcestershire, chopped onion, chopped bell pepper, jalapena—came out a gourmet thing. They ate fine.

As to liquor—Coy kept pouring it as if there was no end in sight. But there was. And Steve worried about what the kid would do when the end came: booze was the glue that held his split world together. He needn't have worried. Once their last bottle was dry, Coy moved in on Brubaker's ample stock. At night when he'd finished studying—he studied at the kitchen table now: Berg and Son had argued but in the end they'd taken back the desk—he led Steve up the steps to the landlord's apartment. The lure was ostensibly Brubaker's color television set. He had invited them to come stare at it any time. But in fact he always offered drinks and Coy always accepted. For both of them.

Steve didn't like it, but he couldn't see how to keep out of it since nothing he said swerved Coy and he couldn't let him go alone. Then it turned out that it made Brubie happy. He didn't have a lot of company—not young, good-looking company. So that, finally, there was no way not to go without hurting his feelings. Especially on Sundays. Brubie, in his baggy-assed Bermuda shorts and floppy straw hat, was always lurking by the rail of his white sun deck, peering down into the patio below, before Steve and Coy had finished their Sunday lunch.

Late March. Sunny and warm. They washed and dried the dishes together at the shiny sink. Steve gazed out between the yellow gingham curtains at the lot next door. A house had once stood there. Only the foundations remained, surrounded by untrimmed shrubs and trees, tumble-down thickets of roses. The roses Brubie watered and they were going to be covered with buds.

"You like to make it outdoors?" Steve said.

Coy, setting a dried plate in a cupboard, looked at him sideways. "What did you have in mind?"

Steve nodded at the window. "Over there. It's dark at night. Lots of shadows."

"In summer," Coy smiled. "Still too cold at night."

They put on their sunglasses and stood grinning at each other for a minute. They did a lot of that. Mostly when they were naked or nearly naked, like now. Mutual admiration society. They kissed. Coy wore little blue shorts with white piping. Steve slid a hand down inside them. Coy shook his head.

"Later."

He took Steve's hand and led him out into the sun-dazzled patio, with Steve wondering if he wasn't getting a lot of *later* these days. Or did he imagine it? God knew, they made out—maybe better now than ever. No maybe about it. He was himself a lot less clumsy and as for Coy—he kept right on delighting and surpris-ing. So . . . if it was happening less often in the past five or six weeks—well, tempos were different. He'd always been a sex maniac. It could never happen too often for him. Coy, after matching him for a while, was probably just back to his natural rhythm now. Sure. Steve smiled his doubts away.

Brubie met them, smiling with his gray false teeth and holding out tall, mint-sprigged, frosty glasses of gin and tonic. Music drifted out through the open doors from the big, boomy stereo in his living room. They sat in chairs of aluminum tubing and green webbing and played Canasta at a round table whose white enamel was pitted with rust. When Coy went into Brubie's to change the record and fetch fresh drinks, the landlord said:

"You know, I own some property down in the southeast part of town."

"Mmm." Steve was hardly listening. Brubie seldom said much worth listening to, and the sun was feeling fine and drowsy on his back. Sexy.

"And I was down there collecting rents this last week. There are signs all over. *Archer for Assemblyman.* Is that a relation of yours?"

"My father. He's a doctor."

"*Is* he?" Brubie nodded, impressed. "Very distinguished looking man. I *thought* there was a resemblance. When I saw the photograph, I said to myself, 'I'll bet that's young Steve's father.' Well . . . that explains a great deal."

"Does it? About what?"

"About you, my dear. I've always said, 'Breeding tells.' And you're a remarkable boy, you know."

"How so?" Steve yawned.

"So reliable," Brubie said. "So mature. I never got my rent on time from Coy until you came along. I couldn't explain it to myself. You're even younger than he is. And you're . . ." He choked slightly and his red face got redder. "I mean to say, you're . . ."

"Black," Steve said. "And financial responsibility is not a quality the American Negro is celebrated for in song and story. Right?"

"Well . . ." Brubie shifted uncomfortably in his chair. "Certainly Smith Tyler was no paragon regarding money. I—"

"You mean, my father must have trained me differently. He did. He wants to change the image. Even if no one else pays their bills on time, he must and I must. Because in the great white public mind all jigs look alike: if one is a slob, they're all slobs. Quite a position to put a kid in—making him responsible for everybody in the world with excess skin pigmentation. Any more questions?"

"Oh, dear." Brubie lifted his sunglasses and blinked anxiously. "I only meant to tell you what a nice, steady boy I think you are. And to congratulate you on your father's . . . candidacy. And now I've made you angry."

"Negroes don't get angry, Brubie. They laugh and dance all day. You know that." He pried out the cigaret pack he had tucked into his trunks. "Here. Relax. Have a smoke." He pushed the pack across the table.

"Thank you." Brubie's smile was a little like a wince. When he held out his butane lighter the flame jittered. "I do hope your father wins."

"He will." Steve lit his cigaret. "Thanks. Winning is his habit pattern. Assemblyman now. Governor later. Then President." Coy came out golden into the sunshine. Ganymede. The drinks he brought on the little bentwood tray looked like cylinders of ice. Steve leaned forward, took his, and told the gaping Brubie, who was a little slow on jokes:

"It's the far future that worries me. Say about 1990 when he's had his two terms in the White House and then he finds out you can't run for God."

Three nights later, when Steve reached home from the Library, the front door was locked. Coy had waited for him that way once or twice. Naked. Surprise. But not this time. When Steve turned the key and pushed inside, the apartment was empty. Nobody came to him, softly laughing, sliding arms around him, plastering him with kisses. It was a little chill and very deserted.

Without taking off his jacket, he walked into the kitchen. No smell of anything cooking. The range was cold, all dials at zero. He hung his jacket in the bedroom closet, looked at his watch, looked at the white telephone. It was 5:50, the same time he reached home every day. So Coy would be calling in a minute. Something had kept him late at Galilee, something he'd forgotten to mention.

Steve set a record on the stereo. Almeda's intelligent guitar, Shank's moody saxophone. He listened to it, waiting for the phone. At the end of the side, his watch said six-twenty. He went back into the bedroom and lifted the receiver. It hummed. But to make sure it was working, he dialed the library. The answer came, so it was working all right. He kidded with the switchboard girl for a minute, and hung up. Coy must be on his way. Buses were undependable. He'd probably counted on being here before Steve, then had to wait on some corner where there was no phone.

Steve turned the record. Hungry now, he took eggs from the refrigerator, cracked them into a red and white bowl, added bits of cream cheese with chives, beat them. He cooked them slow over a low fire the way Coy had taught him, moving them around with a wooden fork. He fixed toast, poured himself a glass of milk. He ate standing at the kitchen counter, watching night happen to the sky over Los Angeles. Below, the streets became long neon gouges down the darkness to the black humps of the Baldwin Hills, where red lights winked on lonely towers.

He didn't know what to do. Something was wrong. This had never happened before. He took a chance on leaving the phone and ran up to Brubie's. After he pressed the button, he had a nervous wait. Finally the door opened and Brubie stood there in a mauve Paisley dressing gown. His hair piece looked a little crooked. Steve had interrupted something. The smile he got was polite but not welcoming. No, Coy wasn't there, hadn't been. Brubie closed the door. But not before Steve saw a sandy-haired, middle-aged man step into view through the white jalousie doors of Brubie's bedroom. He was naked. Freckles. He backed out quickly. The man came around fairly often. Brubie had introduced him once. Lasswell? Steve would never have suspected Lasswell of being anybody's love interest, but he was glad Brubie had one.

Back in the apartment, he walked into the bedroom again and stood staring down at the phone, absently rubbing his hands, palms together. The number of Galilee College would be in the book. But Coy had said never to call there. It made sense. So who should he call, then? Hospitals? Jails? The morgue? Shit. He was scaring himself like some *Reader's Digest* parent. He shrugged into his jacket, wrote a quick note and, leaving the lamps on, pulling the door tight, went down to Sunset for a drink and company.

Norquist said, "You're damn near a stranger."

But he remembered what Steve drank. Steve paid for it and began to tilt and revolve the stubby glass, watching the golden oily swirl of the whisky around the ice cubes.

"Move out of the neighborhood?" Norquist asked.

"No. Just broke, is all." Steve wished Jaime was here. He wished the piano player was here. They weren't. And he was the only customer. So if he wanted company, Norquist was it. He lit a cigaret and sipped the whisky. "Quiet tonight." Brilliant conversational gambit.

"It'll pick up." Norquist was studying him. "You—uh—say you're still living in the same place?"

"I didn't say," Steve said. "But yes. We are."

Norquist looked down the black and white room and saw nobody and looked at Steve again. "Who's we?"

"You know my buddy," Steve said. "Little blond kid."

"Yah," Norquist said, "only . . ." He walked to the small metal sink hidden under the bar and began drying glasses. "I didn't know whether you were still with him."

"Yup. Waiting for him now."

"Here?" Squinting at it, Norquist held up a highball glass to the light, a fluorescent circle above the cash register. "You expect him to come here?" He set the glass on the back bar with a glittering cluster of others like it, and rinsed another.

"Sure," Steve said. "Something wrong with that?"

Under the gold hair of his forearms Norquist's muscles slid smoothly as he turned the glass and towel in his hands.He came back to stand in front of Steve. His look was level. "You know I don't let hustlers in here."

Steve set down his glass. He felt hollow. "Hustlers?"

"Boys who solicit for money. Pick up customers and charge them for sex. I don't like it. The cops don't like it, but first I don't like it. Didn't you know that?"

"So I knew it," Steve said. "What's it got to do with Coy? Are you saying he's a hustler?"

"Didn't you know?"

"You're out of your crazy Swede skull," Steve said.

"Not me." Norquist smiled regretfully. "It was Jaime that caught him. Ask Jaime. You know, your boy never used to come in here except with you—or with that other colored kid he had before you. And when he came in with you it was always late at night. Then, about six weeks ago he started coming in the afternoon. Two-thirty, three. And every time he left, he left with somebody. Mostly strangers, but one or two old customers. So Jaime watched him. If it's just for love, we don't mind. But he was asking for money. And getting it. So I threw him out, told him not to come back here."

"You're lying," Steve said.

Norquist sighed and turned to line up the clean glass with the rest. "Ask him yourself." He bent and rinsed another glass. "He admitted it to Jaime. And afterward I asked two of his scores. They told me so too. Twenty dollars he got. He's not a bad looking boy. Maybe a little nelly. But he looks young. Like sixteen."

"For Christ sake!" Steve shouted. "I know what he looks like. I know that." And he picked up the glass and threw it. Norquist leaned out of its way and it smashed against the black paneling behind him. Blind and stumbling, Steve ran out of the place.

He waited, lying awake in the dark on the bed. He hadn't taken off his clothes. The alarm clock had green, luminous hands. When the apartment door opened, the hands pointed at 2:35. Steve tensed, sick in his stomach, his heart racing. Coy went softly into the bathroom. When Steve heard him come out he sat up and put his feet on the floor. Coy appeared pale and shadowy in the doorway.

Steve lunged at him, fists swinging. They connected. The kid sprawled backward with a yelp. Steve fell on him, fists smashing down at the dim white face. Left, right, left, right. He'd had dreams like this. He'd never done it, but he'd dreamed it. Only in the dreams it had been hard to move his arms. Now it wasn't. In the dreams, when his fists finally struck, what they struck was like mist. Now they struck flesh and bone. It made a bad sound. Coy screamed, screamed again.

"Whore!" Steve grated the word between clenched teeth. "Whore, whore, whore!" Then he heard something. Thunder overhead. He stopped and looked up. Brubie. He opened his hands, couldn't see them in the dark. He rubbed them and they felt wet and sticky. He groped for the light switch and the little white hall glared. His hand had left a crimson smear on the wall. Scared, he looked down.

"Coy?" he panted. "Coy?"

The kid's face was a bloody blur. "Don't," the cut mouth whimpered. "Please, no more, Steve."

Steve pushed himself to his feet. "Get up," he said grimly. "Get up, hustler."

Shakily, cowering, the kid did as he was told. "Steve, he wouldn't let me go." The words came out with a spray of little red drops, in a thin, hurried voice. "I couldn't help it. His place is way down in Malibu. And there's no bus or anything. He wouldn't let me phone and he wouldn't bring me. Not till he was through with me, he said. He kept me till after midnight. But . . . he did give me . . ." He scrabbled in his pocket, took out a crumpled bill. "Fifty dollars. Here, Steve."

"Shit! What am I—your pimp, now?"

The doorbell buzzed. A fist pounded the door.

Steve grabbed Coy's arm and pivoted him into the bathroom. "All right, hustler. Wash your face." He clicked the light on and shut the door.

He looked down at himself. The shirt he wore had been white.

Now it was like some madhouse bandana. He tore it off and flung it behind him into the blacked-out bedroom. He trotted fast through the dark living room, switched on the light on the terrace and yanked open the front door. Brubie stood there, baggy-eyed, alarmed.

"What happened?" he asked. "Are you all right?"

"We're okay," Steve said. "It was the television set, Brubie. Something went wrong with the sound. It got very loud all of a sudden. We were watching *The Blue Dahlia*. The beatup scene. Alan Ladd, William Bendix. You remember."

"Oh? The television?" Brubie peered. "It wasn't . . . your voices? You and Coy? I felt sure—"

"No, it's okay. Sorry it woke you, though."

He shut the door and went back to the bathroom. Coy was kneeling on the floor and leaning his head against the wash basin and crying. Steve ran water hard into the basin, soaked and wrung out a washcloth, knelt and began to sponge the face that was already swelling and turning color. He was gentle but he hated the gentleness almost as he'd hated his rage before. "What in Christ's name is the matter with you? Shut your eyes." He washed around them. Blood still leaked from the kid's nose and the corner of his mouth. Steve stood and rinsed the cloth in the bowl and the water went sick crimson. He let it drain out and filled the bowl again. Coy just crouched there miserable on the bathmat, chin on his chest. "What did you do it for, baby? Don't you know how I love you? Don't you care what you do to me? Jesus . . . you want more sex, is that it? I can give you more sex, chicky. All anybody needs. You know that."

"It's not sex," Coy mumbled. "It's money."

"But we're getting along." Steve crouched beside him again. He had the cloth cold now. He bathed the bruised face once more. "We're making out all right. I get paid, you get your checks from Sister Myra—"

"No." Coy lifted his head and pushed the cloth away. His eyes were swollen nearly shut now, the flesh around them turning ugly purple. They needed an ice bag, Steve thought. Coy said, "The checks stopped. She had another stroke, Steve. Middle of February. Hospital. Big bills."

"But there's insurance for that."

"You don't know her. Insurance is an insult to God's grace. Shows a person doesn't trust in Jesus."

"You're putting me on," Steve said.

"No. It's costing her a fortune. Even now, when she can walk a little again. At first it was like eighty dollars a day just for the room. She had somebody write to me, give me the bad news. No more money. My tuition's paid up for the rest of the year, so I was supposed to go back and live at the dorm. I didn't want to, Steve. I want to be with you."

"Dear God!" Steve laughed in despair. "And this is how you figured to earn enough to pay your part. Hustling."

"It was working." Coy stood up. Hurtfully.

Steve turned him. "Don't look in the mirror. Not now. You'll only scare yourself. Sit down there." He opened the cabinet for aspirin. The kid sat on the closed toilet. Steve shook four tablets into his hand and filled the yellow plastic glass with water. "Take those."

Coy nodded and inserted the tablets carefully, one by one, between his puffed, discolored lips, and swallowed the water in small sips. "It was working," he said again, handing back the glass. "Steve, what else could I do? I've only got a couple free hours a day. And . . . well, people do want sex with me. Have, ever since I can remember. And they'll pay. And I could go on studying and . . . it wasn't supposed to hurt you, Steve. You'd never have known if this hadn't—"

"Except Norquist told me," Steve said flatly. "And if he hadn't, sooner or later you'd have brought home a case of V.D. And I'd have found out the hard way. Right?" He took disinfectant and cotton from the cabinet and knelt in front of the kid. "Easy, now. This'll sting." He dabbed at the cuts and scrapes his knuckles had made. "Coy, you don't want to do things like this. It's true, you don't have time to work. But I have. I can moonlight. They need kids to pump gas at night at the big Hanes gas station up Sunset."

"Steve, it's not fair. You do it all."

"Yeah, I do it all," Steve laughed bitterly. He capped the disinfectant, threw away the cotton. "Look what I did to you, you poor, ignorant hillbilly. Ah, baby. . . ." And he folded Coy in his arms and the kid clung to him, sobbing.

20

C OY DIDN'T GO BACK to Galilee College for the rest of the week. He reported in by phone. Steve made up the lie for him. The bus he'd been riding on had hit a car. Coy had been thrown forward and struck his face on the steel rail of the seat back ahead.

They told Brubie the same story, but the landlord didn't buy it. He made no comment, but Steve could see that he connected the damage to Coy's face with Wednesday night's brawl. The next Sunday, when they went up to play cards—Coy wearing big black wrap-around sunglases—Steve noticed Brubie looking knowl-edgeably from Steve's raw-knuckled hands to Coy's cuts and bruises, with a kind of dry, cynical satisfaction.

Well, let him think what he wanted. They were okay. No, they weren't having sex. Coy was too battered for it and Steve, after eight hours at the library and six more in the glaring night forest of white gas pumps that was the Hanes station, when he hit the steaming shower at home at two A.M. to wash off the grease and the gasoline smell, was too tired for it. He was like a very small, exhausted child. He needed only to be waited for and wanted and to sleep held close.

And what he needed, Coy gave. Tenderly. He must eat, he must sleep. Gentle wakings: "I'm sorry, baby, but it's that time again. Here's your orange juice." Apologies. Assurances: "You won't have to go on working like this. Sister Myra's getting a lot better." He read Steve his mother's letters from Dead Oak with their progress reports on the lady preacher. "You'll see. She'll start sending my checks again. Soon as the doctors are paid." And Steve, fighting sleep at the supper table, too tired to eat but making himself chew and swallow, would reach out and touch his face. "Baby, are you better? Is your face better?" It was. It didn't hurt at all now. Honest.

Coy would have to go home for Easter vacation. Before he went, Steve wanted to repay Shep's and Ross Wheatley's hospitality at Christmas.

"Steve," Coy wailed, "I can't feed them lentils."

"Nope. You can spend money. God knows, I'm knocking myself out for it. Come on. Let's go see Mrs. Terry. I'll buy beautiful booze and you can run wild in the grocery department. Whatever you want to feed this Sunday, you can feed. Check?"

"You mean it?"

Steve meant it. And Coy took him at his word. That Sunday they ate big, succulent chunks of lobster in thick oyster sauce, wild rice with tender slivers of almond, tiny green sweet peas steamed in their pods, a heaping basketful of golden toasted sourdough bread drenched in garlic butter. There were tall green bottles of chilled Chablis, crisp and bright to the tongue.

"My God," Shep groaned, getting up from the table. "And *you* are training to become a minister!"

"What a chef the world is losing," Wheatley said.

"Don't worry," Steve said. "On church supper night, it won't be the parish ladies in the kitchen. It'll be the reverend himself. In a frilly apron."

They laughed.

Steve had worried that the men might be bored. But it was going to be a good evening. They sat on the couch and the basket chairs to drink their coffee and brandy. In the soft glow of the handsome blue lamps he and Wheatley talked about the end of the Metropolitan Opera House, the fiasco of the Lincoln Center Repertory Company. Shep and Coy talked diction. Arguing excitedly, they left for the empty back bedroom where from the closet Coy hauled out the never-used tape recoder. The two of them sat on the floor and Coy talked into the microphone and Shep wound the tape back and played it.

"Here what you say?" he rumbled. "Splaish!"

"But I don't," Coy protested, laughing.

"Now, listen to it again. . . ."

He said *splaish*. He also said *caint*. Shep proved it to him with the tape. Steve grinned, watching them, and said to Wheatley, "Comes the rude awakening."

"Shep with a tape recorder is a public menace." Smiling, Wheatley took a pipe from his pocket. "We won't hear from either of them for hours." He began stuffing the pipe bowl with shag tobacco from a calfskin pouch. "Which means I'd better fill you in on our curious news—since Shep is sure to forget."

"What's that?"

Wheatly folded the pouch shut and slipped it into his jacket pocket. "It's about the robbery the night of the cast party."

"Incidentally," Steve said, "you weren't there. I wondered about that. How come?"

With a wry smile and a shrug, Wheatley set the pipe stem between his teeth. "Mrs. Shepherd and I . . . well, let's say we've learned to be civil over the years, but we're mutually happier apart."

"I dig," Steve said. "So, what about the party?"

Wheatley's lighter poked a finger of flame into the pipe bowl. Between puffs of aromatic smoke, he said, "First, in January . . . we had a telephone call . . . from Mrs. Hayes Brown. Actually . . ." He dropped the lighter into his pocket. "The call came to Mrs. Shepherd. Mrs. Hayes Brown received her brooch back. The one that was stolen."

Straight-faced, Steve said, "Wild. How?"

"By mail. Plain brown wrapper, that kind of thing. No message. But she's pleased and says the how and why don't matter." He bent forward, picked up the little globe of his brandy glass and swirled the amber stuff. "Then, a week or two ago, Bob found an envelope in the mail with no return address and inside three ten dollar bills wrapped in a sheet of blank typing paper."

"The bread from the handbags," Steve said. "Crazy."

"Apposite expression," Wheatley chuckled. "We appear to have had simply a somewhat unorthodox borrower, not a thief at all." He finished off his brandy.

"Looks that way." Steve stood and reached for his glass. Walking to the kitchen to pour another splash into it from the bottle of Martell's, he grinned to himself. There was nice irony to the fact that the thirty dollars had been part of that miserable fifty paid Coy for overtime sex by his score in Malibu.

The Sunset bus was crowded. Steve stood. Numb, at least half asleep. It had been a long day. It was going to be a longer night. Then he noticed a man shoving up the packed aisle. Good-looking topcoat, black and white hounds-tooth check. He'd noticed that coat twice today. Its wearer was a Negro but without the color. He had sat near Steve at the drugstore lunch counter and

Steve had caught him staring at him in the mirror. When their eyes had met the man had looked away. Later, Steve had seen him again—standing in the doorway of the library Literature Department. This time he had started to walk toward Steve. But a patron had spoken to Steve at that moment, a pimply girl, worriedly tapping a pencil against her braced teeth, unable to locate Millgate's *William Faulkner*. By the time Steve had found it for her, the man in the topcoat was gone. Now, as the bus surged out into traffic, its frame groaning with the weight of its home-going load, he touched Steve's arm.

"Stephen Archer?"

"That's my name."

"I'm Jackson, Clive Jackson." His eyes were golden, like a lion's, but without a lion's gentleness. "Been wanting to talk to you. About your father."

Steve stiffened. "What about him?"

"You tell me."

Steve turned away. "This is where I get off."

"Funny thing," Jackson said. "So do I."

Steve halted. "Then I guess I'll ride on a while."

"I can do that too," Jackson smiled. "I can ride to Hawaii, if that's where you're going. But you're going to Fairfax Avenue. Isn't that right? That's where you get off. That's where you live."

He meant the place above Bernie's. Steve only stared.

"With your wife and new baby. Correct?"

"Who the hell are you? Why should I talk to you?"

Jackson mentioned a major television station. "We're doing biographies on all the candidates in the upcoming primaries. Your father's running for assembly. We've already got him and you mother on film. You're his only son. We like to get the whole family."

"I'm camera shy," Steve said.

Jackson said, "That baby would be a selling point in your father's campaign. Don't you want to help him?"

"Man," Steve said. "You're a liar. You haven't got my father on film. If you'd seen my father, you'd know—" He broke off. "Look. Just leave me out of it, okay?"

"You don't want your father to win?"

"I didn't say that." The crowd was tight around him, but he had to get away from this man. He told the fat woman with the bleeding mascara next to him, "Excuse me, please," and began shouldering through. Bruised, his coat half off one shoulder, he reached the rear doors and yanked the cord. When the doors hissed open, he dived out and hit the sidewalk running.

There was a school yard there. Under old pepper trees kids were playing on the tarmack. They stopped and stared through the chainlink fence at Steve running. And he made himself stop. Not because of their stares, but because it was a fool thing to do. The man Jackson could catch him—anywhere, any time he wanted. He'd better talk to him now. He had got off the bus at the next corner and was standing there by the bench, smiling, waiting. Steve walked to meet him.

"Sorry," he said. "I get a little panicked at publicity. You want to show me your credentials?"

Jackson's golden eyes narrowed for a second. Then the smile came back. "Will this do?" He opened the houndstooth coat, reached inside and brought out a paper. He unfolded it and handed it to Steve.

It was a carbon of the Restraining Order his father had brought against the play back in November.

"That look familiar?" Jackson asked.

"Where did you get it?"

"Out of a file someplace," Jackson said carelessly. "It's what made me think you probably don't want your father to win this election. Or anything else. I thought, after he did this to you, you'd probably have a lot to say about him. None of it favorable." He cocked a friendly eyebrow. "There's a Chinese restaurant across the street. Be my guest. We'll have a martini, nice quiet meal. And you can tell me all about your father."

"Thanks, but no thanks." Steve folded the paper and handed it back. "You're wrong. My father was perfectly right to do this. The play was . . . irresponsible. Childish. He did what he had to and I agree with him. One hundred percent."

"But he did stop it. In a pretty drastic way. Why? Why the court order? Couldn't he talk to you? I mean, you're the man's son. Unless, of course, you and he—"

"Jackson," Steve said, "not that I give a damn, but who do you really work for?"

Jackson shrugged. "Politics is a big field."

"And dirty," Steve said. "Go away and leave me alone."

He turned his back and stared along Sunset into the flash of a thousand passing windshields reflecting red, dying sunlight.

There would be another bus. Sometime. To take him home to the empty apartment on Kean Terrace. Coy was down in La Paz Valley. It was Maundy Thursday.

"All right," Jackson said finally. "I'll go away. Now. But you're Stephen Archer, son of Abel Allen Archer, candidate for State Assembly. You haven't got a chance of being left alone. . .".

The building was on Spring Street, twelve stories, gloomy gray stone on the outside, stained marble on the inside. The elevators still went up and down shafts fronted with wrought iron tracery. The elevator cages themselves were paneled in wood. The place smelled of too many winters tracked in on the wet shoes of lawyers, dripped in on the wet briefcases of lawyers, too many summers sweated out by the guilty, the greedy, the aggrieved, too many disputed days, too many filed and forgotten nights. Hell would smell like this.

Steve got off at the eighth floor. It was a big building. He followed the sickly lighted corridor for a while before he found the door with J. D. BIXEL, *Attorney at Law* lettered on its frosted glass. Also *Enter*. The doorknob was built for a giant hand, a grapefruit-size sphere of solid brass. Tarnished. He turned it and pushed open the door.

Under a big poster scotch-taped to the wall, ARCHER FOR ASSEMBLY, a Negro girl in a brown knit outfit with orange beads and earrings, rattled the keys of a Selectric. She looked up, smiled, and turned to face him across a glossy expanse of reception desk, where nasturtiums laughed in a round blue jar.

"May I help you?"

"Mr. Bixel in?" It was Good Friday. The Library had closed at noon. Steve had come straight here. "He can't be in court."

"He's at lunch. You just missed him. I'm sorry." She glanced at her watch. Her nails were enameled orange. "I expect him back at two." She tilted her head. "You look familiar. Do I know you?"

It couldn't be a come-on. She was the wrong type.

With a wry smile he nodded at the poster. Her chair worked on a swivel. She turned it and looked up at the photograph of his father, then swung back with a laugh.

"Another Archer," she said.

"Steve," he nodded. "Look. I think this is important. Where does Mr. Bixel eat lunch, usually, do you know?"

"Oh, yes, of course. But . . . well, he's with a client. I don't think it would be . . ."

The door opened behind Steve.

The girl said, "Oh, Dr. Archer. See who's here?"

Steve turned. His father stopped short and stared while the door wheezed shut behind him. It was a wooden stare. He looked tired. His eyes were bloodshot. From the sleeve of his beige topcoat a button dangled loose.

"What do you want? No, don't tell me now. Come in here."

He didn't take off the coat. He walked to a door marked *Private*, opened it and entered the room beyond. Steve followed, shutting the door. His father sat at Bixel's desk.

"Steve," he said, "I have a lot of matters on my mind. Your grandmother is sick. Wiley's left me at the clinic. Worst time he could possibly have picked. Handling his patients in addition to my own, just when the campaign is going into high gear. . . ." He sighed and shut his eyes and rubbed the lids with thumb and forefinger. "What do you want?"

"I didn't mean to bother you," Steve said. "That's why I came here. I was going to tell Bixel."

"Tell him what?" The lean, black fingers, with their pink nails, drummed on the desk. "I warn you that so far as I am concerned, you are still—"

"I know what I am still," Steve said.

A pair of pigeons landed on the ledge outside the closed window. His father stared at them.

Steve went on, "But there's a man you better know about. Clive Jackson."

"Never heard of him."

"He's heard of you. And me. He's got a copy of that court order that stopped my play."

His father looked at him. His carved face twitched.

"From that," Steve said, "he concluded I must hate you and that I'd tell him a lot of dirt about you. You sure you don't know him? Very light-skinned. Sharp dresser."

"I don't know him, but he obviously works for Naylor."

The pigeons opened their wings and dropped off the ledge out of sight.

"Naylor the man who's running against you?"

His father's smile was mocking. "I can see you've followed my career with interest." The smile died. "What did you tell him?"

"That you were right about the play. And to go chase himself. He went. But he said I wouldn't be left alone. If you can stop him, I think you should."

"Yes . . ." His father blinked thoughtfully. "I think I should too. Thank you. I wasn't aware you had any decent instincts. I'm gratified."

"Don't mention it." Steve turned to walk out.

"You'd better go see your grandmother," his father said. "She's asking for you. She's in Parkway Hospital. She's dying."

Steve kept walking. "I'll go," he said.

21

H IS GRANDMOTHER LAY VERY BLACK in the white bed. She
looked terribly small and shrunken. Her eyes were shut
when he stepped into the room. She might have been dead
already. There were flame-colored gladioluses in a vase on the
white dresser. Reverend E. Mason Howard sat close beside the
bed, Bible open on his knees, reading aloud—an old man now,
hair a white fringe around his polished mahogany skull. He
looked up and smiled at Steve, gold in his mouth. He leaned
forward, gently touched the bony little hand on the coverlet, and
murmured something.

She opened her eyes and they looked enormous and burning.
"Steve . . ." she whispered and reached out feebly.

Steve went and bent over her, took her hands, kissed her. She
smelled of antiseptics. It had always been some kind of lilac soap
since he could remember. Always.

"Grandma. How do you feel?"

"I just waitin'," she smiled. "Just only waitin'. Glad you come to
see Grandma." Her big eyes turned toward the door. "You alone?
You didn't bring the baby? I wants to see him, Steve. You promised me before."

"I'll bring him," Steve said. "Easter day. Day after tomorrow."

Under the olive tree in the patio now, along with the rusty white
iron furniture, there was a playpen. It was empty except for a
string of colored wooden beads. There was dew on them that
made them glisten in the clear, early morning sunlight. Steve
followed his shadow across the flagstones to Bernie's studio.
Through the window he saw only cameras and lights and props.
Nobody living. The door knocker was a brass Japanese demon's
head. Steve rapped with it. Nothing. He rapped again, then

looked in at the window. Christ, what would he do if they weren't here? But they were here—at least Lacey was. She came through the door at the rear of the studio. She wore tight knee-length shorts and a sleeveless top. He stepped away from the window: he wanted her at least to open the door to him.

She did. "Steve!" Naturally pale, she went really white now. Paper white. She put a hand to her throat. "What do you want?"

"My grandmother's dying. She wants to see the baby. I told her I'd bring it."

"Steve, why? You had no right. . . ."

"Oh, I've got *some* rights." He stepped toward her. Her eyes widened. She reached out a hand to stop him. He brushed it aside and walked into the studio. There was the edgy half sweet smell of photographic developer. He started for the inner door.

"Steve, no!" She clutched at him. "Don't go in there."

"Why not? Bernie not decent?—as if she ever was."

"Bernie's not here. I mean—" She clapped her hand to her mouth. "I mean, she'll be right back. Right away."

That was a lie. Obviously.

"Lacey, what the hell's the matter with you? You act scared to death of me. Why? I only want to take the baby for a couple of hours. Jesus, he's half mine." He tried to smile. "Come on . . . get him ready for me." He went through into the little sitting room, then into the bedroom. There was still only one bed, not yet made up. Under the window stood a varnished crib.

The baby lay in it in diapers and T-shirt. It was working on a plastic nursing bottle of oranje juice. It was a white baby. Blue-eyed. It hadn't much hair but what there was was blondie red.

"What . . . ?" Steve felt his face twist. He turned to Lacey. "What's this? Who's this?" He couldn't find the right words. He grabbed at Lacey and shook her. "Where's my baby?" he shouted. "Where's my baby?"

"Steve, let me go. Let me go!"

"Where's my baby? Lacey, this isn't my baby. My baby is—I saw my baby at the hospital. It's a brown baby. Black hair, black eyes. It's—Where is it? Tell me!" A hand came from nowhere, his hand, and cuffed her.

"No, no, no, no." Lacey tore out of his grip and backed away, crouching, spitting like a cat. "It's not your baby. There is no brown baby. You don't have any baby. That's my baby. That's Bobby Wilson's and my baby."

Steve gaped at her. "Bobby Wilson? Who the fuck is Bobby Wilson?"

"A boy at school who got drafted."

Steve remembered him. Bushy red hair. Motorcycle. Rough cat. "You . . ." His throat was dry. He swallowed hard. He shook his head. "You're lying."

"Am I?" she jeered. "Am I? Maybe you better take another look at that baby."

"Lacey?" This wasn't happening. This had to be a nightmare. It couldn't be real. "Lacey, what are you talking about. You told me . . ."

"I know what I told you." She sneered the words. "I told you I was pregnant. Well, I was. But Bobby was gone. He wasn't about to help me. And you were there and you were so easy. You were so anxious to get a white girl."

"Lacey, shut up."

She laughed. It was an ugly sound. "I won't shut up. I've been dying for ages to tell you what a dumb jerk you are. What a sucker. So proud of your brains. All those books you read. But you were stupid. I was the smart one. Dumb-Lacey-Nobody-White-Trash. Me. I turned out to be the smart one." She stood leaning toward him, hands on her hips, mouth working ugly over the pretty little teeth. "I got you and held onto you while I had to. You got me away from home so I don't ever have to go back because they're finished with me for marrying a—"

"Lacey!" He had to get out of here. He stepped forward.

She backed away. "Don't you touch me!"

"I don't want to touch you."

"Oh, yes you do. You'd love to stick it in me again. But you never will. I've *had* you. I don't need you any more. I was going to get Jimmy Pike. I could have too—he was here again just yesterday. But I've got Bernie now. She's better. With her there's nothing for me to worry about. Ever. And I don't have to hear anybody snickering about me being married to a nigger."

All he wanted was out. But she was standing in the doorway to the studio, gripping both sides of the doorframe.

"Will you get out of the way, please?"

"Nigger!" she shrilled at him. "Nigger, nigger, nigger!"

He hit her then.

He sat alone at a table in a back corner of the bar called the

Tinker Toy, two blocks from the Parkway Hospital, where his grandmother had died at 3:49 this sunny Easter afternoon. She'd been in a coma when he got there at ten. So at least she never learned she had no great-grandson. Abel Allen Archer had been tied up at a political rally. Steve had glimpsed him hurrying into the hospital as he left. Too late. But that was something else she'd never know.

He worked on a double bourbon, slowly but meaning it. The jukebox screamed as if someone had stood it against the wall to be shot. There was a hard wooden clatter from the skiball machine, hard wooden laughter from the faggots lining the bar. Then somebody stood beside him.

"Steve Archer. I'm really shook."

It was Smith Tyler. Steve stared up the smiling, half-forgotten face, with its smooth, milk-chocolate color. He worked up a smile.

"Sit down, Smith. Good to see you."

"You too." Smith set his draft beer on the table, dragged out a chair, sat close. It was a little table. Under it their legs touched. Once more—would it ever fail to happen when they met?—Steve got a bright, hot vision of how they used to be, naked together. "Thought you hated gay bars."

"I get thirsty," Steve said, "once in a while."

"I'm hitting every gay bar in town," Smith said. "It's my last day of freedom."

"You mean," Steve said, "freedom came while I wasn't looking?"

"I go in the Army tomorrow. Five A.M."

"Oh . . ." Steve said. "Bad scene."

"It's Nixon's answer to the street crime problem. All blacks back to the jungle. White America." Smith took a swallow of beer and wiped his mouth with the back of his hand. "How come you're alone? You and Coy split up?"

Steve shook his head. "He's with his family down in Dead Oak for Easter vacation."

"Oh, yeah. That's right. He told me."

Steve looked at him. "Told you? When?"

"When he came to the office at Central College. To give me the tape. When was it . . . ?" He squinted one eye, calculating. "Friday a week ago."

"Tape?" Steve blinked. "What kind of tape?"

"Recording tape, man. What'd you think—adhesive tape?" Amiable scorn.

"Recording of what?"

"Don't you know?"

"Would I be asking you if I knew, for Christ sake?"

"Man, don't yell at me." Smith look hurt, then concerned. "What's bugging you, Steve? You don't look right, you don't sound right. Something bad happen to you?"

"Oh, shit." Steve bit his lip, bent his head, shut his eyes, covered his face with his hands. It would be so easy to cry: he wanted to so badly. But who was Smith to cry to? Smith had big trouble himself. Steve dropped his hands, forced a smile. "Sorry. Tell me about this tape deal."

"Well . . . I can't tell you much." Eyeing him worriedly, Smith pulled cigarets from his quilted yellow parka and shook the open pack at Steve. Steve took one, Smith took one. He lit them both. "It's just a roll of recording tape in the box it came in. No marks on it. Coy says for me to stick it in one of the storage files over in the big quonset but where nobody will be liable to find it. So I stuck it there first chance I had. That was at noon. He came about two-thirty and I told him where I'd shoved it and he wrote down the file number. That's all. . . ."

Steve scowled into his drink. "Weird," he said. He took a swallow.

"He's a weird little cat," Smith said. "I know you're the wrong one to say this to—but I was glad to get out of that mess. He'll do anything, Steve."

Steve grinned, switching meanings. "And so well, too!"

Smith drew his mouth down. "Fancywork faggots are a dime a dozen. Just remember—anybody knows all those tricks, they've had a lot of training. Which means they've had a lot of other studs before you. Ever think of that?"

"No," Steve said, "but it doesn't matter. I love him. He loves me."

"What about fat Marvel? She still around?"

"Now and then."

"What did he do—cry to make you let her stay?"

"Smith," Steve said, "I've already had a real bad day. What do you want to make it worse for?"

"Sorry," Smith said. "I'm just trying to help. I mean—get rid of her. Did you ever meet that husband of hers?"

"Once. I'll try not to let it happen again."

"You do that." Smith mashed out his cigaret in the black plastic ashtray. "He is a wild beast, baby. Look *out* for him. Did you ever see her bait him?"

"She kissed me right in front of him."

"Did he get bugged?"

"No."

"Well, watch out when he does. He goes crazy. I mean, he's gonna end up killing somebody. If I hadn't dragged him off, he was gonna kill Coy there one night—one very drunk night. After that, I told Coy to shake her. But he wouldn't. So I cut out. That man Bunk—he scares me. Give me the Viet Cong, any time."

"Looks like that's what they've bought you," Steve said.

"Yeah . . ." Smith glanced at his watch. "And I got a lot more bars to hit, a lot more friends to tell goodbye." Then his hand was on Steve's crotch under the table and with his other hand he gripped Steve's jaw and pulled his head around. He kissed him. Deep.

"Man," he whispered shakily, "why don't we go some place and make it quick? We used to be so—"

Steve pushed his chair back, breathing fast and shallow. He needed somebody to hold right now, somebody to hold him. He'd never needed it more, never been so sad and empty and lost. But this wasn't the way. Even if there wasn't Coy, Smith would be a mistake. Tomorrow, for God's sake, he'd be drilling at some dusty fort, who knew where? A few weeks, and he'd be on the other side of the world, lying out in a tangle of jungle vines, slapping at bugs. Or maybe not able to sleep. Maybe dead. Which was all he, Steve, needed now. He shook his head.

"So long, Smith," he said. "Take care."

22

HE SHOWERED. It had to be almost pure steam to wash the grease, grime and smell of the service station off. He lathered and lathered again, scrubbing hard. Not only to get clean but to make himself feel better. He felt bad. Tired, yes. Hung over, yes. But more than that—grieved and disgusted and sore. And now what the hell was going to happen? Because there was that tape. And what did it mean? When he had picked Coy up at the bus depot this morning and dropped him at Galilee, he'd felt too sick to question him. Anyway, a public bus was no place for it. He'd let the kid chatter. *Well a bunch of us were setting up grandstands in the hills for Easter sunrise service when who should ride up on horseback but Laurette, your friend from the motel. It was hot and I had my shirt off and, Steve, she stared at me as if her eyes would fall out.* . . . So Steve hadn't asked about the tape. And it would have to be now, when all either of them wanted was sex: it had been a long, lonely week.

He turned the head for needle spray and cranked up the Cold. Then he got out and toweled himself. He should dress, but why, since later he'd have to get back into the white pants, the white shirt with HANES on it, and return to shoving the phallic nozzles of the gas pumps into the sheet-metal wombs of automobile tanks, polishing windshields, checking water and oil, making change—thankful they hadn't fired him for refusing to work on Easter. He'd put in eight hours already this Monday—his day off from the Library. He had six more hours to go. Whatever happened to all that talent? He gave himself a wan smile in the steam-fogged mirror, knotted the red towel around his hips and left the bathroom.

He had overbought and Coy had been gone, so there was still some gin left from the visit of Shep and Wheatley two weeks ago.

And now Coy came smiling from the kitchen with martinis glistening in each hand like glass flowers. He wore only his little blue shorts with the white bands. There were fine smells of food in the air. He'd been cooking and the heat had made him sweat. Sweat lay like polish on the neat planes of his body. The La Paz Valley sun had silver-plated his hair. It had darkened his skin, too, so that his eyes looked very blue. Unreal. He put one of the glasses into Steve's hand and gave him a quick kiss.

"Come on." He went to the couch and sat on it.

Steve followed but didn't sit down. "Baby," he said heavily, "there's something we have to talk about."

But Coy wasn't having any. With a grin and a quick headshake, he sat up, grabbed Steve's arm and tugged. Steve fell onto the couch. "Hey, my drink!" He set the wet glass on the table and reached to wipe his dripping hand on the towel. But it wasn't across his lap now. Coy had unknotted it. He threw his arms around Steve, laughing.

"You prickteasing bastard." The words came muffled against Steve's chest. The fair head lifted for a second, the grin impudent. "You know you can't stand around in front of me like that and not get raped." The face turned away again. "Oooh! Look at that. Isn't that pretty?" Cool, strong fingers. The bright head slid downwards over Steve's dark belly. Soft laughter, a warm mouth. . . .

It was a great way to avoid a conversation. Once he would have said it was so great that nothing else mattered. But now, while his body exulted in it, and he gave it back, exulting, feasting on the kid's keen, sweet tastes, his mind brooded. Because it would be all over in a few minutes. And what kind of mindless mess was Coy in now? He was. Steve was sure of it.

He watched him go, naked, gilded by the sunset light, to bring back new Martinis from the kitchen. It was a pretty thing to watch. It made his head hurt. And so he held back his question. They sat and drank wordlessly, while the fire faded out of the sky over the sprawl of the city. At last, Steve sighed and lit a cigaret.

"Okay," he said. "So what's this tape bit?" He wasn't looking at the kid. He had leaned forward to drop the match into the ashtray. But he felt the couch jar as Coy stiffened. "Yeah, I know. You don't know what I'm talking about. You want to play it that way. Well, don't bother."

"Steve, listen . . ."

"You listen. I haven't got time. I've got to eat. I've got to go back to work. So sit there and listen. I ran into Smith Tyler last night and he told me you gave him a tape to hide. Why?"

"You don't have to go back to work," Coy said.

"I don't . . ." Steve stared at him. "Oh, no. Not another money-making scheme, baby. Not that."

"Steve, Sister Myra can't send any more checks, not for a long time yet. And, sweetheart, it's killing me to see you working like this. You'll get sick, Steve. You're so thin!"

He ran a hand along Steve's ribs. Steve shifted out of reach.

"Hadn't you heard? Hard work is good for niggers. They thrive on it. Besides, it keeps them out of trouble."

"Don't, Steve. I hate it when you talk like that."

"I don't want to talk. I want you to talk. What's on that tape?"

"Well, it's . . ." Coy gave a scared little shrug. "It's somebody's voice."

"Surprise. I thought it was Beethoven's fifth. Whose voice?"

"Somebody who wouldn't want it heard."

"God damn it!" Steve's hand lashed out. The slap sounded loud in the hushed and dusky room. "Answer me. What's on that tape, Coy? Who are you blackmailing?"

Coy was on his feet, hands to his face. "Steve, you have to stop hitting me all the time."

"Sit down. I don't hit you all the time. I only hit you when you do crazy things."

"But it's not crazy. It's smart. Why should you have to sweat your balls when . . ." He sat on the coffee table, leaning forward, talking fast. "What do you earn? Like today. Twenty dollars for fourteen hours work. Steve, why, when there's somebody who can pay it and never miss it?"

"Because it's wrong. Blackmail stinks, Coy. It's a filthy thing to do. You stuck that microphone under the bed, didn't you, when you had some score here? Coy, it's sickening. Why can't you see that?"

"It wasn't like that. No score. Nobody I brought. He came himself."

"Who—that rich cat from Malibu?"

"No." Pause. Headshake. "I . . . better not tell you." But Steve raised his hand again and Coy blurted, "Shep. Bob Shepherd."

"What!" Steve stood up.

So did Coy, edging away from him. "He came back the morning

after they were here. You'd gone to the gas station, I was getting ready to leave for school. He said he'd lost his attache case, thought maybe he'd left it here. ..." Steve nodded glumly to himself, remembering that it had been his clipboard Shep had supposedly forgotten that October night after rehearsal. ". . . But it wasn't his attache case he came for. It was me. He was all over me ten seconds after I'd opened the door. I couldn't stop him, Steve. He's too big."

"Yeah..." Steve bent wearily and stubbed out his cigaret. "I know. Shouldn't have introduced you to him. Should have figured he'd . . . But Christ, Coy, that still doesn't make it right to do this to him."

"Why not? His mother's loaded with money. You saw how she lives. Why shouldn't you have a little of it? Why should you slave while—"

"We went over that," Steve said. "How much did he pay?"

"He hasn't started yet. I only phoned him this morning. Didn't have a chance before I left for home. He's going to send checks. His mother's checks, of course. A hundred a week."

"Shit!" Steve kicked out at one of the basket chairs. It bounded down the room like a shadow animal. Coy dodged. "You get that tape back!"

"I can't. Nobody can get it now."

"What are you talking about?"

"It's locked up in a file. Smith could get the keys. But he's gone now. In the Army. And I don't know anybody else in the office. Only a school official can—"

"I get the picture. Shep pays, or you tip off the Dean. Beautiful." Steve lunged for him, grabbed his naked shoulders, shook him so his teeth rattled. "Smith said that file has a number. Where is it? Get it!" He flung the kid, staggering, toward the hall door.

"Steve, stop. Don't you understand—"

"Get that number." Steve let go a flying kick and Coy ran. Snapping on the bedroom light, he rummaged shakily in the chest of drawers. When his hand brought out a folded slip of paper, Steve snatched it. Scribbled on it in pencil was 230-579-A, Tier VI.

"What are you going to do?"

"Get that tape and destroy it. Then I'm going to find myself somebody decent to live with."

"Aw, no. Steve, please. I love you, Steve. I was only doing it for you. I—"

Steve shoved him aside and yanked open a drawer of the chest for clean clothes to put on. "Something's burning," he said. "You better turn it off." Coy gasped and ran for the kitchen. Steve heard him opening windows and doors to let out the smoke. He dressed. He shoved the paper into a pocket of his red orlon jacket. He looked at the phone. No. He'd go out and call.

The living room was still dark. Coy sat on the couch, still naked. He looked up, scared and forlorn as Steve passed. Steve kept walking. Coy's voice, boyish, begging, followed him.

"Steve? Come love me."

"Sorry." The front door stood open. Steve hesitated, looked back at him. It was hard not to go to him, do as he asked. Very hard. But that would be wrong. It would only mean more pain later.

He left. There was nothing else to do.

At the foot of Kean Terrace his hand went into his jacket pocket for cigarets and he remembered he'd left his pack lying on the coffee table. Also he'd need change to telephone. He turned and jogtrotted up Sunset. The market was still open.

"You're in a hurry," Mrs. Terry smiled. "Or are you training for the Olympics?"

"What I'm training for," Steve panted, "they don't have at the Olympics." He dug out his wallet. "Tareytons, please. And could I have the change in dimes? I've got to make a lot of phone calls."

"Sure thing. Won't Mr. Bell be pleased?" Mrs. Terry handed him the cigarets, picked up the bill and punched the cash register. "Say, did that fellow find you?" She spilled the dimes into his outstretched hand.

"What fellow? When?"

"Oh . . . this afternoon, about three, I guess. Very light complected colored fellow. Yellow eyes. Don't think I ever saw eyes that color before. Except on a cat, of course."

"Black and white topcoat?" Steve asked. "Houndstooth check?"

"Why . . . now that you mention it, yes. Believe so."

"What did he want?"

"To know where you live," Mrs. Terry said.

"Did you tell him?"

She shook her head. "I figure if a person wants somebody to know where they live, they'll tell 'em. Thing was, Mr. Brubaker was here. I made faces at him to try and shut him up, but he's a little slow, you know. Must have thought my girdle was pinching, or something. Anyhow, he told the man."

"Oh, fine."

"Bad news?"

"This is my bad news day. Week. Month. Year." He ran for the door. "Thanks for the change."

He ought to charge back up Kean Terrace and find out what Coy hadn't told him about Clive Jackson's visit. And why. But it would have to wait. There wasn't time. Not now. Tomorrow.

Telephone booths, glass and aluminum, stood in a row outside the market. He pushed into one, slammed the door and began dialing. First he got the Hanes station to say he couldn't make it back tonight. Then he tried Shep's apartment in the hills. He let the phone ring twenty times but no one answered. Same result at Wheatley's bookshop. Then he remembered that Ross closed the place Monday nights to go buying books and swapping stories with the other dealers. Steve called the stage at Central College. Against a background of hammering and sawing, the grouchy voice of Andrew Harbison, the stagecraft teacher, answered. No, Shep wasn't at rehearsal tonight.

Under the phone booth's metal shelf, fat directories, dogeared and gritty, hung on chains. He looked up Mrs. Shepherd's number. Not that he'd tell her what it was all about: Shep might have asked her for the check already but Steve doubted he'd have told her what for. He tried the number because Shep might be there. He wasn't, though, nor was his mother. Only the Mexican maid, who didn't know where anybody was or when they'd be home.

Steve hung up the receiver and sat hanging onto it for a minute, head resting against the instrument, eyes shut, mouth clamped grimly. Then he sat straight, tore the cellophane off the pack of Tareytons and lit one. Okay. The main thing, anyhow, was to get the tape. He pushed out of the booth.

The quonset building hunched shadowy under dark trees in a neglected corner of the campus, half a block from the brightly lighted new buildings where night classes were in session. He edged between the bushes crowding the path and pawed out for the door. The knob felt rusty under his hand. He turned it and pushed at the door with his shoulder. No good. His fingers slid up and touched the round brass surface of a springlock keyhole. Higher, and something rattled. A padlock. Lots of protection for outdated student records, really no more than tons of wastepaper. Well, there were windows, he remembered—three to a side, set in dormers. Running his hand like a blind man along the corroded iron siding, stumbling over the roots of trees and bushes, he found the first one. A screen of coarse heavy mesh covered it, bolted in place. But when he locked his fingers in it and shook, it rattled. Rust had done its work since World War II when this place had been set up. He jerked hard on the screen. No luck. He braced his feet against the curving wall and tugged. But the bolts held.

The screen on the next dormer was even tighter. A tree branch hung low over it and had kept the rain from reaching it, rusting it. But the last window on the side was exposed. And when he yanked on the screen it gave with a rusty shriek and swung loose as if it was on hinges. He stumbled backward and sat down. Hard. But he got up quickly to try the window. Locked. Well . . . it was only glass. He stripped off his jacket, wrapped it around his fist, and punched the dirty pane. It shattered with a sound like the falling of fragments in a kaleidoscope. The smell of musty paper came out. He reached through the jagged hole to unfasten the lock so he could raise the sash.

"Hey!" A shout.

He jerked his arm back, spun around, crouching. At the far corner of the building, silhouetted against weak streetlight, he saw an old man in a guard's uniform.

"What's going on back there?"

The man was fumbling for the revolver in the holster on his thigh. In his left hand he held a flashlight, but he must have been nervous because the beam of it was jumping around crazily.

Steve threw himself into the bushes. Scrambling, tripping, branches lashing his face, he ran—hunched over, using his hands almost as much as his feet. The guard shouted, but he wasn't following. He yelled that he'd shoot, but no shot came. Steve broke out onto a path. Where? The back wall of the wooden temporary building that housed the campus bookstore. He ran along beside the place, ducking to avoid the light from the windows.

Not till he reached the far side of the campus, the deep wedge of shadow cast by the ramp leading to the big scenery doors at the back of the auditorium, did he stop. Panting, heart racing, he shook the dust and dry leaves from his jacket, put it on, slapped the dirt off his white Levis. Then classes broke and he joined the swarm of kids on the lighted paths and lost himself among them.

He was still shaking when he walked into the bar on Melrose near La Brea. He had got on the first bus that came after he'd left the campus and had ridden it as far as his nerves would let him. Now he pushed through the standing crowd of drinkers to the bar. As he moved, a hand squeezed his genitals. Teeth grinned. The jukebox played "The Shadow of Your Smile." There were no empty stools at the bar and when he had his drink he wedged through the standees looking for a table. A hand caressed his ass. A voice caressed his ear: "You're something new, and I mean something." Pancake makeup, a writhing mouth. *And you're something old,* Steve thought, *and I mean. . . .*

He found a table. Its red formica top was wet with circles left by vanished beer glasses. He dragged out a red bentwood chair and sat down. Still shaking, he drank. If this was bonded whisky, he was the Imperial Wizard of the Ku Klux Klan. All right—look at it this way: because it was nothing proof he could drink it faster. He drank it and it helped to stop the shaking and it let him laugh at himself. Not happily. Just laugh.

What a crazy thing to have tried. If he'd been caught—and it couldn't have come much closer—there'd really have been trouble. What the hell—he could give Shep the file number. Shep was on the faculty. He could think up some excuse to get the keys for the quonset hut tomorrow and dig out the tape. Nobody was going to find it between now and then. Coy sure as hell wasn't going to tell anybody about it. Steve shook his head, mouth tight at one corner. Sometimes he acted as if he didn't own a brain.

His glass was empty. He looked at his watch. 8:40. There was a pay telephone screwed to the scarred red wall beyond an open doorway labeled RESTROOMS. He went to it and tried all of the numbers again. Every time some stud passed on the way to the toilet Steve got his ass stroked. And nobody answered any of his calls except for the Mexican maid who hadn't learned anything since he'd talked to her at 7:00. He went back to the bar for a refill, making sure this time that it was hundred proof.

The jukebox was playing a soupy orchestral arrangement of "I Left My Heart in San Francisco," and as he eased through the pack this time he heard a quiet baritone sing "I got VD in San

Francisco . . ." Back at the table he drank the real booze slowly. It was 9:35 when he finished it, stubbed out his cigaret and went to phone again. Still no Shep. Picking up a third drink, he went back to the table and found a boy sitting there.

He was slender, with brown, sunstreaked hair cut like an English schoolboy's, and eyes like a deer's. "You can't be real," Steve said, sitting down. "Because at the present moment I am the most unlucky son of a bitch in the world, and you would be a very good thing to happen to anybody, even if they were very, very lucky." The boy had a bottle of Champale, just one bottle, and just one frail, hollow stem glass to drink it out of. Steve glanced at the crowd and then looked at the brownhaired boy again. "You're with somebody."

The boy's mouth curled. He shook his head.

"All right, you're waiting for somebody."

"I was," the boy said. "I think it was you. Could I have a cigaret?"

23

THE LITTLE ROOM HAD moss green walls. Bare. There were windows all along one side but the daylight was shut out now by broad movable upright moss green slats. The table had steel legs and a formica top. There were three straight chairs. An air conditioning vent gave the soundproof ceiling a tin navel.

The cold white glare of fluorescents glinted off a three-cell flashlight that lay on the table. The flashlight was bent. Its glass was shattered, only a few slivers left sticking in the frame that was beaten out of shape and clotted with dried blood and hair. Blond hair. Coy's hair. Around the end of the flashlight the Police laboratory had looped an identification tag.

"Is it yours?" Cummings asked.

Steve shook his head. "No."

"Because your fingerprints are on it."

Steve's heart slammed against his ribs. "It's not mine."

"Well, let's put it this way," Dieterle said. He was the man in the rumpled blue suit. "Did you have it in your possession. Did you use it?"

"No."

"I suppose you never saw it before?" Cummings asked.

At the apartment, while Dieterle's big, gentle hands had patted his clothes, searching for hidden weapons, Cummings had told Steve he didn't have to answer any questions and that if he did what he said would be a matter of record.

He said carefully, "I don't know."

Cummings had also told him he could call a lawyer. He only knew one. He had let Cummings call. Cummings had said Bixel was going to call back. Now the door opened and a man with a pockmarked face said, "Cummings—telephone. I'll stay." And he folded his arms and stood leaning against the wall. Cummings went out and shut the door.

Dieterle sat down and lit a cigaret. "After you killed him, where did you go?"

"I didn't kill him."

"Your landlord says he heard you fighting. He heard somebody fall down."

"Nobody fell down," Steve said. "I got sore. We were having an argument. I kicked a chair. It fell down."

"What was the argument about?"

Steve looked away at the slits of window light.

"Your landlord also said you beat up on the Randol boy. A few weeks ago. Gave him two black eyes."

"That's not murder," Steve said. "I thought this was the Homicide Division."

"Did you beat up on him?"

"Not last night," Steve said.

"But you knocked him around sometimes?"

"Cummings said I don't have to answer questions."

"It will make things a lot easier if you do."

Cummings came in, the pocked man left, shutting the door carefully.

Cummings sat down and tilted back his chair. "Your lawyer Bixel isn't coming. He says it's because of his close association with another client whose name you know. He says that client objects that it would damage him."

Steve felt hollow and sick.

"You don't need him," Dieterle said. "Just give us the facts. If you're not guilty we—"

"I walked out of the apartment a little before seven o'clock and I was sore and I went and got drunk," Steve said, "and I met somebody and I spent the night with them."

"Except when you came back, about ten, ten-thirty."

"I didn't come back," Steve said. He looked at Cummings. "I want a lawyer."

"You tell us who to call," Cummings said, "we'll call."

"I don't know any other lawyers."

"Who was this you spent the night with?" Dieterle asked.

"I don't know his name. Somebody I met in a bar."

"Which bar?"

"The Blue Barracuda," Steve said, "on Melrose near . . ."

"We know where it is." Dieterle looked at Cummings.

Cummings raised his pale eyebrows. "A gay bar," he said.

"Right?" It seemed to please him.

Steve looked at him expressionless.

"And you're a homosexual." He set the syllables out in the air immaculately, one by one. "Correct?"

Steve said nothing.

"And your little buddy, Randol—he was a homosexual too. Isn't that true?"

"He was a student at a religious college—Galilee. Very religious. Very strict. He was an honor student. He taught Sunday school at Third Evangelical Church. He was president of his Christian Endeavor group. Go ask them if he was a homosexual."

"I don't think they could tell us. I think you can."

"If you arrest somebody," Steve said, "don't you lock them up?"

"If that's what they want."

"That's what I want," Steve said.

"You know . . ." Dieterle leaned forward and crushed his cigaret out in the ashtray on the table. "If you tell us where to find this . . . man you stayed with, we'll ask him if you stayed with him and if you did, that clears you."

"He lives in a rooming house on some street in the hills a few blocks above Hollywood Boulevard. But I don't know the address. I don't even know the name of the street."

In his mind he stumbled again across the weed-grown yard in the darkness. The kid had brought him there on the back of his Honda. Steve remembered clutching him tightly around his narrow middle, laughing in the wind, and when they'd hit dark streets, letting a hand slide to take hold of the boy's crotch. He remembered the big, oldfashioned California frame house with its deep, night looming caves, the rafters poking out, the porch overgrown with vines, the open front door yawning on the dark, empty hall, the staircase, the room with its rain-stained ceiling and the bed that came down out of the wall. But where? Where?

"Maybe," he suggested lamely, "if I could walk back . . ." But it wouldn't work. He'd been too drunk going there, too hung over leaving this morning. Too hung over, too preoccupied with thoughts, too hurried. He shook his head. "No. Only I was there. I never went back to Kean Terrace, the apartment. I left there at seven. You can ask Mrs. Terry—Terry's market. Sunset at Byron Terrace. I bought cigarets from her. I asked her for change for the telephone."

"Who did you telephone?" Dieterle asked.

"I didn't get any answers."

"If you did, it might help clear you."

Steve shook his head. "Mrs. Terry will clear me."

"For seven o'clock," Cummings said. "But Mr. Brubaker says you came home at around ten, ten-thirty."

"He's lying."

"Suppose we tell you he saw you?"

"Then he'd be lying or you'd be lying. He couldn't have seen me because I was at the Blue Barracuda with this brownhaired kid. They'd tell you I was there till nearly ten. Ask the night bartender. Guy with dead eyes. He'll remember me. I made him open a new bottle of Old Crow Bonded."

Dieterle took a tattered little notebook from his pocket and wrote something in it with a ballpoint pen. He pushed the notebook and pen away again and said, "We'll check."

"But you still could have done it," Cummings said. "Medical examiner tells us he was killed between ten and eleven."

"I was with this kid," Steve said. "All night."

"Prove it," Cummings shrugged.

"Even if you find him," Dieterle said, "is he going to want to tell the Police he spent the night with you?"

"Sorry to disappoint you," Steve said, "but all we did was sleep." And the sad and funny part of it was it was true. The kid was hung up on Bette Davis. He had a dozen Bette Davis scrapbooks, over three hundred photographs of Bette Davis. Steve had to look at them all and the kid had to tell him about them all. They were drinking champale. And finally Steve passed out. Naked. In bed. But passed out. Till morning. "There's no law against sleeping."

"You weren't sleeping," Cummings said. He picked up the grisly flashlight and swung it by its tag. "You were back at your apartment hammering Jesse Coy Randol's head to jelly with this."

"No," Steve said.

"Your fingerprints are on it," Dieterle said.

Steve looked at the floor. It was shiny black composition specked with white. *Like,* he thought irrelevantly, *the population of Rhodesia.* He looked up at Cummings who was still swinging the flashlight like the body of a hanged man. "Look . . . will you phone a friend of mine and ask him to get me a lawyer?"

"All right," Cummings nodded. "What friend?"

Steve gave him Ross Wheatley's number.

The detention cell was another little moss green room but smaller and with a glass front and a toilet and a bunk. He lay on the bunk, sweating and whimpering in a dream where Coy stood holding out his hands, tears running down his face, saying *Steve, you have to stop hitting me all the time,* and he was naked and very beautiful and the top of his head was all bashed in and blood was streaming down over his ears and over his shoulders and chest like the long hair of the princess in the fairy tale. . . .

"Come on, Archer." Somebody shook his shoulder.

He opened his eyes and light glared into them. A heavy-bellied man in a starchy brown uniform bent over him, gave his shoulder another shake, then stood back.

"Come on. You're wanted upstairs."

Groggily Steve sat up. He glanced at his wrist but he didn't have his watch. It was in a manila envelope, along with his wallet and keys, filed away in the shiny booking room at the end of this row of cells.

"What time is it?"

"Twenty till two in the A.M.," the guard growled. "Put your shoes on."

Steve pushed his feet into them, thinking sourly that this was how they were going to work on him—cut into his sleep, wear him out till he'd tell them he killed Coy. Corny. Outdated fiction, warmed-over Arthur Koestler. Shit. That nobody lawyer, Kahn, that Ross had sent—what was he doing? Steve pictured him, hairy, barrel-shaped, asleep now, snoring in his Beverly Hills bedroom. Tying his shoelaces, fingers clumsy, he told the guard:

"Your security is lousy. I could have hanged myself with these."

"While I watched you through the window?"

Steve stood up. "Let's go."

They climbed the stairs. At the top was a big, bright room with glossy desks where men who all looked like Cummings and Dieterle worked, filled out arrest reports, telephoned, or stood talking. At one desk, a Negro detective sat with his feet propped on a half open drawer. A paper cup of coffee stood in front of him and he was munching a hamburger and reading a newspaper, a Negro newspaper, sleazy and sensational. He had it folded vertically and was holding it up and Steve saw a two-column headline:

ARCHER SON, WHITE BOY

IN QUEER HOUSEHOLD

He stopped dead.

The guard nudged him. "Keep moving."

He moved, but stunned. Clive Jackson. He had gotten to Coy, then. His father hadn't been able to stop him. And now the story would be all over the heavily Negro district where his father was running for office. And tomorrow! Christ, what a headline they'd print tomorrow:

ARCHER SON ARRESTED FOR MURDER

"Hold it." The guard knocked on a door.

It was another little moss green room, maybe the same one. The guard took his arm and steered him inside. There was the scrape of a chair as Cummings stood up. He looked very tired, collar wilted, necktie loosened. Dieterle had taken off his blue jacket. There were sweat stains under the arms of his shirt.

"Thanks, Foley," he said.

The guard grunted, stepped out into the hall and shut the door. Steve didn't hear it. He stared. Because at the end of the table sat the brownhaired boy. He smiled. Nervous, timid, but a smile.

"Hi," he said.

Cummings asked him, "Is this the man?"

The boy nodded. "He's the one."

Cummings took a deep breath, let it out, and smiled. His mouth smiled. "All right. Thank you. We appreciate your cooperation."

The boy stood up. "You mean . . . that's all? It's all over. I can go?"

"Yup," Cummings said. "It's all over."

"How long did they keep you here?" Steve asked.

"They had a lot of questions," the boy said.

"Sorry to do it to you," Steve said. "How did they find you?"

"You told Mr. Kahn, the lawyer, about my Bette Davis collection. Mr. Wheatley guessed I must have bought it at Eddie Lawrence's store on Sunset. . . ."

Steve remembered the nervous little man at Shep's and Ross's Christmas party.

"Eddie Lawrence has my address so he can let me know any time he gets new Bette Davis stills and Mr. Wheatley . . ."

"Look," Cummings cut in, "could you talk it over later? We have to go through a few formalities here."

"Oh . . . sorry." The boy gave a little flinching smile.

Cummings opened the door and propelled him out. "Good night, Mr. Rice. Thanks again." He shut the door and turned to

175

Steve. "Sit down, Archer."

"What do you mean, sit down? I'm cleared."

"Yup, and I wonder if you know how lucky you are. Lucky that little flit has guts. Lucky Wheatley knew how to trace him for you. Lucky the bartender at the Blue Barracuda has eyes and a memory. Lucky you and Rice were strangers."

"What do you mean?"

"If you'd been friends, we could have assumed you'd fixed the alibi beforehand. We would have. Those fingerprints were on that flashlight. They're still on it."

"How do you know we're strangers?" Steve asked. "We could be Siamese twins."

"You don't give us much credit, do you, Archer? Why do you think we held him there for hours? We asked his friends, his landlord, the people he works for. You posed for pretty portraits down in the booking room, remember? None of them ever saw you before."

"All right." Steve turned for the door. "I'm cleared. So check me out."

"You're cleared," Dieterle said, "but your friend Randol is still dead. And somebody killed him with a flashlight that had your fingerprints on it. You must know who that somebody is. We'd like you to tell us."

Steve shook his head. "No."

Dieterle stood up slowly. "You won't tell us?"

"I can't tell you because I don't know."

"You handled that flashlight sometime," Cummings said.

"I must have," Steve shrugged, "but I don't remember."

Dieterle narrowed his eyes. "You know what a frameup is, don't you, Archer?"

Cummings said, "Someone killed your buddy and then tried to pin the rap on you. Why cover up for them?"

"Or maybe you're scared," Dieterle said. "Scared they'll kill you too if you tell who they are."

"I don't know who they are," Steve said.

Cummings stared at him bleakly for a minute, then wiped a hand down over his face and turned away. His jacket hung on the back of a chair. From one of its pockets he pulled a small manila envelope. His fingers pried up the clasps and opened the flap. He shook the envelope and a button fell out on the table, a pale tan button with a couple of long threads attached.

"Ever see that before?"

Steve felt cold in the pit of his stomach. "How do I know? It's just a button."

"Not quite. It was under the coffee table in your apartment. Next to the body. The deceased. Randol."

"Maybe it's off something of his or mine."

"It's not," Dieterle said. "We checked."

"Okay," Steve said, "so you've got a clue. You must be anxious to work on it. Don't let me keep you. Just give me back my stuff and I'll leave."

24

M EDICAL CENTER 24 HOURS. The sign glared high and white against the pre-dawn sky. Below it, the sharp-cornered shape of the clinic slept dark. Except for its door. This was glass and hard yellow light poured out through it. Beside it, a push-button was labeled with a little square of black plastic, the lettering incised in white: FOR NIGHT SERVICE RING BELL.

He pressed the button and shivered. Three in the morning was a cold time. He pushed his hands into his jacket pockets and jigged grimly while he waited. It took a while, but finally she came—the night nurse, a motherly colored woman in rimless glasses. A big police dog tugged at a chain by her side. A light went on over Steve's head. The thick glass muffled her voice.

"May I help you?"

"I have to see Dr. Archer," Steve called.

He wasn't here, wouldn't be till eight, and then he'd be on his way to the hospital. He had surgery tomorrow.

"I need him now," Steve said. "I'm his son."

The woman stared. "I don't understand."

Steve took out his wallet, slid from it his city employee identity card from the Library. On it were his name and his photograph and his right thumbprint. Steve held it against the glass for the woman to look at. The dog growled and heaved at the chain. The woman blinked at the card, at his face, at the card again. Then she smiled, but it was a puzzled smile and her head tilted doubtfully.

"Why don't you go home? He must be home."

"So would my mother be home." Steve put away the card and the wallet. "I don't want to frighten her."

"Are you sick or hurt?" She looked concerned.

"Very sick," Steve nodded. "Very hurt."

She went away for a couple of minutes then and when she came back she didn't have the dog. She unlocked the door and pulled it open. Steve stepped inside. She locked the door again.

The waiting room was warm and smelled of antiseptics. The pumpkin-colored walls and chalk-blue naugahide couches still looked new. There were black iron racks of magazines. Lush artificial greenery filled the corners. The business office, with its white desks and cabinets, lay beyond a counter of white formica specked with gold. She leaned across the counter and picked up a white telephone.

"Wouldn't you like to call him yourself?"

Steve shook his head. "I'm too sick."

"You're not sick." His father stood in the doorway to his private office. Steve sat at his father's desk, in his chair, and stared. His father was wearing the beige topcoat. Steve pointed at it.

"There's a button missing from your sleeve," he said.

"What?" His father lifted an arm, scowling.

"The other sleeve," Steve said. "The right arm. The arm you kill people with."

His father's head snapped up. "What did you say?"

"Beat people over the head with, smash in their skulls. Did you know, slivers of glass from that flashlight, some of them, went two and a half inches deep?" His voice cracked. Tears ran down his face. He brushed at them savagely. "Did you know that? Did you know they counted more than twenty sharp little broken bits of his skull buried in his brain—"

His father kicked the door shut and started toward Steve. But he stopped dead when he saw the gun. It was his own gun, flat, black, ugly, kept in the top desk drawer. This was a shiny new clinic, but the neighborhood around it was sullen, restless, hungry. That was the why of the dog at night. It was the why of the gun. Steve didn't point it at him. He just held it.

"Did you have to hit him so hard, for Christ sake? Did you hate him so much? I wish I had the photos they made me look at, so you could see what you did to him."

"You killed him," his father said. "Bixel phoned me they'd arrested you for murder."

"It was a mistake."

"What kind of mistake? It didn't surprise me. I knew you'd turn out rotten. I told you so a year ago."

"But you're surprised I'm here."

"I'm not surprised . . ." his father eyed the gun ". . . that you've come to kill me."

"I haven't come to kill you," Steve said. "They've got a room for that at San Quentin. It's a gas." He tried to laugh but it didn't work. "Only before I phone the police, I want you to tell me why you did it. Sure, I know about this . . ." He had bought a copy of the Negro newspaper from a coin rack downtown. He yanked it from his hip pocket and tossed it on the desk. "But if you wanted to stop that, why go to Coy? He'd already talked to Clive Jackson. If you had to smash somebody's skull, why not Jackson's? Why Coy's? Because I loved him, and you have to wreck whatever I love?"

Archer reached for the phone. "I'm calling the police right now."

"You don't want to do that." Steve pointed the gun and backed the chair on its smooth wheels. "They don't want me anymore. They know I didn't kill him because I wasn't even there. But you. You were there. You left that button, and they found it. Right by his body, for Christ sake. I thought you were always so thorough."

"I tried to be."

The room tilted. The gun almost fell. Steve gasped for air. "You . . . tried to be?"

"As a doctor." There was a chair for patients. Archer sat down in it heavily. "It must have been close to midnight when I got there. I tried the doorbell but no one came. The doors and windows were open, so I stepped inside. He was lying on the floor. I knelt down by him to see if I could help. I couldn't. He was already dead."

"And you phoned the police?"

"No. I got out. I couldn't afford to be connected with murder."

"Yeah. I guessed that from your fatherly response to my cry for help to Bixel yesterday."

His father didn't hear. "I never missed the button. It had been loose for a long time. But I was busy and . . ."

"What did you wait till midnight for?" Steve asked.

"It wasn't until late that a member of my staff brought me that newspaper story. The ink was still wet. There was no way to stop it, but I wanted to stop anything like it happening again. I wanted you to leave, get out of town, both of you, until the election was over. I'd brought money. I thought you'd . . . enjoy a trip to, say, Mexico."

"So you had been on to Jackson, then?"

"Yes. Too late. You neglected to tell me you'd left your wife." His mouth twisted. "So I had a man watching her address. He headed Jackson off successfully. But by the time he'd learned you didn't live there any more, and where you'd gone, Jackson was ahead of him."

"I never thought of telling you," Steve said. "It happened quite a while ago. Back before the play, even. The play you killed."

"I didn't kill your friend," his father said.

"No . . ." Steve sighed. "You never owned a flashlight like that. Not that I handled anyway." He slid open the drawer, laid the heavy gun in it, shut it again. He stood up wearily. "I guess I knew you didn't kill him. Otherwise I'd have told the police who that button belonged to, wouldn't I?"

He slept at Billy Rice's again. The brownhaired boy had told him to come there when they'd stood talking outside the night-glaring Police Building after Steve's release. The kid could have hated him for getting him into trouble. He didn't. He not only had guts, he was kind. Steve hadn't wanted to go back to the Kean Terrace apartment, for several reasons, the best being that Cummings had told him Coy's parents were in town. They'd be going there to pick up his clothes and stuff. Steve didn't want to face them, or try to. Brubie would take care of it and love the excitement. Brubie—that loose-mouthed old bitch! Steve thrashed angrily in the pulldown bed, rattling it. But he was through sleeping and he knew it. The pills he'd pocketed at his father's clinic had kept him knocked out for six hours. Now it was noon. He got up and headed for the gruesome bathroom. . . .

Billy had ridden the bus to work, leaving the Honda for Steve. Wobbling on it through the hulking steel and glass of Hollywood traffic, he felt scared and naked. But when he left Cahuenga Pass for Mulholland Drive, climbing, it seemed a great way to travel. The sun was high and warm, the sky blue. Spring green carpeted the hills, yucca jutting out of it, cream white. Golden poppies edged the road, lavender joepye among the rocks, red shooting-star.

He tilted down the steep tarmac drive. The carport was under the apartment joists. The Austin-Healy was gone, but the red Sunbeam was there. He climbed to the gallery, pushed the button at the door marked 3, and stood waiting. Quiet. Down the slope a meadowlark spilled song. The air was heavy with the sleepy smell of sunwarmed eucalyptus. A sudden scream jolted him. He turned sharply, then grinned. A bluejay sat on the gallery rail, cocked its head at him, squawked again, then flew off, scolding.

He pressed the buzzer once more and heard it sound in emptiness. Hands cupped against the day-glare, he put his face to the window. No sign of life in the big, handsome living room. Then he heard a door open and he turned in the direction of the sound. A young woman in a bandana bikini looked at him from the end of the gallery. Smooth and breedy. Deep tan. Taffy-colored hair. Actress, model, call girl? She held a glass of grapefruit juice.

"You delivering something?"

"Sure," Steve said. "A half million dollars in pure heroin. Can I leave it with you?"

"I forgot," she said. "You're all comedians now."

"We're not," Steve said, "but we're not all delivery boys either."

She gave a little bow. "I'm sorry. Stand corrected."

"I'm Steve Archer. I wrote a play Shep—Mr. Shepherd— produced at Central College back in November.

"Mmm." She nodded. "Of course. I saw you there. I saw the play. It was great-great-great."

"Thank you," he said. "Do you know where they are?"

"I'm afraid I do." Her eyes went grave. "Police arrived at noon. They took Bob in their car. Ross went in his own. I couldn't believe it. I just stood at the window letting my bacon burn and stared. I mean, they are but *the* nicest *guys*. It's got to be a mistake."

"Sure," Steve nodded, feeling sick. "Sure. It's got to be."

The moss green sun slats stood open and bright daylight glinted on the clear plastic reels of a steel-cased tape recorder. They turned with a steady electronic hiss. The voices had stopped. Cummings shut off the machine.

"You still think it's a mistake?" he asked.

"It doesn't mean he killed him," Steve said.

"It means he had a motive," Dieterle said.

Steve stared at the dead loudspeaker. "Where did you get it?"

"It took a while." Cummings sat down. "On Monday night somebody tried to break into the warehouse at Central College."

Steve felt as if he'd been kicked in the stomach.

"A campus security guard scared him off. But he dropped a slip of paper. It was off a college office memo pad and it had a number written on it that turned out to be the number of a storage file. The guard turned in the slip. The college called in the L.A.P.D. Our men checked the file. The tape looked out of place among a lot of I.Q. test results for 1958."

Cummings lit a cigaret.

"The warehouse keys were kept in the college office so that was the first place the officers showed the tape around. Sure enough, a typist had seen a blond kid give the tape to a student clerk named Smith Tyler. Well, Tyler's been drafted. He's in the Army up at Camp Roberts. But the officers got in touch with him. He told them it was Jesse Coy Randol who asked him to hide the tape. He wrote the number down on a slip Tyler gave him. When the other officers heard Randol's name, they turned the matter over to us. It was a break."

"Why? Why wasn't it a frame-up?" Steve asked. "If the one who killed Coy got the slip, he could have made a lot of noise breaking the screen and smashing the window and then dropping the paper when the guard showed up."

Dieterle asked, "Who said anything about broken screens and windows?"

Steve stared at him, then at Cummings.

"Shit!" he said. "Oh, shit!" He leaned forward, elbows on knees, and looked at the floor. "All right. Yeah. It was me. Smith Tyler's a friend of mine. I ran into him Sunday night and he happened to tell me about Coy giving him this tape. Coy wasn't back home till Monday. That night I asked him what was on the tape. When he told me—that was when we had the fight Brubie heard. Not fight—argument. I left and tried to telephone Shep and tell him not to worry. I couldn't get him. That was when I got this half-assed idea about breaking into the quonset hut. Shit!" He stood up. "I didn't even know I'd dropped the stupid slip." He turned out the pockets of the red jacket. Nothing but cigarets and matchbook. "It must have fallen out when I took this off to wrap around my fist to break the window."

"Just like in the movies," Cummings said.

"Yeah . . . What do I do—get arrested for attempted burglary now?"

Cummings and Dieterle traded ironic looks.

"Do you know Judge Clayton Herter?" Cummings asked. "Deputy District Attorney Melvil McGriff?"

Steve nodded. Powerful Negroes, friends of his father.

"They phoned us this morning. They'd like us to leave you alone. They're worried about your father's election. And we're certainly not going to make any waves where we don't have to. Not and rile up the black community. Not for twenty dollars in property damage. Naturally, when Shepherd comes to trial, you'll have to testify. But that won't happen till after the election."

"It won't happen," Steve said. "But thanks."

Dieterle was fitting the cover on the tape recorder. He said, "So Randol admitted to you that he was blackmailing Shepherd."

"He was like that," Steve said glumly. "Short on ethics. He got crazy ideas sometimes. This was the worst."

"Yup." Dieterle snapped the fastenings on the machine. "It was the one that killed him."

"No." Steve shook his head. "Shep didn't do it."

"Why?" Cummings was suddenly caustic. "Didn't he own a three-cell flashlight that you'd had your hands on?"

They were both looking at him hard. He looked at them the same way. "No. He didn't."

But he felt cold in his belly.

25

S HE WAS WEARING A BLUE-GREEN pleated smock and a straw hat with a tall crown and a turned down brim. Cotton gardening gloves covered her hands. And when she turned to look at him across the handsome upstairs sitting room, she was an old woman. The eyes that had been the finest part of her beauty the night of the cast party were dull now. But she made herself smile earnestly, and her voice was still lovely.

"Stephen," she said. "It's good of you to come. I'm sorry for your loss. And your trouble."

"Thank you. I'm sorry for yours . . . Shep's."

On the long balcony with its balusters of turned and painted wood, she was surrounded by begonias, acanthus—deep pinks, dark lush greens. Bougainvillea cascaded off the balcony roof, a dense tumble of sunlit magenta that cast shadow, coolness. He went to her there. There was the good smell of damp, rich earth.

"He'll be all right," she said. "He didn't do it. I know. You see . . . I was with him."

"With him?"

"All evening." She knelt, picked up a heavy fork and began turning over the earth around the roots of an azalea in a redwood tub. "He came here at noon, very troubled. Not that he had to say so. I saw it in his face. He was sick with it, of course. I insisted he tell me. We've always been very close. Finally he did. And do you know what I advised him?" She glanced up with a worn smile. "I advised him to get in touch with you."

Steve said, "He wouldn't want to do that."

"He didn't want to." From a gaudy sack she poured fertilizer on the loosened soil. While she forced it in, she said, "He felt he had betrayed your friendship, done something quite unforgivable. It was a long time before I could persuade him that, however you might feel about it—and I shouldn't blame you for being very angry—still, you wouldn't allow this kind of thing to happen."

"You were right," Steve said. "I wish he'd called."

"He tried. First the library, but it seems it was your day off. Then your apartment. No one answered."

"I was working," Steve said. "I've got an extra job. Nights. Except Sunday and Monday—then I work all day too. Filling station. Shep didn't know about it, I guess. It was on my dinner hour that I found out what Coy had done. I tried to call you then. Couldn't reach anybody."

"Mmm." Her face was hidden but the straw hat nodded. "When Bobby is troubled, he finds the sea soothing. Always has, since he was a little boy. I drove him to the beach. There's a little seafood place on the pier we both love. But, naturally, it being Monday night, they were closed. So . . . we ended up simply walking on the sand, watching the sunset, talking, debating, trying to decide what to do. Oh, for hours. It grew very dark. At last we made up our minds. We found a cafe open. Very indifferent food, but it didn't matter since we weren't, either of us, hungry. Then we drove back to Los Angeles and straight to your apartment. Hoping you'd be there. It was almost eleven."

"And if I wasn't there?" Steve wondered.

"Then intending to . . . well, persuade the boy to give up his scheme. He is . . . was a religious student. Exposure surely couldn't have helped him, either." She got stiffly to her feet and pulled off the soiled gloves. "Let's have a cigaret, shall we?" She sat in the rubbed plush wing chair, leaned her head back, shut her eyes for a minute and took the smoke gratefully. "I tire so easily these days. That was why I didn't go in with Bobby. Those stairs of yours . . . those terrible, long, steep stairs!"

"I know," Steve smiled. "Too much."

"Too much at my age," she nodded, "certainly after a long walk on the beach. I simply couldn't hurry. Bobby went on ahead. I kept stopping to rest. And I'd scarcely reached the top when out he came. Your apartment was dark but the French windows and the front door were standing open. It was too dark to see his expression, but when he took my arm he was trembling terribly and his voice shook. 'He's dead,' he said. 'Let's get out of here.'"

Steve asked, "Do the police know this? I mean, have they talked to you?"

"Yes, of course. Or rather, I talked to them. But they insist that

Bobby was able to go in and kill the boy and come out again before I caught up with him." She gave a little crooked smile and shook her head. "It's nonsense, of course. Bobby's incapable of doing such a thing. . . . Do you know the play *Hobson's Choice*? There's a charming speech in it, by the girl in love with the big, grubby, young shoemaker. 'You great, soft thing,' she calls him. That's Bobby. A great, soft thing. . . ."

But you, Steve thought, watching her stub out her cigaret and rise from the wing chair, *you're not soft.* She went back to her plants.

"I'd better go," he said. "Let me know if there's anything I can do."

"Thank you, I will." She had put on the gloves and was tinkering with a little red spray pump. "Shall I ring for Maria to show you out?"

"I know the way, thanks."

He stopped in the hall at the linen closet. Heart thumping, he opened the tall doors.

The flashlight still lay on the shelf.

Cummings and Dieterle weren't at the Police Building. They were at the District Attorney's office with Shep and the lawyer Kahn. Steve talked to the pockmarked detective. His name was Van Zandt. He lit a pipe. Its smoke curled in the air-conditioned sunlight of the big, busy office. Men came and went. Typewriters rattled. Phones rang. Van Zandt rocked back in his swivel chair and shook his head.

"It doesn't mean anything."

"It means it wasn't Shep who killed Coy."

"It means there's a flashlight there. But who says it's the same one you handled the night of the party?"

"I say so."

"But how do you know?"

"My fingerprints are on it. Go get it. Test it."

Van Zandt sighed and laid the pipe in the ashtray. He leaned forward, elbows on the desk. "Let me put it this way. Was there something to prevent your going out to a hardware store today and buying that flashlight and putting it in that linen closet?"

"I didn't have to," Steve said. "It was there."

"Fine." Van Zandt nodded. "But you see my point."

"I see a hard nose," Steve said.

Van Zandt shrugged. His pale eyes smiled. "Standard equipment on all detectives," he said.

He was dirty. He needed a shower and a shave and a change of clothes. By now, the apartment should be empty. It was. He went straight and fast down the long white room because he didn't want to see any of it or think about what he saw. . . . Clean again, feeling maybe not quite so sick and beaten now, he opened the drawers of the chest. Their half-emptiness made him hurt. All Coy's stuff was gone. He got into narrow black corduroy Levis and a black shirt with an op white stripe and a roll collar. He had a charcoal tweed jacket in the closet. He opened the door.

Coy's little Mod suit hung there, brass buttons twinkling. That one they hadn't taken. The blue serge, yes. Christ, they'd bury him in that! It broke him up. He sat down on the floor and cried. It was bad and took a long time but at last he wore it out. He got weakly to his feet, went back to the bathroom, washed his face. He threw shaving stuff into a kit, zipped it, and started to leave.

But Brubie was standing on the front terrace. Naturally—he'd have heard the shower. Well . . . Brubie he didn't want to see. He went through the kitchen where there was still the smell of burned food. Bitter, like his memories. He let himself out the back door.

The property sloped up steeply to June Street. Between geraniums and trees, white wooden steps climbed all the way. Seldom used. He used them now. Halfway up, at a jog, stood a dark cedar. One branch had lopped across the steps at face level. He knocked it aside and saw something flutter down out of it. He stopped and picked it up. A feather. A long, brown feather with black stripes. A pheasant feather.

He had blacked Lacey's eye. It would be a long time before he got over hating himself for that. The flesh around it was still discolored, but the swelling was down now and both her eyes watched him, bright with fear. She stood in the doorway at the back of the studio room, fresh in yellow-green striped cotton. Beyond her someplace in the apartment the baby made happy sounds. Bernie stood in the middle of the studio room wearing blue jeans and a Russian peasant blouse with a lot of cross-stitching embroidery. She held a camera tripod like a club.

"You take one step in here and, so help me, I'll break your head open. What you did to Lacey—"

"You're confused," Steve said. "I didn't break her head open. That was what you did to Coy. Remember?" He snarled a smile. "You're a rougher stud than I am, Bernice. It's something we both have to face."

"What the hell do you mean?" She narrowed her eyes.

"You know, but if you want me to tell you . . . You came home from wherever you were Easter and found Lacey with a black eye. And you saw red and tore up to my place to kill me. But I wasn't there. Coy was. Well, that was even better. Poetic justice. Sitting there naked, maybe lying there asleep naked. I don't know. Anyway, you beat his head in."

"My," she mocked, "doesn't our little mind operate on a primitive level?"

"Maybe," Steve said. "Where do you keep your hats?"

She turned her head, looked at him sideways. "What? My hats?"

"One hat. The slouch one, sort of cinnamon brown. The one . . ." He had brought the feather inside his shirt. He pulled it out. "The one that used to have this on it. The one you wore when I saw you Christmas at the hospital. The one you wore when you killed Coy."

She lost color. She set the tripod against a chair arm. Carelessly, so that after a second it fell with a clatter. She blundered out past Lacey. Steve followed her into the little sitting room and watched her rummage frantically in a closet. She turned with the hat in her hands, staring from it to Steve's face and back again. Her jaw worked convulsively. "No . . ." she croaked. "No . . ."

"Yes," Steve said. "It caught in a low tree branch up the back stairway from my place."

"I was running away," Bernie said. "Yes, I did come to see you. I'd been in San Berdoo with my mother. She's ill. I didn't get home till late Monday night. Eleven or so. As soon as Lacey told me it was you who did that to her, I went to find you. The windows were open. I barged right in. He was lying on the floor. Well, there were martini glasses and there was the smell of burned food. I thought he must have passed out and forgotten dinner. But he hadn't passed out. I touched him and he was cold. I never felt anything so cold."

She shuddered and wiped a hand on her blouse.

"Then I heard somebody coming. The doors at the back were open, the ones into the little patio. I went out that way and there were those white stairs. I didn't know where they led, but I ran up them as fast as I could. . . . Where are you going?"

The kitchen was brightly lighted. The baby lay there in the playpen. The flashlight hung on its hook by the back door. The baby laughed at him.

He turned sharply to Lacey. "You said Jimmy Pike was here Saturday. Did you tell him where I live?"

"Yes," Lacey said. "It's you he wants—not me. He's a fairy. Did you know that, Steve? A fairy."

Pike said, "It got old. Waiting."

Advertising paid. The place didn't look like a garage any more. Sliding glass front, floor to ceiling drapes, wall to wall carpet, Japanese furniture. Two shoji screens. Beyond one a new bed, low and broad. Beyond the other a sleek, shiny new kitchenette. No messy easel now but a clean white expanse of drafting table. No battered raw plywood chest for paints and brushes but a glossy black lacquer cabinet. One picture on the wall. The portrait of Steve.

"And I'm not a believer in bisexuality. Anyway—Lacey's head is hollow. You couldn't stay with her. Not forever. You've got too many brains."

"Look, will you shut up," Steve said. "I only want to hear one thing from you. Did you go to my place?"

"Steve, what the hell's wrong? Yes. I went to your place. Easter. Morning, noon, night. Nobody home. Monday, after work. Too many people home. Do you two always carry on like that with the curtains open?

"You mean you watched?"

"I went home. Steve . . ." Pain made the blue eyes bright. "Why? Why him? Why not me? You knew I wanted you. I said I'd wait."

"So you went home. And you sat there getting soggy drunk and staring at that picture and feeling sorry for yourself. Right? And then you began to hate me. Right? And pretty soon you went back. And he was there all alone in the dark and you killed him."

"What?" Pike's voice went high and cracked.

"Killed him!" Steve yelled. "Killed him, Jimmy!"

"No . . ." Pike backed away, sick white. "I didn't."

"You didn't take that big flashlight of yours and bash his skull in? That flashlight with my fingerprints all over it. You didn't put on driving gloves to use it and then leave it there so I'd be killed too?"

"Steve, cool it, baby." Pike shook his head, held out his hands. His voice wobbled. "Man, I didn't even know he was dead. Steve, I'm sorry for you."

"He's dead," Steve said. "Show me the flashlight."

Pike walked into the kitchenette, opened a drawer, took out the flashlight and laid it in Steve's hands. It was the old one. Daubed with paint. But there could have been paint on the one Cummings had swung in front of his eyes. The dried blood could have covered it. He handed it back.

"Yeah. Thanks. Sorry, Jimmy. Sorry for everything." He turned away.

"Wait." Pike put the flashlight back and shut the drawer. "I did go back, Steve. Like you said, I got drunk and I got sore and . . . Christ, how I wanted you. Especially after what I'd seen. Talk about rubbing salt in wounds! Anyhow, I went back. I don't know what I thought I was going to do. But I had to go. And I'd just gotten out of my car when this man came running down your front stairs. I mean, running scared, Steve."

"When?" Steve felt his heart jump. "What time?"

"Ah, who knows . . ." Pike raised his shoulders. "Maybe ten-thirty. Maybe not quite that late."

"What did he look like?"

"Kind of fat and squatty but big shoulders. I couldn't see his face. That's a dark street. He must not have seen me at all. He went past so close I could hear him breathing. It was like sobbing, almost. I could smell him. Sweat, cold sweat. It scared me. Jesus, if I'd known. . . ." His eyes widened for a second. Then he gave a sorry headshake. "I was too stoned. All I knew was I wanted out of there. I got back in my car and took off."

He ran up the strip of broken cement between the facing rows of scabby stucco cottages. It was warm. Lighted windows and doors were open. The scream of television commercials came out, the screams of married quarrels, the screams of kids. A dog yapped at him from inside a torn screen door. An empty beer can clattered. A woman gave a shriek of laughter. A door slammed. Back in the darkness somewhere cats fought.

He didn't knock. He went in. Two men in swim trunks stood up with little scared cries. One was old and bony. Leathery skin, grizzled body hair, little eyes looking out of deep sockets. The other was younger, thick-bodied, with short legs and arms. They

191

held drinks. So did Marvel, who wore a sleeveless pink leotard that looked as if it could crawl to the laundromat by itself, given the chance. She turned the color of vegetable shortening.

"Steve!"

"Where's Bunk?"

"At sea. What's the matter with you? You look—"

"At sea since when?"

She turned the men a look of pained apology. They kept trying on little frightened smiles and taking them off again.

"Answer me, Marv!" Steve shouted.

"Steve, darling—" She reached out. Fake tenderness. "I know how you loved Jess. I loved him too." Small, crooked smile. Biting of the lower lip. "And I don't blame you for being this way. But . . ." She stood up. "Look, let me get you a barby." She turned.

He grabbed her arm. "When did he go to sea, Marv? Answer me or I'll break your fat neck."

"Tuesday, Tuesday, Tuesday!" she yelled.

He let her go. The men knew the back way out. They took it, stumbling over each other in their hurry. Steve heard Bunny's voice: "Auntie Archie, Auntie Phil—are you going? Bye!" Then an electronic rip as a tone arm skidded across a record. Then the tormented screams of the Beatles.

"What ship?" Steve asked.

"Some freighter. What difference does it make?"

"He killed Coy. The police will want to know."

Her eyes opened very wide. "He couldn't have. He was here Monday night. With me and Bunny."

"He was there, doll," Steve said. "A friend of mine, Jimmy Pike, saw him leaving. He's ready to report it. I asked him to wait till I saw Bunk first."

Marvel sat down on the greasy couch. "Oh, no."

"Oh, yes. So you might as well tell it straight."

"We had a fight. . . ." She talked looking at nothing, voice flat. "He wants Bunny in Catholic school, of all things! He only goes to church once a year, at Easter, and right away he's a devout Catholic." She lifted her lardy shoulders and let them fall. "You know how fights are. You start with one thing and pretty soon it's half a dozen others. You say a lot of things you shouldn't. We were on vodka and hitting it pretty hard. And I got sarcastic and he got mean. He can. You wouldn't think so, he's so sweet most of the time. But he started snarling about all the gay boys I hang around with and calling me a whore. And worse. I flipped out. I told him little Jess was hung better than he was and I said . . ." She broke off, looked up at Steve quickly, then away again. "What does it matter? He went there."

"It matters," Steve said. "It must have been pretty rough to make him commit murder."

She said in a low, quick voice, "I told him going down on Jess for five minutes was better than being screwed by him—Bunk—for an hour."

Steve wished he hadn't asked. "Was it true?"

She nodded. "Jess let me. Once. I begged him and he let me. He was so beautiful, Steve."

"I know that, for Christ sake."

"But he wouldn't do anything else. Nothing to me. And it was only once. He said women didn't know how."

"When was this? When I was around?"

She shook her head. "No, before. Smith was around."

"Yeah. Okay, so you told Bunk."

"But he didn't do it. He got there too late. Jess was already dead. Bunk told me so next morning. He was so shook he didn't come home till then. I never saw him so shook. He cried, Steve."

"And you still think he didn't do it."

"He'd have gone and confessed. Steve, he hated himself when he got violent. I know. Once after he beat me up, he tried to shoot himself. He's really gentle and kind." She picked up her drink moodily. The ice was melted. "It's me that makes him run wild. I do it to him. I bait him. I don't know why, but I can't stop myself. I'm just a bitch. Bitch! Bitch! Bitch!" And she began to cry and it was real now. The words jerked out broken and helpless. "But he didn't kill him, Steve. You've got to believe that."

He believed it. After he found the flashlight. It was in the Volkswagen, among beer cans and crumpled cigaret packs and soiled paper napkins in the dirt under the driver's seat.

26

ALFWAY THROUGH THE ROCK-WALLED PASS on the Honda, he met the funeral procession. Broad black Cadillac hearse, broad black limousine. He glimpsed Coy's father, face like broken gray stone, Coy's mother, face like a crushed flower, Coy's sister. She was chewing the inside of her cheek. Next came Myra Lusk's big Buick station wagon with its slogans. She drove eyes front and vacant, face like a painted mask. It wouldn't have mattered if she'd look straight at him. In Billy Rice's crash helmet and green plexiglass visor, he might have been anybody.

He began counting cars. But he quit when he reached the bright morning end of the pass and saw them in an ant line along the curving road through the orchards, all the way to the far end of the valley, where the steeple of Berea Church glinted among the live oaks. A lot of cars. A lot of people had made the same mistake he had—loving Coy Randol. He sloped down into Dead Oak. The cars left gaps now and then. He waited at the road edge and cut through the next one to get to the motel.

He'd come nonstop from L.A. Three hours on the bike. Getting off, he was stiff and sore. The snarl of the little engine had been loud in his ears. Now, even with the passing cars, the quiet was scary. He unlatched the helmet, lifted it off, hung it on the handlebars. He wanted Laurette to know him. But the office was locked. He peered inside. Bright reflections from the swimming pool rippled on the ceiling. That was the only movement. He knocked loudly. Nobody came. Noting that there were no parked cars, he went along the covered walk, squinting through the cabin windows. Deserted. Beds made. Everything neat and tidy, but no sign of life.

The filling station was closed too. When he chopped to a halt there, scattering gravel, he saw that the yellow pumps were padlocked. So was the station door. Puzzled, he went around back for a look. There was a paddock fenced with raw wood rails sheltered by ragged old eucalyptus trees. At its far side was a stable building made of corrugated galvanized iron. Bales of alfalfa were stacked against it, half covered by a tarpaulin. The doors stood open on a dark interior. The smell of horse came out, the clop of a heavy hoof, the snort of big nostrils.

"Mr. Morris?" Steve called.

Heck Morris came to the door, a big coarse-bristled brush in his hand. He blinked in the sunlight, smiled.

"Why, it's you again. Need some gas? You I'll sell it to." He came across the paddock on his round-heeled cowboy boots. Same pot belly, same sweaty Stetson. He shrugged, winked. "Hell, I'll sell it to the rest of 'em . . ." He nodded in the direction of the road. "But only if they make a fuss for it. The general idea is I'm closed out of respect of the dear departed."

"Who's that?" Steve asked.

"Young fella grew up here. Randol by name. Was going to college up in L.A. Killed in a car accident."

"Too bad." So that was how they were telling it. Steve looked toward the road. "Where are they going?"

"They held a funeral at Berea Church. But there's no cemetery here. Got to drive to Escondido to bury him."

"And Laurette," Steve said. "Why is she closed?"

Something happened to Morris's stubbly, good-natured face. No tears came to his eyes. He didn't look away. His voice held flat and steady. But he was in pain. "Laurette's dead," he said.

"No." In the warm sun, Steve chilled. "I'm sorry . . . She was good to me when I was down here Christmas."

"She liked you," Morris nodded.

"How did it happen?"

"Horse threw her. Busted her head on a rock."

Steve winced. "When? Where?"

"Tuesday morning. Far end of the valley." He pointed.

"Were you with her?" But Steve knew the answer.

"Nope. Had a pickup truck I was reboring. Hodges had to have it soonest, like they say. Anyway, whatever it was she went for, it was some kind of secret. She was all bright-eyed and excited. But she wouldn't say why. Said she'd tell me later. Something about that building scheme of hers. The bar and all. Did you know about that?"

"She showed me the plans," Steve nodded.

Frowning, blinking, Morris picked his teeth with a wooden match. "Queer thing. Can't figure it out. Come in here." He turned for the stable. Steve climbed between the fence rails and followed him across the paddock. Inside the dim building, Morris halted in front of the first of three big, shadowy horses. "This is Karl," he said, and stroked the dark muzzle. The horse turned its head from under Morris's hand to stare at Steve. Soft, brown eyes, brushy lashes. "Go ahead. You can touch him. Gentle as a kitten. Gentler. Never knew a steadier horse."

The big animal's breath was warm and sweet with hay. The shock of mane down its forehead was rough to the touch. In the dark rear of the stall the black tail swished flies.

Steve said, "But he's the one who threw her?"

Morris nodded. "He's got more sense than nine average humans. And Laurette was a good rider—natural born. But . . . accidents happen. Something scared him. Could have been a rattler. We've got 'em around here. He reared and threw her off. Right into the barranca. It's full of rocks, you know. Karl, here—"

The horse's ears went up.

"He wandered down into the orchards. They phoned me. I went and got him. Started to look for her then, of course."

"Did you find her?"

"Couple kids found her. Radio station was the nearest place. They legged it there and Sister Myra, she phoned the Sheriff." Morris clumped in his worn-out boots back to the doors and stood gazing out at the bright sunshine. "Funny thing, her and that young Randol boy dyin' so close together. Him Monday, her Tuesday."

"Funny thing," Steve said.

The church looked deserted. He buzzed the Honda across the tarmac under the trees and stopped it by the door into the right rear wing. He tried the door and to his surprise it opened. Then there had to be somebody here. Putting on an inquiring smile, he leaned inside. "Hello?" No answer. He walked in. The office, the printshop, the shipping and storage rooms were empty of life. He opened the windows because he wanted to be sure to hear approaching cars. A mockingbird sang. That was the only sound. He began to search. He tried every drawer of every desk. He poked among the shelves of supplies, the shelves of printed matter. He let his gaze wander along the walls. Painted plaster religious mottoes, cheap color reproductions of Bible scenes, a purple felt banner with gold fringe: BEREA CHURCH BRASS CHOIR. So it wasn't in a drawer, it wasn't on a shelf, it wasn't hung on a hook. In the storeroom he set up the ladder and climbed it. He pushed up the trap door of the loft and looked in. Right beside the opening lay the flashlight.

The Dead Oak Market occupied an old one-story frame building with a covered wooden walk along its front. Bins of fruits and vegetables stood out here under a pair of hanging scales with rusty white dials. Inside, the long single room was crowded. To the right were groceries, shelves of canned goods, brightly boxed breakfast foods, waxpapered bread and the rest, a freezer of meats in cellophane, a lighted icebox with glass doors— milk, eggs, butter, soft drinks. In the center of the store were counters of clothing, overalls, underwear, straw hats, shoes. Cotton housedresses on a rack. To the left was the hardware department—nails, paint, rolls of wire mesh, shovels, rakes, saws, Steve moved that way.

The man who said, "Howdy"—Charlie, hadn't Laurette called him?—was tall and gaunt and wore sleeve garters like a character out of Rick O'Shay in the comic strips. "Almost didn't open today, on acount of the funeral. What can I do for you?"

"I've got a motor bike outside," Steve said. "The headlamp's burned out. Heck Morris didn't have one to fit. He thought you might."

"You got the bulb?"

Steve reached into his jacket pocket. Empty. He tried the left pocket, the inside one. He shook his head, puzzled, apologetic. "Sorry. I had it. Must have dropped it along the way."

"You don't know the size?"

"Gosh, I'm sorry. I'm afraid I don't. It's not my bike. I just borrowed it for this trip. And I don't know much about these things."

"Well . . ." The man stepped from behind the counter and shambled toward the door. "We'll just take a look."

Steve didn't follow him. He reached for the sales book that lay on the counter, its used pages rolled back, tucked under and held with a rubber band. He pulled this off and thumbed quickly through the used slips, keeping watch on the door. It appeared that every sale, no matter how small, was recorded in the store-keeper's big sprawling hand. But all he'd sold in the last four days were lengths of pipe, panes of glass, bags of fertilizer and so on. Steve snapped the rubber band back as he'd found it, laid down the sales book and walked to the door.

The man was coming up the steps from where the Honda was parked on the road edge. "I can give you a bulb'll fit that socket, I think," he said.

In Escondido, Steve began with the stores on the broad, high-curbed main street, the route a driver would normally follow to the coast highway or coming back from, say, San Diego to La Paz Valley. There were two big hardware stores, windows full of power tools and kitchenware and dead flies. No luck. There was a sunbaked lumberyard that sold hardware as well. No luck. He tried Grant's, Woolworth's, Newberry's, a cavernous Rexall drug-store—all of them so cold that each time he came out onto the sidewalk the heat slammed into him like a wall.

The hardware department of Sears Roebuck was cold too. It was in the basement—bright, broad and empty. Except for one middle-aged man in shirt sleeves who was fiddling with a fishing rod. There was no business this Thursday afternoon at 1:30. He was enjoying himself.

"Excuse me," Steve said. "I'm on an errand for Sister Myra Lusk, the pastor of Berea Church in La Paz Valley."

The man didn't look at him. He kept watching the rod, weigh-ing it, testing its flexibility. He gave everybody else's answer. "Sure, I know Sister Myra."

"Well, she bought a flashlight here Tuesday," Steve said. He had it by rote now. He'd repeated it all over town. "And she forgot to get the sales slip for the church records. She wondered if you'd be so kind as to make out a copy for her."

"I gave her the slip," the man sighed. He set the fishing rod back in its rack. "She lost it. All right." He had a bad limp that tilted him to the left at every other step. He lurched toward the wrapping counter. "I'll write her out another one."

Construction junk still lay around the radio station, broken lath, old cement sacks, chicken wire. The place stood all alone among rocks and dry brush on the top of the mountain. White stucco. New. Its tall sending towers looked fragile against the hot blue sky. Sister Myra's Buick was parked beside the door. Steve left the Honda next to it and pushed inside.

Cold air and organ music came at him. And Sister Myra's voice. Through a loudspeaker above a door in the far white wall, a door where a red sign glowed ON THE AIR, a door that was open. Beyond it he saw her. She sat in a leather swivel chair. Her back was to him. In front of her a microphone hung above a gray, slope-fronted control panel. White dials, black knobs. To her left was a tape deck. To her right a turntable revolved, the tone arm on a record. Mournful hymns.

He walked to the doorway, leaned in it and listened to her.

". . . But that fine boy's name is going to live on in this green valley of God that he so loved. The Jesse Coy Randol Memorial Summer Youth Camp will keep his memory alive—a place where our wonderful Christian boys and girls can come and have their good times during vacation, prayerfully, far from the liquor and cigarets and dance halls and movies of this sin-sick world.

"The Jesse Coy Randol Memorial—up here in these sunlit hills of God. Oh, it's going to be beautiful, too, dear listeners in Christ. I've seen the plans. Dormitories, dining hall with a big stone fireplace, swimming pool, a pretty little chapel in the pines. So you help us, now. Help us to build. Send in your dimes and dollars. Remember this wonderful, dedicated little boy of ours that Jesus has called home to be with Him in paradise. You know who this is talking. You know where to send your donations: Sister Myra Lusk, Box Number One, Dead Oak, California. God bless you all. . . ."

She touched a switch on the control panel. The red light above his head blinked out. That meant the microphone was off. She twisted a knob. The organ music swelled.

"Beautiful," Steve said. "Very touching."

She swiveled the chair. A cane had leaned against it. The cane clattered to the floor. She gaped at him. The right side of her face was badly dragged down now. The eyelid drooped almost shut. The lower lip hung loose at the corner. "No!" she gasped. She bent and frantically clawed for the cane. "You're supposed to be locked up!"

"Why would I be locked up?" Steve walked toward her.

"Because . . ." She wasn't watching him. Her eyes were on the cane she was straining to reach. "You killed him. You killed my Jess!"

"He wasn't yours," Steve said, "and now he isn't anybody's." He flicked the microphone switch so that they were broadcasting again. This would sound pretty with an organ music background. " . . . Because you killed him. You took that flashlight I'd used in the church loft and beat his head in with it. No, don't tell me the flashlight's still there where I left it. You bought a new one and—"

She got the cane, straightened in the chair, and struck out with it. It caught him under the ear and sent him hard against the wall. Then, clutching the turntable stand to keep her balance, she was on her feet, beating at him with the cane. "It was God's command. You'd smutted him, you black beast of Sodom. Smutted him, besmirched him!"

Steve grabbed at the cane and missed. It lashed across his cheekbone. He pawed out for it again. But he couldn't get it away from her. She was too fast, too furious. She wrenched it back and swung with all the strength of her lumpy body. Pain seared his skull and he went down.

"There's power in me!" she screamed. "God's power. This is *His* arm, His strong right arm, to smite evildoers!"

Christ, he thought, *she's going to do it to me—what she did to Coy.* He tried to stand. She struck him down. Blood was running into his eyes. He lunged for the door, scrambling on hands and knees. Down came the cane again. Down came blackness. But it didn't last. He opened his eyes. Through the red mist he saw her bending over him, her ruined face writhing, the cane held ready.

"That woman came to me, that woman Laurette, that whore of Babylon." Her breath rasped in and out hoarsely. "She said Jesse Coy Randol slept in your bed with you when you were down here that time. She found his medal in your bed, his little Christian Endeavor medal. She said you'd claimed it was yours. Then she saw Jess wearing it at Easter. Oh, she'd guessed what you were. You'd lisped and flounced like a woman to make her laugh but you never tried to take her in carnal knowledge."

Steve made a sound to keep her talking.

"I said it was a lie. But I had to know. God gave me the strength. I drove to Los Angeles and found that place of yours. I'm sick. God's trying to help me, like Job. But somehow I dragged myself up those steps. It was sundown nearly. Those tall windows were open and there were the two of you. . . . What I saw was unspeakable, an abomination in the sight of the Lord."

The blood was pooling under his face on the floor. Her voice was fading. He was going to pass out.

"A young man came, young man with a beard. He didn't see me. I'd heard him coming and hid myself around the corner of the house. He didn't stay. And when he'd gone I got back to my car. I drove to a Gospel Church and I prayed. 'Lord,' I said, 'let this cup pass from me.' But I'd known before I left here, known Laurette was telling the truth. That was why I'd brought the flashlight. And I went back and slew Jess. My little boy. It was the same sacrifice God asked of Abraham. But . . ." Her voice went high and reedy and sad. ". . . This time, no angel came."

High and reedy and sad he heard far off the sound of a siren.

"And then there was Laurette. I'd told her I was going to see Jess. When she found out what happened, she'd have told. She hated me. The wicked hate the righteous. I had my ministry, my life for my God. I phoned her the next morning, made her think I'd let her sell her rotten liquor like she wanted to. I told her to meet me up here by the wash. She came on horseback. I knew she would. I smote her with a stone. Crushed her head like a serpent's and rolled her body into the wash. I—"

She broke off, straightened, turned. The siren ripped the air. There was a snarl of tires on dirt. Car doors slammed. Steve heard the building door torn open. Shouts. Footsteps. He heard Sister Myra saying over and over again, "Agh, agh, agh . . ."

He slid steeply into darkness.

EPILOGUE

I T WAS HOT. THE BOY with the sunstreaked brown hair lay on the
window seat again, naked again, but not asleep. He was reading a movie magazine. Above him, the big window with its stained
glass trim stood open, propped by a wooden coathanger. Outside
it, honeysuckle climbed. The smell of it was heavy in the room.

Steve stood in the doorway. After five long days—maybe good
days in the sense that they'd let him forget a little, heal a little in his
mind as well as in his skull—after five long days he'd been allowed
to leave the hospital in Escondido this morning. He had come
back on the Honda. But by slow stages. His head still hurt and he
had taken a lot of rests. It was nearly six now.

"Hi," he said.

Billy Rice turned his head and smiled at him. "Hi."

"I brought your bike back," Steve said. "Thanks. Didn't mean
to keep it so long."

"It's all right." Billy sat up, dropping the magazine. He frowned.
"Hey, that's quite a bandage. You look like Ali Baba or somebody."

"So you won't think I'm one of the forty thieves," Steve said,
"here's a few bucks for the gas and wear and tear." He laid them
on the battered dresser.

"Forget it," Billy said. "Steve, that's a bad cut. Stitches! What
happened to you?"

"A broadcast interview," Steve told him. "I guess I said the
wrong things." He stopped. A woman was standing in the corner
of the room. Wrapped in white lace. A woman. With Billy naked?
He squinted at her and saw she was a cutout photo blowup. Life
size. Bette Davis in *The Letter.* "Shit!" he grinned. "Where did you
get that?"

Billy jumped up, ran to the cardboard thing and draped his

arm around the shoulders. "Isn't she marvelous? Eddie Lawrence found her for me. Twenty dollars."

"Jesus," Steve laughed.

"You want a beer? You must be pooped."

"Not so much pooped as hot," Steve said.

"Take off your clothes," Billy said, "and stay a while. I've got a sixpack in the refrigerator downstairs. Unless some cheap faggot's run off with it."

"Any soft drinks?" Steve was peeling off his shirt. "Alcohol makes my head hurt."

Billy pulled on little gingham shorts. "Bubble-Up?"

"Fine," Steve said, "anything."

"Back in a minute." The boy went out and shut the door.

When he came back, Steve had pulled the bed down and was lying on it naked. "Do you mind?"

Billy set the tall green wet bottles on the dresser. He slid off his shorts. "All I've minded is the wait." He knelt on the bed. "I wasn't cut out to be a nun."

"I was kind of busy," Steve said. "But now I'm not busy any more." He reached up.

But Billy's beautiful brown eyes had opened wide. He pointed at the corner. "You turned her around!" he cried. "Why?"

"I've taken a dislike to people staring at me while I'm making out." With a sad laugh, Steve pulled the boy down to him.

Published in paperback.
There is also a special edition of ten numbered copies,
handbound in boards and signed by the author.